the only thing worse than me is you

the only thing worse than me is you

LILY ANDERSON

ST. MARTIN'S GRIFFIN ⚓ NEW YORK

This is a work of fiction. All of the characters, organizations, and events portrayed in this novel are either products of the author's imagination or are used fictitiously.

THE ONLY THING WORSE THAN ME IS YOU. Copyright © 2016 by Lily Elena Anderson. All rights reserved. Printed in the United States of America. For information, address St. Martin's Press, 175 Fifth Avenue, New York, N.Y. 10010.

www.stmartins.com

Designed by Anna Gorovoy

The Library of Congress Cataloging-in-Publication Data is available upon request.

ISBN 978-1-250-07909-1 (hardcover)
ISBN 978-1-4668-9172-2 (e-book)

Our books may be purchased in bulk for promotional, educational, or business use. Please contact your local bookseller or the Macmillan Corporate and Premium Sales Department at 1-800-221-7945, extension 5442, or by e-mail at MacmillanSpecialMarkets@macmillan.com.

First Edition: May 2016

10 9 8 7 6 5 4 3 2 1

For Erin and Liz
Because you're never alone when you're part of a trio

acknowledgments

a top-ten list of thank-yous

1. **My Family**: For your love, your encouragement, and your understanding that I will miss holidays when I'm breaking a story.

2. **The Harbor Family**: Teddy, Elizabert, J-Tho, Kiddo, Hailo, V-Luu, Brig, Nic, KB1, KB2, Gnat, Magic JJ, Abby Fabby Funk, Monks, and Lady Bon Bon—my super friends, who put up with being incessantly nicknamed. Thank you again and always, for absolutely everything. *I do love nothing in the world so well as you. Is not that strange?*

3. **Laura Zats**: My agent and my champion, who got this book immediately. Thank you for pushing me to be nerdier and for believing that I could juggle three manuscripts at the same time. You make me a stronger writer and a stronger person. I could not be more thankful for you. I owe you a beer and a hug.

4. **Sylvan Creekmore**: The coolest editor in the world, who changed my life in the span of one e-mail (and every e-mail since).

I can't thank you enough for making this book possible. Beer and hugs for you, too!

5. Everyone at St. Martin's Press, especially Michelle and Karen: For believing in me and this book and for guiding me through the mess that was achieving my greatest dream.

6. The Sweet 16s: The sweetest and most talented group of people on the Internet. I can't believe how lucky I am to be debuting alongside of you all.

7. The Harleys (Mellissa, Rich, Aidan, and Spencer): For your amazing support and insta-love.

8. Brandon, Sylvia, and the overlords: For being on my team for so many years.

9. Erin: My best friend and first fangirl whose rants about the X-Men proved to be quite useful. Thank you for bringing me mugs of tea and reminding me to eat, for reading YA when you really didn't want to, and for introducing me to *Saga*. You're the world's best lying cat.

10. My students: This book started as a love letter to my students. Without their enthusiasm for sharing their fandoms with their school librarian, the Messina Academy would be unpopulated. Endless thanks to every Bee and Falcon who stopped at my desk to talk about *Doctor Who, Star Wars*, Marvel, DC, *Lord of the Rings*, and *Harry Potter*. Thank you for handing me books that you loved and reminding me that stories change lives. You all make my job a blessing.

And none for Gretchen Wieners.

There is a kind of merry war betwixt Signior Benedick and her: they never meet but there's a skirmish of wit between them.

—William Shakespeare, *Much Ado About Nothing,* I.i

the only
thing worse
than me is
you

✸ 1 ✸

Ben West spent summer vacation growing a handlebar mustache.

Seriously.

Hovering over his upper lip—possibly glued there—was a bushy monstrosity that shouted, *"Look out, senior class, I'm gonna tie some chicks to the train tracks and then go on safari with my good friend Teddy Roosevelt. Bully!"*

I blindly swatted at Harper with my comic book, trying to alert her to the fact that there was a mustachioed moron attempting to blend in with the other people entering campus.

"I know I should have made flash cards for the poems that Cline assigned," she said, elbowing me back hard, both acknowledging that she wasn't blind and that she hated when I interrupted her monologues about the summer reading list. "But I found Mrs. Bergman's sociolinguistics syllabus on the U of O website and I'm sure she'll use the same one here."

The mustache twitched an attempt at freedom, edging away from West's ferrety nose as he tried to shove past a group of nervous freshmen. It might have been looking at me and Harper, but its owner was doing everything possible to ignore us, the planter box we were sitting on, and anything else that might have been east of the wrought iron gate.

"So," Harper continued, louder than necessary considering we were sitting two inches apart, "I thought I'd get a head start. But now I'm afraid that we were supposed to memorize the poems for Cline. He never responded to my emails."

Pushing my comic aside, I braced my hands against the brick ledge. The mustache was daring me to say something. Harper could hear it, too, as evidenced by her staring up at the sun and muttering, "Or you could, you know, not do this."

"Hey, West," I called, ignoring the clucks of protest coming from my left. "I'm pretty sure your milk mustache curdled. Do you need a napkin?"

Ben West lurched to a stop, one foot inside of the gate. Even on the first day of school, he hadn't managed to find a clean uniform. His polo was a series of baggy wrinkles, half-tucked into a pair of dingy khakis. He turned his head. If the mustache had been able to give me the finger, it would have. Instead, it watched me with its curlicue fists raised on either side of West's thin mouth.

"Hey, Harper," he said. He cut his eyes at me and grumbled, "Trixie."

I leaned back, offering the slowest of slow claps. "Great job, West. You have correctly named us. I, however, may need to change your mantle. Do you prefer Yosemite Sam or Doc Holliday? I definitely think it should be cowboy related."

"Isn't it inhumane to make the freshmen walk past you?" he asked me, pushing the ratty brown hair out of his eyes. "Or is it some kind of ritual hazing?"

"Gotta scare them straight." I gestured to my blond associate. "Besides, I've got Harper to soften the blow. It's like good cop, bad cop."

"It is nothing like good cop, bad cop. We're waiting for Meg," Harper said, flushing under the smattering of freckles across her cheeks as she turned back to the parking lot, undoubtedly trying to escape to the special place in her head where pop quizzes—and student council vice presidents—lived. She removed her headband and then pushed it back in place until she once again looked like Sleeping Beauty in pink glasses and khakis. Whereas I continued to look like I'd slept on my ponytail.

Which I had because it is cruel to start school on a Wednesday.

"Is it heavy?" I asked Ben, waving at his mustache. "Like weight training for your face? Or are you trying to compensate for your narrow shoulders?"

He gave a halfhearted leer at my polo. "I could ask the same thing of your bra."

My arms flew automatically to cover my chest, but I seemed to be able to conjure only the consonants of the curses I wanted to hurl at him. In his usual show of bad form, West took this as some sort of victory.

"As you were," he said, jumping back into the line of uniforms on their way to the main building. He passed too close to Kenneth Pollack, who shoved him hard into the main gate, growling, "Watch it, nerd."

"School for geniuses, Kenneth," Harper called. "We're all nerds."

Kenneth flipped her off absentmindedly as West righted himself and darted past Mike Shepherd into the main building.

"Brute," Harper said under her breath.

I scuffed the planter box with the heels of my mandatory Mary Janes. "I'm off my game. My brain is still on summer vacation. I totally left myself open to that cheap trick."

"I was referring to Kenneth, not Ben." She frowned. "But, yes, you should have known better. Ben's been using that bra line since fourth grade."

As a rule, I refused to admit when Harper was right before eight in the morning. It would lead to a full day of her gloating. I hopped off the planter and scooped up my messenger bag, shoving my comic inside.

"Come on. I'm over waiting for Meg. She's undoubtedly choosing hair care over punctuality. Again."

Harper slid bonelessly to her feet, sighing with enough force to slump her shoulders as she followed me through the front gate and up the stairs. The sunlight refracted against her pale hair every time her neck swiveled to look behind us. Without my massive aviator sunglasses, I was sure I would have been blinded by the glare.

"What's with you?" I asked, kicking a stray pebble out of the way.

"What? Nothing." Her head snapped back to attention, knocking her glasses askew. She quickly straightened them with two trembling hands. "Nothing. I was just thinking that maybe senior year might be a good time for you to end your war with Ben. You'd have more time to study and read comics and . . ."

Unlike the tardy Meg, Harper was tall enough that I could look at her without craning my neck downward. It made it easier to level her with a droll stare. Sometimes, it's better to save one's wit and just let the stupidity of a thought do the talking.

She rolled her eyes and clucked again, breezing past me to open the door.

"Or not," she said, swinging the door open and letting me slip past her. "Year ten of *Watson v. West* starts now. But if one of you brings up the day he pushed you off the monkey bars, I am taking custody of Meg and we are going to sit with the yearbook staff during lunch."

"I accept those terms." I grinned. "Now help me think of historical figures with mustaches. Hitler and Stalin are entirely too obvious. I need to brainstorm before we get homework."

Messina Academy for the Gifted—the Mess—was the only nondenominational private school in a fifty-mile radius. At some point in the mid-seventies a bunch of disgruntled academics from the local university had taken over a foundering Jesuit school, turned the chapel into the state's first high school computer lab, and started only letting in students who passed the three-hour entrance exam.

From the outside the Mess seemed like any other private high school—four hundred kids in uniforms whose tuition had one too many zeroes. But inside we were even weirder than the poor saps at the Catholic school across town. Sure, we had sports and proms and cliques, but we also had electives devoted to the physics of *Star Trek* and the chemistry of emotions.

In short, we were the smart kid school, Xavier's School for Gifted Youngsters minus the mutant abilities—unless you counted the polyglots and concert violinists as mutants, which wouldn't be entirely unfair. The Mess was where parents stuck their prodigy kids when they didn't want them attempting nuclear fission in the garage or going off to college at twelve.

The school handbook included a lengthy list of regulations, the first of which was a gag rule against any discussion of the results of your entrance exam—to keep IQ-based bullying to a minimum. Legend had it that Mess kids used to walk around with their IQ numbers pinned to their uniforms so they could only associate with "their own kind." Since that sounded like the beginning of a *Battle Royale* kind of dystopia, no one complained about the gag rule. It was bad enough that they publicly ranked us once a month.

Senior year was not going to be a picnic. Just because we'd spent last year prepping our college applications did not mean that we got to slack now, as proven by my schedule: Calculus, Russian literature, Programming Languages, the Economics of the Third World, and— my first class of the day—the History of the American Immigrant.

Meg had opted out of the American Immigrant class, insisting that having to do any in-class discussions of the *Joy Luck Club* would end in her crying her mascara off and calling her grandmothers to apologize for being an ungrateful second-generation child. This left me and Harper without our usual third seat to save. I settled into a desk in the center of the room and took off my sunglasses, stuffing them into the front pocket of my bag and resuming blending in with the rest of the khaki-pants-and-white-polo-clad members of the senior class.

Our teacher, Mr. Cline, started ticking off the roll sheet. The whiteboard behind him had his name scrawled lopsided across it like a poorly thought out marquee.

"Cornell Aaron?" he read, his pencil poised to make checkmarks.

Over the sound of Harper's heart going pitter-pat next to me, a familiar voice said, "Here."

I peeked over my shoulder and saw Cornell sitting a few seats behind Harper, his arm raised in the air. If you went in for that young Lando Calrissian, future-prom-king kind of thing—which Harper did—Cornell Aaron was pretty much perfect, from his shaved head to his penny loafers. He spotted me and waved.

I waved back and turned around. Harper tried to shrink in her seat.

"You look kind of greenish," I whispered to her.

"It's nothing."

"Nothing, huh?" I asked under my breath. "Nothing sure got taller over the summer."

"Shut up," she hissed back.

As Mr. Cline continued reciting the names of our classmates, I looked around the room, waiting to see an unfamiliar face. TV and movies would lead you to believe that the first day of school was the day a handsome stranger walked in, possibly in a leather jacket or harboring some kind of deep dark secret, like an abusive family or fangs.

But there were no handsome strangers. Mike Shepherd was sitting in the front of the room, picking at a zit with a vacant expression. Brad Hertz and Nick Conrad were already passing notes back and forth. Mary-Anne France was putting on more lip gloss than was medically advisable.

"Beatrice Watson?" Mr. Cline read.

"Trixie," I corrected automatically.

Call me vain, but being called Beatrice made my skin crawl. I don't care how much my parents had loved my great-grandmother. I had nothing but respect for GG Bea, who had been a pilot and liked to refer to Amelia Earhart as "Eleanor Roosevelt's girlfriend," but that didn't change the fact that Beatrice was a terrible name.

"Trix, not recommended for kids," Ben West said loudly from somewhere behind me.

I craned around in my seat, leaning into the aisle so that I could see him from around the girl sitting between us. It was hard to focus on his face with that thing under his nose, but I managed, focusing instead on the mop of unbrushed hair on his forehead.

"How did you get in here?" I asked.

He scoffed and his mustache spazzed out. "Through the door, Trix. Did you climb in through the window? I would have paid to see that."

"Ben West?" Mr. Cline asked, ignoring us.

West half-raised his hand in a limp salute. "Right here, friend."

"Yes, thank you." Mr. Cline frowned before gesturing to the pile of textbooks dwarfing his desk. "Please come check out a textbook and return to your seats."

There was a screeching of chairs as the class swarmed toward the front. The girl behind me shoved her way forward, getting trapped in the traffic jam. I watched as Cornell stood to the side, letting Harper sneak past him. She thanked him breathlessly.

I considered, not for the first or last time, how much easier life would have been if one of them had been born with a backbone. They'd been doing this awkward flirt shuffle since freshman year after an incident involving a pepperoni getting stuck in Harper's hair and Cornell gently retrieving it. Ever since then, it'd been all furtive glances and Harper sighing and Cornell being extragentlemanly whenever she was around.

I'd considered locking them in a closet together when we'd been roped into helping the yearbook staff the year before, but Meg pointed out that it would have been "inappropriate" to barricade our best friend in a closet by piling a bunch of desks in front of it. I still stood by the fact that it totally would have worked and I wouldn't have spent all summer listening to Harper muse about what Cornell was doing at his summer internship in Washington, DC.

"If a look could knock someone up," Ben West muttered behind me, "Harper would be blown up with Cornell's triplets."

I didn't turn around. I was busy throwing up in my mouth. "That is the worst thing anyone has ever said out loud."

He grinned. "That's not even the worst thing I've said in the last half hour."

"Which proves that you continue to excel at being an awful person," I said, glancing at him over my shoulder. I couldn't stop myself from giggle-snorting at his old-timey mustache again. "Seriously, West. The mustache? You look like Mario. You just need a plunger and a self-fertilizing hermaphroditic dinosaur."

I pushed forward, fighting against the tide of people holding the weighty tome that was to be our textbook for the semester. It was a college-level text and didn't even include the extra academic articles and novels we'd be covering. I took a moment to wonder whether or not I should have taken the British Imperialism class with Meg.

"I will take that as a compliment," West said, following behind me. "Mario is a hero. Saving princesses and clearing pipes? The man deserves a medal."

"You deserve a straightjacket. Or a muzzle. Possibly both. You could do it up Hannibal Lecter style and save us all the trouble. You could pay someone to wheel you from class to class."

"How many name drops can you get in to one insult? It's like you aren't even trying. I could easily compare you to—"

I spun to face him again and tilted my chin up so that I wasn't staring straight into the jut of his Adam's apple. "A summer's day?"

"Dry and unpleasant?" he said, twirling the end of his mustache nefariously. The sound of the whiskers crunching together was awful. "I could see that. It doesn't capture the full scope, though. Maybe a summer's day in Death Valley with nothing but yogurt to drink? And a swarm of wasps."

"You always go one too far." I sighed. "I can actually hear you scraping the bottom of the barrel of your limited intellect."

We got to the front of the room and Harper bumped me with her arm, throwing me a warning look that pointed out that I should stop sniping at Ben West. Scowling at her, I scooped up a book and shoved past West on my way back to my seat.

Most of the new senior class at the Mess had started at Aragon Prep, Messina's warm and squishy sister school. From kindergarten to eighth grade, Aragon had spent countless hours teaching all of us how to socialize with our peers and have fun with our education. And then the Mess spent four years making us forget all of that crap and get ready to go to college and/or take over the world.

That's why the class list was posted constantly. Outside of the attendance office, locked in a Poly(methyl methacrylate)— Plexiglas—case, the class lists were posted in order of rank on the first of every month. Just to keep the student body with a healthy— and occasionally nervous-breakdown-inducing—sense of competition.

I had done the Rank Tango with Ben West throughout junior year. One month, I'd be third, then he'd replace me. He'd managed a 103 percent in Statistical Anomalies—beating me by one percent—and I'd stayed firmly stuck at number four for the rest of the year.

We'd been playing this game for as long as I could remember. Despite the lazy insults and his nonstop blathering on, Ben West was always there to sweep a victory away from me. When I won the geography bee in third grade, he'd won the spelling bee. When I'd trounced him at kickball, he'd wiped the four square court with me.

And that didn't even include the incident with the monkey bars.

All I wanted was one win that he couldn't take away from me. If I could dethrone him from the number three spot in our class— Cornell and Harper were one and two, respectively—and stay there until graduation, I would be able to dance out of the Mess with no regrets. A decade of battles with Ben West would be worth it if I won the war.

I retrieved a pencil and my Spider-Man binder from my bag. Flipping the binder open to the first fresh sheet of sweet-smelling college-ruled notebook paper, I dated the top right-hand corner. T-minus 179 days until graduation.

"'Keep, ancient lands, your storied pomp!' cries she with silent lips," shouted Mr. Cline, his voice suddenly booming with theatrical intensity. "'Give me your tired, your poor, your huddled masses yearning to breathe free. The wretched refuse of your teeming shore. Send these, the homeless, tempest-tost to me. I lift my lamp beside the golden door!'"

He looked around the room with narrowed eyes, breathing heavily.

"This is the promise of 'The New Colossus,'" he said in a reverential whisper. "Written by whom, Miss France?"

Mary-Anne cocked her head at him. "Emma Lazarus."

"Correct," he roared, spinning to the whiteboard to scrawl the name under his own. "Emma Lazarus, a Sephardic Jew from Portugal. The voice of the disenfranchised immigrant!"

As he started listing the accomplishments of Emma Lazarus and the symbolism of the Statue of Liberty, my pencil flew over the notebook paper. We hadn't even opened the textbook and I was already a page of notes in.

Just a normal first day at the Mess.

To: Messina Academy Students
From: Administrative Services
Subject: Salutations!

Welcome pupils, new and old, to the Messina Academy for the Gifted.

As you enter this morning with your proverbial clean slate, you may note some changes to our institution. Thanks to a generous donation from the Donnelly family, we have secured a second mass spectrometer with electrospray ionization capabilities. . . .

✬ 2 ✬

Where were you this morning?" Harper asked the second Meg was within earshot of us in the cafeteria. "We waited for you out front."

Meg set her tray down on our table, smoothing her pleated skirt as she sat down. As expected, her glossy black hair had been meticulously curled.

Like short women across the globe, Meg looked like she would be harmless, but she was a pocket-sized ball of fury when you crossed her. We'd called her Pikachu through most of our time at Aragon Prep until the day she started sobbing and told us that it made her sound fat. We'd given up on nicknames that day. And discovered a sync in our menstrual cycles.

"My parents made a huge deal about this being my last first day of high school," she said airily. "There was breakfast with my grandparents and a Skype conversation with my brother. It was a nice thought, but it put me totally behind schedule. Sometimes, they care too much."

"You should try being an only child," I said, laughing. "It's like that every day."

"Pretty much," Harper said.

"I don't know how the two of you survive," Meg said. "Did I miss anything important before the bell?"

"Cornell and Harper continue to try to make out with each other via telepathy," I said, stabbing my fork into the wilted lettuce that the Mess cafeteria mockingly called a salad.

Harper squawked, spewing chicken nugget breading onto the table. Meg covered her plate as Harper flapped her hands, blindly searching for a napkin.

"Untrue." Harper coughed. "That's not what happened at all."

Meg wasn't convinced but she seemed to weigh her options and come to the conclusion that it wasn't worth seeing if Harper would actually lay an egg if we kept talking about Cornell.

"Anything else?"

I scanned around the cafeteria and found West sitting on the other side of the room with Cornell and the Donnelly twins. I pointed at him and Meg clasped her hands to her face, sucking in a gasp.

"What is that on Ben's face?"

"Exactly," I said, shoving a forkful of salad into my mouth. "Good luck eating your chicken nuggets after that."

"Is it real?" she asked.

"I'm not entirely sure." I cringed as I spotted West shoving pizza under the flap of hair. "I considered trying to rip it off of him during first period, but I'm afraid that I'd disturb the family of mice living in it. I wonder what he's doing with the politicos. Doesn't he normally run with the Dungeons & Dragons crowd?"

"Mike Shepherd kicked him out last year," Meg said. "He's on the student council now."

Harper smoothed her soiled napkin on the side of her tray, patting it into place. "He and Cornell had the same internship over the summer."

I raised my eyebrows at her. "Have you been Internet stalking again, Miss Leonard?"

"Is it possible that Peter's eyes got bluer?" Meg asked, squinting into the spotlight that was Peter Donnelly's all-American good looks. "I think being president is making him more handsome."

Harper tried to hide in her hunched shoulders. "Please stop staring at them. It's so conspicuous."

I eyed her warily. "You're lucky we aren't marching over there and telling Cornell to grow a pair."

"You would not," she said. "Especially since Ben is sitting with him."

"That's probably true," I conceded. "I'd like to keep my salad down and West's insults have been superlame today. I think the mustache might be draining his intellect. Which is useful because I am going to take the number three spot before the end of the year."

Meg's face contorted in disgust. "That's your big plan for senior year? You want to be number three?"

"Well, I can't beat Harper or her future husband without giving up sleeping and eating and comics. So yeah, I'll settle for being number three. I'll get a cake shaped like a four and shove it in Ben West's stupid hairy face after he walks across the stage at graduation. And then I'll rip off my cap and gown, revealing a red leather jacket and black skinny jeans and moonwalk all the way home."

"Wow," Harper said after a moment of silence. "That was detailed."

I reached over and flicked a piece of chicken nugget shrapnel from her specs. "I've had time to plan with all of the good TV being on hiatus. Without *Game of Thrones,* I get weird."

"That's why I took classes over the break," Harper said. "And rewatched *Supernatural.*"

"God, I love the Winchester brothers," Meg said. She nibbled on the end of a chicken nugget. "You know, considering it's our senior year, normal people might be thinking about things like the harvest festival."

"What about the harvest festival?" I frowned. "It's the same thing every year. We get dressed up, we're the only girls on campus not dressed up like trampy tramps, we drink apple cider, we eat kettle

corn, and Harper gets a stomachache. It's not even on real Halloween."

"Yes, but we're seniors," Meg said, ever the voice of the obvious.
"Maybe we should try to, you know, go with other people?"

"Other people like the yearbook staff or other people like you
want to turn this into some kind of cliché mating ritual?" I asked.

"Closer to the second one," said Harper.

"Less mating, more dating," Meg added cheerfully.

"Dear God," I said, unable to stop my face from twisting in horror. "And I thought that talking to West would be the lamest thing
that happened today. Did you really just say 'less mating, more
dating'?"

"Trixie, you know that boys are my risk this year," she said loftily.
"Well, boys and manga. I'm branching out emotionally and intel-
lectually."

I tried not to groan. Instead of giving the usual birds-and-bees
talk, Meg's psychologist parents had sat her down with a model of
the human brain. Upon hearing that her prefrontal cortex was developing slower than her limbic system, making her more prone to
risky behaviors—like drug addiction and uncontrollable sexual
impulses—Meg had come to the conclusion that the only way to beat
nature was to decide her own risks to keep her brain preoccupied
from real dangers.

The Great Thought Experiment, as she referred to it, had started
off small enough. She'd pushed herself gently out of her comfort
zone with Internet videos on hair care and the proper application of
makeup. She'd secretly mastered the art of nerd burlesque with the
help of Jo Jo Stiletto's books and blogs. She joined the yearbook com-
mittee for a year to learn graphic design—and then dragged me
and Harper to help with distribution. She spent a year referring to
her parents by their first names.

But on a particularly hot day over summer vacation, as we'd lain
in the sprinklers in her backyard, she'd looked over at me and asked,
"Why don't we have any male friends?"

"We don't have many friends at all," I'd said. Which was true. With Harper stuck in summer school classes at the university, Meg and I had been soaking up the sun alone.

"I can't go to college without having any interactions with the opposite sex," Meg had said, plucking damp blades of grass between her fingers.

"You want a degree in women's studies. You could just go to an all girls' school."

This had been met with spiny silence.

It appeared my beloved best friends were on the fast track to becoming utterly antifeminist. Instead of comparing notes on our classes or comic books or which Joss Whedon show was the best—*Firefly,* obviously—they'd started this secret campaign to get boyfriends. Outwardly, they were the same brilliant, proudly nerdy ladies that I knew and loved. But then there was the boy crazy, scheming part of them that I could not condone.

I was seventeen. I had eyes and girl parts and functional hormones. I was aware that we went to school with a few not-ugly boys. But I didn't want to date them. I just wanted to get into a decent college and escape the Mess with as little emotional baggage as possible. Was that so much to ask?

Apparently it was. Because Harper and Meg refused to let the whole boyfriends thing go.

"You two are more than welcome to throw yourselves at whomever you want," I said drily. "I won't stop you. But I refuse to be party to this."

"Trixie." Meg sighed, but I held up my hand to stop her.

"Look around you," I said, gesturing to the crowded cafeteria. "Look at the bounty of uniform-clad, mid-pubescent, Axe-body-sprayed boys we have been given as our only option for dating. Let's say for one minute that I decided to hop on your bandwagon and tried to lure one of these losers into dating me. I'm not Mary-Anne France."

I pointed to the student council table again. Mary-Anne was

sitting next to Peter Donnelly, smiling demurely behind a bottle of mineral water. Her hair was loosely curled, resting delicately on the shoulders of a perfectly tailored cardigan. There was peach shimmer on her eyelids the same color as the goo on her mouth. The rest of the cafeteria was zit-ridden, nearsighted, and pit-stained. Mary-Anne was starring in her own personal version of a magazine spread, using her genius only to find ways to make her uniform look couture.

Okay, fine. She'd also published two volumes of startlingly insightful poetry, but that's beside the point.

"I am like a twelve-year-old boy with massive boobs," I continued. "Comic books and science fiction? I am not the kind of girlfriend a seventeen-year-old boy wants."

"Well," Harper said, attempting to find the flaw in my logic. Her face lit up and she flapped her hands. "You could find a college guy. You're too mature for high school boys. What about one of the guys from the comic book store? They're nice and nerdy and not in high school."

"No way." I laughed. "Any college guy who wants to date a seventeen-year-old has some kind of massive problem. Creepy pedophiles that can't date girls their own age are not on my bucket list."

"So you're going to die alone without ever attempting romantic love?" Meg asked.

"No," I said. "I am going to get through this year, go off to a good college, and meet handsome, educated sophomores who appreciate Marvel over DC and think that it's rad that I look like Rogue from X-Men. Maybe I'll add the white streak to my hair to hedge my bets."

"So, you won't be finding a date for the harvest festival?" Harper asked.

I chomped another forkful of salad. "Nope."

"Well, I am not Team Spinster," Meg said, shifting in her seat to look at Harper. "You should ask Cornell. And then he can set me up with a Donnelly."

"Either Donnelly?" Harper asked. "Even if it's Jack?"

"Poor life choice," I declared. "Jack Donnelly is a sociopath. He'd probably murder you in the haunted house and then go bob for apples like it never happened."

Also wedged into the student council table, hiding behind a copy of *House of Leaves,* Jack Donnelly seemed oblivious to the fact that his lunch companions were laughing and throwing things at each other. He and Peter were fraternal twins, sharing the same blue eyes and massive forehead. On Peter, the look was charming, if a little goofy. Jack, on the other hand, just seemed sinister. Peter was the class president. Jack had been caught drinking cough syrup for fun in the eighth grade. It made no sense that they'd once shared a womb.

"I heard that the Donnellys donated that mass spectrometer so that Jack could test a *Flowers for Algernon* smart drug without killing lab rats," Harper said.

"That's ridiculous," I said. "Obviously, he'd just kill the lab rats. He was overly enthusiastic about dissecting things in biology."

"He's not a sociopath," Meg said. "It would have shown up on his entrance exam. He's just not chatty. And that's fine. I'll chat and he can buy my kettle corn."

"That sounds like prostitution," I said.

Meg rolled her eyes. "You think all dating sounds like prostitution."

"If it looks like a duck and sells its time like a duck," I said. "How can you guys even consider dates when we haven't nailed down costumes yet? I've decided that I'm going to go as OG Maleficent. None of that Angelina Jolie nonsense. I want to be warm."

In order to get into the harvest festival, you had to wear a costume. And being the largest group of underage geniuses on the West Coast the student body of the Mess always went all out. Yes, there would be plenty of sexy witches, cats, and other farm animals, but generally everyone went to the extreme with it. It was the only thing I liked about the festival, really. I wasn't much for the scary movies, haunted houses part of things. But an excuse to bust out a hot-glue gun and my sewing machine? I was the conductor of that train. All aboard.

The girls relaxed a little, letting the conversation drift away from boys and toward whether or not we should all go as Disney villains. Harper had her heart set on being Supergirl and Meg didn't really care what she went as providing that she could wear heels with it. I agreed to help her craft a Queen of Hearts costume if she would help me papier-mâché my Maleficent horned headpiece.

"We should do it as soon as possible," Meg said. She sent a worried frown toward her backpack. "I'm three classes in and I already have two essays to do."

"Same here," Harper said. "And about fifty pages of reading to do before tomorrow."

I glanced down at my arm, where I'd started writing my homework notes. It looked like I'd have a full sleeve by the end of the day. "And you two want boyfriends?"

The girls fixed me with the same *It doesn't signify* glare. There was no reasoning with them when they were like this.

"Okay," I said, drawing the word out into a snarky warble. "I'm just saying: we're all trapped in a codependent relationship with the Mess until June."

"You can't make out with the Mess," Meg said.

I shook my head, my ponytail wagging against my neck in defeat. "No, my darling Margaret, you cannot. But we have three weeks before the first rank list comes out, so I'm going to try my darndest."

Harper   [4:02 PM]

Can you bring me that Sarah Vowell book about
the Puritans tomorrow? I need a quote for an
essay.

Meg   [4:31 PM]

Sending you ideas for my costume. I think
cleavage is going to be essential to my thought
experiment.

Mom   [4:45 PM]

Dinner in fifteen minutes.

✫ 3 ✫

I flipped over my arm, tracking down the note I'd made there in Russian Lit and crossed it out. Harper had wasted many years giving me planners and calendars for my birthday in an attempt to get me to stop writing on my arms, but with this, there was no way I could forget about any special assignments. Besides, it gave me something to do in class when the teachers went off on unrelated tangents.

I capped the pen and tossed it aside before uncurling myself and padding out of the room. Sherry, our Chocolate Lab, galloped toward me and thrust his head into my hand, taking a tentative lick at the nontoxic remnants of dayglo ink as I walked toward the kitchen.

Mom was standing in front of the slow cooker on the counter, carefully ladling a steaming rust-colored sludge into a soup bowl.

"Lentils?" I asked, holding back the urge to add, *again*?

Dad gave me a nod that commended me on my restraint. "With tomatoes and white beans."

"And okra," Mom said. She thrust the bowl into my hands, swatting Sherry away as he leapt up to try to filch some.

"Sherlock," Dad said firmly.

Sherry lowered his head and trotted over to Dad, who rubbed his ears. I rolled my eyes and sat down at the table across from him.

"It would have been easier just to let him eat some," I said, shaking a napkin into my lap to avoid staining my khakis. "You know he hates okra."

"He hates it because it makes him vomit," Mom said, unironically plopping lentils into her own bowl.

"How was school, Trix?" Dad asked, possibly to keep me from pointing out our meal's resemblance to regurgitation.

"Mess-y." I lifted my arm, showing him the long list of homework. "But it looks like you had an actual slapdash kind of first day."

I twirled a finger in the air, outlining his face. There were tiny blue dots on his right temple.

He reached up and picked at one of the paint spots. It flaked off easily, but immediately fell into his lentils.

"Oh, you know," he said. "The first day of kindergarten. Not a lot of criers this year, but there was an arts-and-crafts incident."

Mom sat down next to him with a soppy grin. She reached over and brushed the remaining paint flecks off his face.

My parents' marriage was its own special kind of statistical anomaly. Mom's income ran laps around Dad's. He spent his free time sitting at the family computer playing World of Warcraft. She knitted and read articles on pediatric medicine. Dad was wide and big eared with my flat grayish-blue eyes. Mom was polished, from her sleek brown hair to the button nose she'd bestowed upon me to her Doc Martens.

And yet, they'd been married for twenty years and remained utterly nauseating. I'd never figured out how it worked. It just did.

"How are the girls?" Mom asked me, smoothing a napkin over her lap.

I wished that we could have started the evening's conversation with something less unsavory like classes or the current state of my hair.

"Boy crazy," I admitted. "To the point of insanity."

My parents shared one of those concerned adult looks, ready to blow my comment out of proportion.

"Not like fellating-guys-in-the-bathroom insane," I amended. "The normal kind of talking about boys constantly. It's starting to feel like being friends with an issue of *Seventeen* magazine."

Mom blew delicately over the top of her laden spoon. "Well, as long as it's *Seventeen* and not *Cosmopolitan*."

"*Cosmopolitan* is lady porn," Dad agreed.

"Really?" I asked. "We're using the phrase 'lady porn' at the dinner table?"

"I thought I handled you saying 'fellating' fairly well." He gestured to his ruddy cheeks. "Note my lack of fatherly weeping."

"Greatly appreciated." I laughed. "In other news, I have been trapped with *Anna Karenina* all afternoon. I have made the command decision to graduate third in my class. Since Harper got extra credit for those college classes she took over the summer—"

Mom's bristle cut me off. "Greg is putting entirely too much pressure on Harper. It's not healthy. I know he wants her to do well, but she's still a little girl. I can't imagine that Sa—" She paused, choking on the name of Harper's mom. Mrs. Leonard had died when Harper and I were in first grade. I didn't remember her very well, but she and my mom had been close.

"Harper's fine," I said, firmly rerouting the conversation. "But she and Cornell Aaron have a ridiculous head start on first and second. So, I will sweep third away from Ben West."

Dad's head popped up. "The boy who broke your arm?"

While my friends thought that West throwing me off a play structure happened too long ago to matter anymore, my parents remembered the incident like it had happened yesterday. It was, to date, the only time I had ever broken a bone. As the medical professional of the house, Mom had taken it fairly well, from what I remembered. Dad, on the other hand, had been more scarred than I was. He'd threatened to send me back to school in a giant hamster ball. Parents who care too much are the plight of an only child.

"The very same," I said with a satisfied grin. "I have decided that crushing him under the heel of my Mary Jane shall be my greatest triumph. At least until college."

Sherry darted under the table, slamming my legs against my chair. My spoon clattered into my bowl.

"Damn it, Sherry!" I shouted at the retreating waggle of his tail. "You are not a puppy anymore. Stop trying to fit into tight spaces. You are the size of a baby ox."

Dad glanced over at Mom with a patient smile. "Dr. Watson, I believe it is time to feed Sherlock."

They chuckled to themselves as though, in the four years that we'd had Sherry, no one had ever thought to make a Sir Arthur Conan Doyle joke. Mom slid her chair back. Sherry followed her toward his food bowl, woofing in anticipation.

"Well, I think that aiming for third in your class is a worthy endeavor, Trix," Dad said, turning his attention back to me. "Even if it means locking yourself in your room with dusty Russian literature."

"It's my own fault," I said, returning to my dinner with disgust. "I could have signed up for the Shakespeare class, but they were focusing on the authorship debate this year and I could give a crap who actually wrote the plays. I just want to enjoy the work."

"'The public have an insatiable curiosity to know everything, except what is worth knowing.'"

"That's Oscar Wilde," I said with a mouthful of lentils. The added okra really brought out a fine sliminess to the dish heretofore unknown in the Watson household.

"It was relevant." He pouted.

I laughed and continued shoveling lentils into my mouth, pausing to pepper the bowl until it was more black than russet, which helped the flavor but not the texture. I made a mental note to scour the Internet for better recipes. It would be worth the pause in studying to have decent food to look forward to, even if I had to set up the slow cooker myself.

I politely declined seconds, grabbed a glass of water, and retreated to my room. My phone, which I had silenced in the name of distraction-free reading, had a series of texts from Harper and Meg about costumes. I told them both to email me pictures of what they wanted and we'd figure out how to construct them at lunch the next day.

Pushing aside thoughts of how to make horns out of wire hangers and papier-mâché, I sat down in front of my desk and cracked open my Calculus book. Maybe if Harper kept worrying about how short to make her Supergirl skirt, I would be able to sneak into the salutatorian spot.

Meg   [5:32 AM]

First comic book day of the school year!!!

Me   [5:33 AM]

WHY ARE YOU UP SO EARLY?

Harper   [5:35 AM]

COMIC BOOK DAY!

✦ 4 ✦

The rest of the first week of school and beginning of the second continued without incident. I found a recipe for white beans that was much less disgusting than the other dinners we'd been enjoying. I worked as far ahead on my homework as humanly possible. My arm stayed covered in an endless list of reading assignments and quiz dates.

After a particularly lengthy classroom argument about the merits of the Linux system in Programming Languages that had ended with Mike Shepherd hyperventilating, Harper, Meg, and I met at the front gate of the Mess. I was itching to pick up two weeks' worth of new releases from Busby Comics and pretend that I didn't have a pile of homework to do.

Harper drove us the three blocks, abandoning her usual overly cautious crawl in favor of a breakneck speed of thirty-five. Meg dug lip gloss out of her bag and smeared some onto her mouth, taking a moment to whine about us always going to the comic book store in uniform.

"So what?" I asked, glancing back at her from the front seat.

"So, it makes it so obvious that we're in high school."

I assumed this meant that she was still considering the employees of Busby as spousal candidates and rolled my eyes at her, choosing not to point out how ridiculous that was.

The three of us walked into Busby, passing a row of locked bicycles next to the front door. The store was cramped with three walls of metal shelves covered in comics, divided by publisher. There were glass cases full of elaborately packaged action figures and limited-edition statues, including a full set of pewter *Doctor Who* figurines that I continually drooled over. They would look rad in my future dorm room, wherever that happened to be.

Meg moved to the heavy wooden table in the center of the store where graphic novels were precariously stacked and immediately started stroking the spines of *The Extraordinary Adventures of Adèle Blanc-Sec*. Harper moved to the DC shelf, her hands fluttering over the preservation packages that housed glossy covers. She smoothed her hair as she read the titles.

"The Powerpuff Girls have arrived," crowed a heavyset bearded man, appearing in the window where the cash register sat. "Is it three thirty already?"

"Three fifteen. We're early," I said, turning away from the Dalek statue that was still calling my name. Well, it was really shouting about exterminating me, but I knew it meant it with love.

The bearded man, who was wearing a massive Transformers T-shirt that was obviously vintage, glanced around at us to make sure that we hadn't brought our backpacks in with us. Busby had a strict "no bags" policy.

"I saved three copies of the new *Buffy* for you guys in case you showed," he said to me.

"We always show," Meg said, clutching a book to her chest. She peered around the corner at the bearded man and her face fell. Obviously, she had been expecting the younger hipster gentleman who occasionally worked the register.

"Fair enough," the bearded man said. He looked over at me. "Are you gonna buy those *Who* statues yet?"

"Are you going to give me a hefty discount?" I asked.

"They're imported."

"From England. And they've been sitting here mocking me for over a year."

"Save up your pennies."

I scoffed at this and moved over to the Marvel shelf, immediately pulling down three comics and tucking them under my arm. Harper slid over to me, clutching her own stack of books.

"Verbal foreplay?" she asked under her breath.

"Failed haggling," I corrected sharply before turning my attention to the shelves.

The door opened and I looked up in time to see Jack Donnelly walk in. He pointedly ignored the bearded man behind the counter—and me, Harper, and Meg—as he made his way over to the indie release shelf. He ripped a book out of the plastic and pulled it close to his face. I cringed at this blatant disregard for comic-book-store etiquette.

The door creaked again. Harper sucked in a breath as Cornell led West and Peter inside. Meg's eyes went wide at me as she retreated a few paces.

"And I said to the senator, 'With all due respect, sir,'" West was crowing, "'I think it might help if you held the chart right-side up!'"

"No way," Peter said, laughing, somehow ignoring the twitching of West's facial catastrophe.

"I promise you, he did," Cornell said, shaking his head. "I thought the senator was going to kill him. We were just supposed to be updating the social media sites for a month."

"Hey, man," West said, veering right to perv my *Doctor Who* figures. "I was doing my part to save democracy. How's that for a piece of fried gold?"

"Good day, gents," the bearded man said. "Ben, still rocking the 'stache."

West's hand shot out and clasped the bearded man's in a firm and somehow pompous shake. "Aw, you know. The chicks dig it."

"Speaking on behalf of my gender," I said as the door closed behind Peter, "I can assure you that we do not, in fact, dig it."

Cornell, Peter, and the bearded guy laughed as West shot me a look of scorn that did not quite succeed in masking his surprise at the sound of my voice.

"Watch that one, Ralph," he said, half-turning to the man behind the counter. "She spits acid."

"If only," I said with an innocent flutter of my eyelashes. "I could burn that thing off of your face. It's so, hmm . . . flaccid?"

Meg buried her face deeper in her graphic novel. Jack Donnelly made a choked sound that might have been the mirthless guffaw of an evil twin. I watched with no small amount of pride as a crimson flush rose out of the starched white collar of West's polo.

Ralph the comic book guy looked from me to West and back again.

"Ah," he said with dawning understanding. "Exes."

"What?" I squawked, nearly dropping my comics.

The very idea that Ben West and I had ever been anything other than bitter rivals was the most horrifying aspersion ever cast upon my character. Even worse than West himself accusing me of being a "fake geek girl" back in the sixth grade. I thought of his mustache getting near me and gagged audibly.

West waved his splayed fingers in wild and emphatic denial, also blustering an incoherent series of "No, no, no." He looked to Cornell and Peter for backup, but they—like Harper and Meg—attempted to appear deaf, dumb, and blind to the situation.

Ralph threw Cornell and Peter a bemused smirk. "All right. Regardless, no turf wars in the store unless it's Risk night. Play nice or bounce."

"No problem," West said, staring at me as though throwing down an invisible gauntlet between us.

"None at all," I said, accepting the challenge with narrowed eyes.

Meg half-lowered the book from her face. "Should we draw a line down the center of the store?"

"No need," I said. "I won't get in the way of West getting the newest issue of *Archie and Friends*."

West grunted, but he let the Archie comment slide. Pleased that I had managed to get the last word in, I turned my attention back to the Marvel shelf. I could sense the boys moving behind me. I had always been distantly aware that Ben West read comics, but I'd never seen him at Busby before. It felt like someone had defecated in my sanctuary. I prayed that it wouldn't become a weekly problem.

Out of the corner of my eye, I watched as Cornell reached over the top of Harper's head, pulling down an issue of *Green Arrow,* seemingly at random. They muttered a greeting to each other, low enough that I couldn't make out the words. There was a clear lack of shocked bumbling on Harper's part, however. While she was fraying the ends of her hair between her thumb and index finger, she did not appear to be stuttering or clucking.

It dawned on me that this was not a coincidence. Harper was utterly prepared to see Cornell—or, at least as prepared as she could be. They must have planned this meeting beforehand. I knew they had a class together sixth period. I never would have guessed that they'd actually talk to each other.

"Yeah," sighed a mind-reading voice to my right. "It's a coup."

I whipped my head and found Peter's towering frame leaning next to me. He blended in easily with the superheroes behind him. He nodded toward Harper and Cornell with a wry smile.

"Isn't this what the kids call a tête-à-tête?" I whispered back, wrinkling my nose in distaste.

"No clue," he said. "I took Mandarin."

I snuck another peek at Harper and Cornell. "I should have known something was up. She refused to stop for Slurpees on the way."

Peter chuckled softly, then winced as he adjusted his weight from his right leg to his left. The sound of his articular cartilage collapsing in on itself slipped through a time wrinkle and echoed in my ears.

"How's the knee?" I asked. There was no way anyone would ever forget last year's basketball playoffs. Peter had crumpled to the court like a felled tree, wearing his knee the wrong way around.

"Maimed," he said. "I won't be playing this year. Or possibly ever again. We'll see."

"I'm sorry."

I'd never been the most athletic of individuals—other than a cricket ability that did not do me any good since the Mess had let me opt out of PE—but Peter had loved playing basketball since we were at Aragon Prep together. He always grinned when he was on the court, completely unstoppable. Now, he was permanently mortal.

"It's okay," he said. "I don't really have time to play this year. I need to focus on my classes and the student council. Are you guys coming to the harvest festival next week?"

I glanced back at Harper and Cornell. She was holding up two issues of *Green Lantern* with her face screwed into a pensive frown.

"I couldn't get out of it if I tried," I grumbled.

"It's going to be pretty cool this year," Peter said. He looked over at West, who was yanking down Marvel titles left and right. "Right, Ben?"

"Oh yeah," West said without taking his eyes off the *Avengers* comic in his hand. "Nothing like the usual kettle corn and bobbing for apples crap we normally do."

"Really?" Meg asked, skipping around the graphic novels table to stand with us.

"No," Jack Donnelly said, striding toward us. "It's going to be exactly like that."

I jumped. I'd already forgotten that he was in the store. He may have been equally as massive as Peter, but he had a habit of clinging to the shadows. I think it was the way his forehead jutted out more than his brother's. It was like a skull visor, providing him with extra shadows.

"Not exactly," Peter said, suddenly sheepish.

"Right," Jack drawled. "We bought a fog machine for the haunted house."

"That's cool," Meg said.

Ignoring this, Jack tucked his single comic under his arm. "Let's go," he said to his brother.

Peter's mouth curved into a frown that was more confused than insulted. "We just got here."

"I'm good to go," West said, his hands heavy with a stack of books roughly the same size as mine. He slammed them onto the counter. "I just need the new *Buffy* and we can roll out."

"*Buffy?*" Jack repeated with a derisive laugh. "Come on. Get your porn off the Internet like everyone else."

"It's not porn," West said with a sneer. "It's Whedon. The man does Marvel and Shakespeare. Joss is the nerd pope and *Buffy* is the first goddamn testament."

"Hear, hear!" cried Meg.

I choked down my disgust. It was bad enough that West was in my comic book store. I did not need him to also start bandwagonning my fandoms. Was nothing sacred anymore?

"Well said, Ben," Ralph said, scooping up the books and drawing them through the window. "Unfortunately, my last three copies are on hold for your female associates."

West's head flopped back, exposing the lump of his Adam's apple. He aimed a groan of frustration toward the heavens.

"Of course they are." He waved Jack in front of him and stepped aside, grinding the heel of his hand over his eyes as Ralph accepted Jack's money.

I stepped into line, examining West's apparent agony with relish.

"See this?" I waved a hand over him, indicating his tense shoulders and clenched jaw. "This is just a fraction of the devastation you'll be feeling in June when I beat you in rank once and for all."

His chin snapped down, the joints in his neck audibly popping.

"Fat chance, Medusa," he breathed, low enough that Jack was the only person who could have heard.

"You can take my copy of *Buffy,* Ben," Harper said quickly, hopping into view with Cornell in tow.

West bowed to her. "You are a gentlewoman and a scholar, Harper Leonard."

"I'm already way past my limit. I'll read Trixie's copy," she said. She turned to Cornell, holding up her pile of books. "Okay, which ones can I live without?"

He gingerly lifted four books out of her pile. "There. Go ahead."

Jack grabbed his receipt from Ralph and jerked his head toward Peter, who followed him out of the store, limping slightly. I paid for my own stack and made Ralph promise to continue putting aside one issue of *Buffy* for me every month for the foreseeable future. West let Harper and Meg go ahead of him in line. I waited for them next to the door, anxious to get in the car where I could demand to know when Harper had planned our not-so-accidental meeting with most of the student council.

Meg joined me near the door and we watched as Harper and Cornell exchanged a painfully awkward goodbye. I started to tell them to make out and get it over with already, but Meg caught me with a tiny pointed elbow in the stomach and I closed my mouth.

Harper adjusted her glasses, smiling dreamily as she followed me and Meg out of the store. Jack and Peter were standing in front of a silver hybrid, appearing—as usual—just as similar as they were different. Peter was drumming his fingers against the hood. Jack had buried his face in his comic again. I squinted at the cover and leaned over to Meg.

"Vault of Evil," I murmured. "That's comforting."

"Bye, guys," Harper said, eyeing the door as though waiting for Cornell to burst through and declare his undying love for her.

Jack didn't move, but Peter waved.

We started to walk back toward the yoga studio, but Cornell did, in fact, burst through Busby's door, calling Harper's name. Hair whipping around her like a ship's sail, she turned, unable to stop herself from looking delighted. She seemed to shake herself, her face settling into a slightly unnatural reserve.

"What's up?" she asked, her face flushing the same pink as the frames of her glasses.

Meg and I backtracked toward the boys as West walked out of the store. He jerked his head, indicating that we move away from Harper and Cornell. Meg grabbed my wrist and yanked until I obeyed, moving to stand in front of the hybrid.

A bright-blue plastic bag swung from Cornell's fingers. From its depths, he withdrew the four comics he had removed from Harper's original bounty. He held them out to her with a shaky smile.

"You needed all of them," he said softly.

"Cornell," she said, gasping. "You didn't have to . . ."

He grinned. "I know. But I wanted to."

Meg made an involuntary sound, somewhere between cooing and moaning in jealousy.

"Dear God," Jack grumbled into his comic. "Someone let me into the car."

Peter shoved him, but Harper and Cornell didn't seem to notice that any of us were standing barely six feet away from them. Harper was staring up at him with wide eyes like a cartoon rabbit about to be trampled. She took the books, hugging them to her chest without looking away from him once.

I glanced over at West, who seemed vaguely queasy at the proceedings.

"Okay," I muttered. "You were right."

He quirked an eyebrow, glancing at me sidelong. "Usually. But about what in particular?"

I jerked my head to indicate Cornell and Harper's saccharine expressions. It was as though an invisible hand had cranked up their adorable quotient to the breaking point.

"Triplets," I said simply.

West snorted and I was momentarily afraid that the pressure would suck his mustache right up his nose. "I think we have progressed into sextuplets."

"You always go one too far." I sighed. "That was a cheap pun."

"All puns are cheap," he said. "It's still accurate."

"We could attempt to distract them," I offered. "I bet if I ripped that thing off your face, they'd mellow out."

His hand flew up to his face protectively. He seemed to realize that I'd found the chink in his armor and he glowered at me as he smoothed his fingertips over his whiskers.

"I'll be working for the first half," Cornell was saying to Harper. "But maybe we could meet up after I'm done?"

"That would be—" Harper faltered, unable to access the thesaurus that lived inside of that massive brain of hers. I guessed it would be difficult to find a word that encapsulated all of her dreams coming true. She settled on, "Wonderful."

"Yeah?" Cornell exhaled a shocked laugh through a toothy grin. "Great. I'll um . . ."

"See you tomorrow," Ben prompted.

The moment ended like it'd been doused in ice water. Harper and Cornell scuttled away from each other, registering that they were being watched by five other people.

"Nothing ruins a tender moment faster than the dulcet braying of Benedick West," I said.

West whirled on me. "It's Benedict, Dr. Freud."

"Is it?" I tapped my chin with my index finger, scrunching my forehead as I pretended to think about this. "I could have sworn it was Benedick."

"It was in sixth grade." Peter chuckled.

"Have you sunk so low?" West asked. He was doing his best to remain cavalier, but I could see that the renaissance of the school yard nickname was starting to creep under his skin. I didn't go in for DC analogies, but it was kryptonite, pure and simple. "What's next? You want to find a set of monkey bars? I'd gladly throw you over—"

My hand shot out and two fingers wrapped around the edge of his mustache. I yanked, just once. He yowled like a jungle cat and staggered away from me.

"Hmm," Meg said. "It is real."

I nodded. "Who knew, right?"

"Of course it's real," West snarled, stretching his face as he rubbed the injured portion. "God, you miserable harpy. I haven't reached out and grabbed your—"

"If you make one more comment about my chest," I said, brandishing a threatening finger, "so help me, West, I will end you."

Peter slid his cell phone out of his pocket and consulted it thoughtfully. "Five minutes. That's a new record for you guys."

"It was four minutes too long," West said. He glared at Cornell. "Geronimo, dude."

"Yes," I agreed, taking Meg's elbow and giving her an indelicate shove forward. "Let's go."

"Finally," Jack said to no one in particular.

Cornell reached into his pocket and withdrew a set of keys. He pushed a button and the silver hybrid's doors unlocked with an electronic whirr. Jack and West threw themselves inside without another word. Peter waved again before sliding into the backseat.

Harper, failing at concealing the crestfallen set of her mouth, gave a single sad cluck. Cornell smiled at her, rocked forward on the balls of his feet for a second as he debated following through on some kind of physical contact. He thought better of it and retreated toward the car, bidding all of us a fond farewell.

Two chickens in love.

Meg and I walked arm in arm with Harper shuffling behind us. We silently climbed into the car and buckled our seat belts. Three plastic bags rustled as they were set on the floor and shoved into backpacks. Harper was taking shallow breaths in through her nose, her hand hovering over the ignition.

"So," I said, wedging my tongue into my cheek. "Slurpees? The park? Or should we just hightail it to the fabric store so I can start sewing your wedding dress?"

"Oh my God, Harper!" Meg strained against her seat belt and shook Harper's seat with both hands. "Oh my God! Oh my Superman, Sandman, and Thor!"

"Multiple pantheons, even." I giggled.

Harper closed her eyes, biting down hard on her lower lip. Her jaw was trembling. For a minute, I was terrified that she was going to dissolve into tears. It'd been so long since I'd seen her cry that I couldn't really tell the signs anymore.

"Harper?" Meg asked, tapping on the back of the driver's seat again. "Hello? Harper?"

Harper opened her mouth. A breath of air went in silently and then a squeal rushed out. Her arms flailed against the steering wheel and her feet stomped a hollow report against the floor. Her hair flew around her face until even her freckles seemed to vibrate. It was the battle cry of the newly not-single nerd girl, the polar opposite of every furtive sigh she'd sacrificed to the altar of unrequited love for the last three years.

Meg bounced in the backseat, giggling uncontrollably as I bent over laughing. Harper came back to herself, staring blindly ahead at the yoga studio, where the dozen contorted sweaty people squinted back in horror. She adjusted her glasses.

"I am going to the harvest festival with Cornell Aaron," she said tremulously. "He bought me comic books. I don't think I can even read them. Okay, no, that's crazy. I'm totally going to read them. But that does not diminish the fact that he bought me comics."

"I know!" Meg crowed.

"The festival isn't for another week, though," I said, carefully trying to avoid pricking the bubble of joy that had filled the car.

Harper turned to me. Her face was alight. "Then we have time to put together costumes. I know that you have a ton of homework, Trix, but can we please go to the fabric store and start picking out patterns?"

"Sure. I finished *Anna Karenina,* so I'm ahead of the game. I can bust out all three of our costumes over the weekend."

"Thank you," she said, running her fingertips over the steering wheel before she turned over the engine. "Thank you so much. I'll pay for the fabric and keep you in Slurpees every day from now until forever—"

I interrupted her with a laugh. "It's okay. Find a way to keep me and West as far away from each other as possible and everything will be peachy."

"He's not that bad," Meg said. "Ben, I mean. You guys managed to have a fairly civil conversation while Harper and Cornell were talking. You were the one who decided to try to rip off his mustache."

"I tested a hypothesis," I said. "Turns out the mustache is real. Come on. We were all wondering about it."

Harper waved an unconcerned hand, too flush with girly joy to be bothered with chastising me. "Stay close to Peter. He's a good buffer."

"It is his civic duty as our president to maintain domestic peace," I said.

Harper made a vague sound of assent, watching the road with a goofy grin. I could almost see the big Valentine hearts swimming in her pupils.

"We've lost her," I said to Meg.

"Oh yeah." She nodded. "It's okay. Now no one will roll their eyes when we point out that DC is a vastly inferior brand—"

"June 1938," Harper said into the rearview mirror. "Action comics number one. The introduction of Superman. Detective comics number twenty-seven, May 1939, the introduction of Batman. And when, pray tell, was the first Marvel comic released?"

Meg lifted her chin, twirling her hand in the air. "The Human Torch. October 1939."

"And there is your answer. Marvel is completely derivative," Harper said. "DC invented the superhero and then Marvel came along like it was their idea—"

Well, maybe she wasn't completely lost.

Not that I was going to let that dig against Marvel stand.

Harper [8:03 PM]

I don't think I've stopped smiling. Am I broken?

Me [8:05 PM]

Yes.

✯ 5 ✯

Anyone who says that uniforms mean you don't have to think about what you wear to school is a filthy liar. It wasn't quite cold enough yet to have to worry about whether to wear a pullover sweater or a cardigan, but there was still the endless supply of khaki pants, skirts, and shorts to thumb through. I thought about how much worse things must have been for Harper that morning. She would be standing in her bedroom across town, trying on polo after polo trying to find the perfect collar to match her mushy smile.

I snickered to myself at the thought and grabbed the closest pair of long khaki shorts in the name of soaking up the last few days of summer. I took a moment to daydream about a world where I could walk into school in jeans. Soft, stretchy jeans and shoes that were not made of patent leather.

College, I mused as I wandered into the bathroom, would be wonderful if for no other reason than getting to look like myself every day. I had a dresser teeming with beautiful, barely worn T-shirts. As much as I wanted to go to a good college and devote myself entirely to whatever major I decided on, I really just wanted to escape the Mess and be the kind of girl who came to class in a Princess

Peach shirt and still managed to decimate everyone in an argument about Kierkegaard. Because that's the girl that I was in my head. Proudly geeky, not only about comics or sci-fi but about everything I loved.

I patted the remnants of face wash from my cheeks with a fluffy white towel and wrinkled my nose at my reflection. I wasn't adorable like Meg or a lost Disney princess like Harper or elegant like Mary-Anne France. I had brown hair and overcast eyes and small lips. Nothing particularly exciting unless you counted my being two inches above the national average height for Caucasian women.

The elastic band holding my ponytail slipped down. I grabbed two ends of my hair and yanked until I felt the ponytail secure itself to the base of my skull. It was shameful to be dissecting my own appearance. I blamed Cornell Aaron and the way he stared at Harper, as though he'd picked her out of a claw machine and couldn't believe his luck. I wasn't jealous, exactly. I certainly had no designs on Cornell for myself. He was a nice guy and good-looking, but nothing like the vague idea I had in mind for a male companion.

But that was the problem. Harper only wanted Cornell. Meg only wanted to see what the hype was about without letting her limbic system get the best of her. And I didn't really want anything. Not anything concrete. I didn't want to waste my time. I didn't want someone who wouldn't understand when I referenced Tony Stark, Mal Reynolds, and Alexander Hamilton in the same breath—all handsome rogues, obviously. I wanted someone who didn't need me to backtrack and explain everything. Someone who would escort me to midnight showings but never ask me to dress up to attend. Someone who knew that I always, always, always wanted a Slurpee, but especially when it was snowing.

A boyfriend, I concluded, should be like a new best friend. Which didn't help me at all considering I hadn't made a new best friend since I was eight and Meg transferred to Aragon. Even in a world full of people as smart as I was, there weren't that many people I wanted on my team.

I pushed the thought away. It didn't do any good to spend too much time dwelling on it. I was content to be a singular kind of person, to focus on comics and homework and surviving senior year. If I went the way of Harper and Meg and started prematurely melting down about the harvest festival or the spring fling or any of the other Messina Academy social events, our group would undoubtedly explode in an array of hormones and prom dresses. I had to hold down the sanity quadrant.

And yet, a prickle of wistfulness crept across my shoulders like the feeling of trying to remember the details of a dream that remained elusive. It lasted throughout my walk to school. I tried to shake myself like an Etch A Sketch, but the feeling persisted, fraying my patience. Maybe Harper's and Meg's boyfriend-centric insanity had started the same way. Had they gone to bed normal and woken up unable to think about anything else? Perhaps it was a communicable disease and I'd spent too long being infected by their chatter.

The Mess came into view, a blooming series of brick buildings half-hidden behind the open wrought iron gate. I sat on a planter box near the gate, my Mary Janes sinking into the immaculately cut grass. I flipped open the front of my bag and pulled out my sunglasses and the *Buffy* comic. Scanning pages, I finally found the point where I'd left off the night before and started reading.

"You haven't finished it yet?"

Ben West had moved out of a line of other Mess kids and was leaning against the planter a few feet away from me. His polo was wrinkled and he hadn't brushed his hair. I glared at him for a second and then turned my attention back to the comic.

"No spoilers," I said.

"Ah," he said, staring at the groups of incoming classmates. "So, you haven't reached the point where Xander dies?"

"Damn it, West." The glossy pages gave a pathetic crinkle as I closed the book.

He laughed loudly. "Kidding. Don't freak out."

"Why don't you leave me alone?" I growled at him. "There is absolutely no reason for us to ever have a conversation."

He gave me a sardonic look out of the corner of his eye as he reached up and twirled the end of his mustache.

"I was just trying to uphold the school ordinance," he said. "Everyone is required to try to be pleasant to you in the name of making you seem like less of a dangerous loner."

"Go to hell," I said with a groan, stuffing the comic into my bag. "Or whatever hellish dimension you prefer."

"I'm partial to the world without shrimp. I'm allergic."

"Name the episode or stop sullying my fandom," I said. There really should have been a rule about unworthy jerks making *Buffy the Vampire Slayer* references. I shoved my sunglasses farther up my nose.

"'Superstar.' Season four, episode seventeen," he said drily. "You're extra shrewish today. Did your friends finally realize that they could do better?"

"Did yours?" I asked, turning to look at him dead-on. "Why are you skulking around alone?"

He gestured vaguely to the front gate. "Waiting for the guys."

"Then wait with your mouth shut."

Someone called my name and I spotted Meg bobbing toward us, her shiny black hair leaping around her cheeks. She landed in the grass faintly out of breath.

"Good morning, Trix," she said. She gave West a confused wave. "And Ben West."

"Margaret Royama," he said, inclining his head.

"You guys aren't going to, like, duel or something, are you?" Meg asked me, cocking her head.

"I submitted the challenge years ago," I said blandly. "But appealing to his sense of honor is useless."

"We're divvying up hell dimensions," West said. "Trix is taking the world that's nothing but shrimp."

"But you don't eat meat," Meg said, blinking at me. She brightened suddenly and said, "Oh! Did you guys read the new *Buffy*? Isn't it cool when—"

"No spoilers," I huffed, holding up a staying hand.

"Beatrice is a little behind," West said in a loud whisper. "There were some very big words in this issue."

"I have some very short words for you, West. Shut your damn mouth, for a start." Taking in a deep breath, I turned to Meg. "I was up late starting our costumes."

"Oh," she said. "That's okay, then."

"What will you be dressing up as this year?" West asked me. "Something with a mask, I hope?"

"Maleficent," I ground out.

"Ah." He paused. "So, just scraping off your makeup and going in your true form."

"Perhaps you could follow suit and put on a pair of donkey ears."

"Oh look," Meg interrupted with false cheeriness. "Peter and Jack are here."

The Donnelly brothers were, in fact, walking toward us. Jack sped ahead of Peter, leaving his brother limping behind as he rushed through the gate without a backward glance.

"Asshole," I breathed.

West nodded in pleasantly mute agreement as he stepped forward. He and Peter clasped each other's forearms in greeting like a pair of Roman soldiers in white cotton polos.

"Good morning, Mr. President," I said.

"Hey, Trix, Meg." Peter grinned, casting around for a second. "No sign of Harper and Cornell?"

"Not yet," I said.

"The poor saps are probably off somewhere gazing deeply into each other's eyes," West muttered. He stared off into the parking lot as wistful wind played at the corners of his mustache. "At least with Cornell distracted with composing sonnets I've got a chance of getting valedictorian."

Meg looked appalled. I'm sure I did, too, but only because I hated hearing my own secret desire to up my place in the ranking coming out of Ben West's mouth.

Peter laughed, ever the picture of amiability. "Whatever keeps you from getting in their way, Ben."

West's mouth twisted into an unconcerned smile. "I told him that if he let his guard down, I'd sweep him. I'm not going to get distracted by some chick."

"And all of the chicks on Earth thank you kindly for that," I said. "What could be worse than being courted by that mustache? You could start prospecting for gold any minute."

He flushed to a pernicious shade of scarlet. "You really should examine your obsession with my facial hair, Trix. It's becoming a problem for you."

"It seems wise to keep an eye on anything that could gain sentience and go on a killing spree," I said, peering at him over the tops of my sunglasses. "It wouldn't be difficult for it to surpass your diminutive IQ."

"Hey," Peter said, dragging the syllable out into a heavy warning. He glanced around for eavesdroppers before lowering his voice. "The gag rule."

"Eff the gag rule," West snarled. He took a threatening step toward me. "You want to throw down numbers, girly? We aren't on campus yet. Let's do this."

"We're on school property," Meg squeaked. She shuffled her feet against the grass in a sort of manic jig. "See? Official Messina Academy grass. Our tuition pays the landscapers."

"No," I said, jumping off the planter. "We've been dancing around this for years. Go ahead, West. Inflate your IQ points to try to win this once and for all."

"I'll tell the truth if you will, Beatrice," he growled.

"The IQ test really isn't a reliable test of intelligence," Peter said imploringly. "That's why the entrance exam is so long. It measures more than the standard—"

"Meg, count to three for us," I said.

"I knew this was going to turn into a duel," Meg whimpered. "You could both be suspended for this, you know."

Peter scrubbed a hand over his forehead, mussing his hair. "I really shouldn't be a part of this. Ben, you could lose your seat on student council—"

"Worth it," West barked, not taking his eyes off me. "Meg, count us off."

"Okay," she sighed. She gave Peter an apologetic frown. "Unos, duo . . . tres."

"One hundred and seventy-eight."

I paused at the sound of the echo. My voice had never been on the dulcet side of things, but I was sure that I hadn't woken up as a baritone. I tilted my head at West, who looked as though he'd been slapped.

Peter and Meg stared at us in abject horror. I reached up and pulled my sunglasses off, squinting through the sunlight.

"You're a damn liar," I said.

He slapped a hand to his chest. "I'm the liar? There is no way—"

"You have the exact same IQ," Meg breathed, holding onto her cheeks.

"That explains some things," Peter murmured.

There was absolutely no way that it was true. What were the chances of having the exact same score? It defied imagination. I doubted that even our old statistical anomaly teacher could have given us the odds on it.

"It explains nothing," I said. "Because it can't be true. West is just a—"

"A what?" He laughed, but there was no color in his face. "We're at the Mess, not Hogwarts. I'm not a gorram wizard."

Blistering heat rose to my cheeks. I clenched my hands into fists. "Then you snuck a look at my file or—"

Cornell appeared out of the crowd moving toward the front gate, holding onto the straps of his backpack as he approached us. He frowned. "What's going on?"

"Nerd duel," Meg answered. "Where's Harper?"

"I thought she'd be here with you guys." His frown deepened and he rubbed a hand over his shorn scalp. "What's a nerd duel? I don't see any Magic cards or polyhedral dice."

"The gag rule," Peter said.

"Oh." He swung his head to look at me and West. "Who won?"

"It's a draw," West said numbly.

My brain was lagging, as though the proceedings had somehow shorted a circuit in my head. I had never assumed that I had the highest IQ on campus, far from it. I was above average, but not in the mad-genius range of 190 or above. And there was no logical way for Ben West to have hacked into my file. The only answer was the most impossible—we were exactly the same.

I walked away without a word, unable to endure everyone staring at me for another minute. I heard footsteps behind me and assumed it was Meg, but as I climbed the steps toward the front door, I saw West's face reflected in the window. He followed me silently into the American Immigrant classroom. We sat down in our usual seats, feigning ignorance of each other's continued existence.

I took out my binder and set it down on my desk, going over the previous day's notes in case Mr. Cline decided to spring a quiz on us. After a few minutes, Harper slid into the empty seat next to me. As I'd expected, she was more coiffed than usual. Her hair was pulled back with a handmade Batman logo headband and she smelled vaguely of raspberries.

I glanced over at her. She gave me a tentative smile that plainly said that someone had updated her on the results of the nerd duel. Cornell skulking to his seat and folding his hands guiltily on his desk confirmed this suspicion.

"Don't," I grumbled, turning back to my notes.

"I had no plans to," she said lightly.

"Uh-huh." I reached into my bag and extended the *Buffy* comic across the aisle to her. "Take it and swallow your gloating."

She took the comic and tucked it into the pocket of one of the many folders in her binder. "I'm not gloating. Just thinking."

I rolled my eyes and did not ask her to elaborate. Whether she was thinking about Cornell or the best way to force me to keep my mouth shut, I didn't need to know.

For the first time, I was thankful for the Mess staff's undying love of pop quizzes and spur-of-the-moment essays. There was very little time to dwell on my morning when I was digging through my notes on the national debt of Zambia and struggling to remember the metaphorical significance of the train in *Anna Karenina*.

Of course, after I was excused from Russian Literature, I faced the long walk across campus to the cafeteria. Alone with my thoughts for the first time in hours, I considered the events of the nerd duel. Now that the shock had mostly worn off, I was left with an unshakeable determination. More than ever, I wanted to crush Benedict West. Now I knew that beating him in the ranking would be a true victory. We'd grown up in the same town. We'd had the exact same education. And, apparently, we had the exact same IQ, give or take an unknown decimal.

This was so much bigger than the monkey bars. This was the Rebels versus the Empire. This was the Doctor versus the Daleks. This was Ripley versus the Xenomorphs.

This was a real, true, full-scale war.

With the strap of my messenger bag slung across my chest, I slipped my sunglasses on and stepped into the open-air quad in the center of campus. Dozens of other students were zigzagging across the mosaic *M* emblazoned into the concrete, some scurrying out of the chemistry labs, some heading toward the library for lunchtime studying.

I spotted Kenneth Pollack shoving a small dark-haired boy against one of the many decorative sycamore trees that dotted the edges of the quad. The smaller boy went rigid as Kenneth's hands braced into his shoulders. There was a rolling backpack toppled on the ground beside them.

Swerving slightly, I moved toward them. Hazing was, of course, forbidden at the Mess, but that didn't mean that meatheads like Kenneth didn't occasionally rough up the freshmen. As my shoes tread against the grass, the frosh made a pathetic whimper of dissent, his round face pinched.

"I didn't," the frosh protested. "I don't even know—"

"Kenny," I said, coming up behind them. There were only about a hundred people in our class and Kenneth had gone to Aragon with us, so I was fairly sure he at least knew who I was. "Isn't it a little hack to push around the freshmen? It's so expected."

If we'd had a football team—instead of basketball, cricket, and chess—Kenneth would have been a linebacker. As it was, he'd taken Peter's place on the basketball team, but he lacked the natural grace that the sport required.

"He told Cline that I cheated," he snarled at me.

"I don't know who that is," the frosh protested, remaining against the tree as though he hadn't realized he'd been released. "I don't even know my lunch number."

"Kenneth," I said, resting my elbow on top of my bag. "Cline doesn't have any contact with the lowerclassmen. He doesn't even have office hours this year. He went back to teaching poetry at the university."

"The email came from this kid's account," Kenneth blustered. His cheeks were blistered with impotent fury, pushing a whitehead on his chin into the foreground. "B. Calistero at Messina Academy. There aren't any other Calisteros on campus."

"We have school email?" B. Calistero asked.

"How do you know he sent the email?" I asked Kenneth. "Cline wouldn't have told you."

"I just know," Kenneth said darkly. "He emailed Cline and said I copied Mike Shepherd's Ellis Island essay. They're threatening to bench me."

Of course his outrage was unrelated to the sullying of his academic record—a mark of cheating would almost undoubtedly revoke any incoming college acceptances. No, it all came down to basketball. Why did his parents even bother writing his tuition checks?

"B. Calistero," I said, peering over Kenneth's shoulder at the frosh. "Can you name the gentleman who introduced the back of your skull to that tree trunk?"

The frosh's eyes were wide and raced between me and Kenneth as though trying to figure out which of us was more likely to hurt him in the event that he gave the wrong answer.

"I don't," he spluttered. "I mean, this is only my second week here. I was in public school before and—"

"It's okay," I said, mostly to keep him from vomiting down the front of his polo. I looked back at Kenneth. "See? He doesn't know anything. And the freshmen are still turning in hard copies of all of their homework."

"So?" Kenneth asked.

"So he doesn't know who you are and he hasn't touched his shiny new email account," I said, a tad exasperated. Honestly, sometimes talking to my classmates made me wonder how useful the entrance exam was. "Someone probably hacked him as some kind of start-of-term prank. We are at a school for geniuses. Stuff happens."

Kenneth considered this, his forehead indenting around a smattering of zits.

"But who would have done it?" he asked finally.

"How should I know? I'm no Veronica Mars."

He stared at me with vacant, glassy eyes.

"She's a detective on TV. And there was a movie," blurted the frosh. And then, in a much smaller voice, "The movie was really good. . . ."

I offered him a grateful smile. "Thanks, sport. Now, run and be free."

He bobbed his head to me, scrambling to grab the handle of his rolling backpack. It leapt behind him as he charged toward the cafeteria. Kenneth watched him go.

"But I still don't know who told Cline I cheated," he said with a smidge of petulant whine lurking underneath.

"Did you cheat?" I asked.

He blew a raspberry of disdain. "No. And even if I had, it wouldn't have been off of Shepherd. He's an idiot."

"Well. Best of luck to you. Try to stop roughing up the newbs. They're delicate."

"Whatever," he grunted. "Put a few of them in line and the rest will learn not to screw with their betters."

Gee whiz, why was it so hard to find a suitable male companion when there were gems like Kenneth around?

"Wow. You would have been a swell slave owner."

I turned on my heel and walked into the cafeteria, where I promptly put together a spinach-and-egg salad. I found Harper and Meg whispering together at our usual table, tucked into the corner as far away from the door as possible to keep from being interrupted by traffic.

I set my tray down across from Harper, doing my absolute best to ignore how she and Meg had stopped speaking at the sight of me. I was sure that they'd been discussing the nerd duel and I had no intention of prompting them to continue.

"Why, Miss Harper Leonard," I said, cracking open a can of cola. "I didn't expect to find you here. Shouldn't you be claiming your position as the senior class's Second Lady?"

Meg tittered into a potato chip. "Does she count as the Second Lady if Peter's still single? I mean, if the president doesn't have a First Lady, doesn't that automatically make her First? There isn't any precedent for it in history. James Buchanan used his niece."

I laughed. "Maybe we could vote on an incumbent if Harper isn't feeling up to the job."

Harper couldn't stop herself from giving her glasses a telltale adjustment of embarrassment. "We're just going to the harvest festival together. It's not like he's my boyfriend now."

"Well, there hasn't been enough time for him to pin you." I smirked.

"I've never considered how dirty that sounds." Meg giggled. "Pinning."

"We don't have pins," Harper said.

"Oh, we could find some pins." I said. "If that's what it takes to get this show on the road."

"Again," Meg said with a snicker. "Dirty."

"Anyway," Harper said loudly. She gestured to my heaping plate of greens. "What kept you?"

"Oh, I had to stop Kenneth Pollack from braining some frosh. Nothing particularly interesting." I paused and took a bite of salad. "Explain to me again why you didn't go sit with Cornell when you got here? He bought you comics yesterday."

"Four comics." Meg nodded. "That's totally like a dowry's worth of comics."

Harper pushed a pizza crust around her plate with her index finger, letting it slide through a smear of orange grease.

"Because," she said, "I'm not his girlfriend. And the student council is starting to plan the winter ball."

I caught a piece of spinach as it tried to escape my lips and shoved it back in. "The what?"

Meg's face lit up like a kid on Christmas who descended the stairs to find a unicorn sitting next to the tree. "You haven't heard?"

I raised my eyebrows at her. "I've had three pop quizzes today, so unless this winter ball is being thrown by Tolstoy or the struggling people of Yemen, no. I don't know anything about it. Aren't we still waiting for the harvest festival?"

"Yes," Harper said. She also seemed to be dangerously excited about this news but was holding it back better than Meg. "But you know how there's a lull between the harvest festival and the spring fling?"

"The lull known as finals?" I asked.

"Right," Meg said. She braced her hands on the table and leaned toward me. "They're adding a third dance this year."

"Why?" I asked.

In the name of us having a "normal" high school experience, the Mess allowed us to have the spring fling and the prom. The spring fling was more of a sock hop—no formal wear, lots of punch. Meg, Harper, and I usually went to it as it was more group dancing and less requiring of a date than the prom. We'd spent junior prom eating candy and having a movie marathon in my bedroom.

"It'll be more like prom than the spring fling," Meg said, hurt by my lack of enthusiasm. "It's formal, but it'll be here on campus instead of at the fancy ballroom downtown."

"And there's going to be a live band," Harper added.

"Do you think they know the Electric Slide?" I asked between bites.

Harper and Meg exchanged an unamused glance. I could feel their combined excitement for this exercise in torture pounding against my temples. Or maybe that was a stress migraine.

I allowed myself ten seconds of mental cursing and temper tantrum throwing before I said, "You're going."

"Of course we are," Meg said. "It's an important school event. We went to basketball games."

"And stopped," I said.

"The tickets won't be that expensive," Harper said. "When Noni was telling me about it in Latin, she said that it wouldn't be more than twenty-five apiece."

"Do you have any idea what I could do with the money I'd be wasting on a prom dress?" I asked, lowering my fork. "I could buy my *Doctor Who* figur—"

"Trixie," Meg interrupted. "This is our senior year. Wouldn't it be nice to have one night where you got dressed up and—"

"And?" I asked, turning on her swiftly. "What am I going to experience at some dance that I can't feel right here in my uniform? I will go to the harvest festival because I like costumes and kettle corn, but there's no way you two are going to talk me into going to a ball."

"Okay," Harper said, cutting across Meg, who was primed to keep arguing. "Really. We won't hassle you about it, Trix. It just seemed like it might be a nice thing for the three of us to do together."

But it wouldn't have been the three of us. None of us had to say it, but we all knew. Harper would go with Cornell and be crowned the snow queen or whatever the winter ball award for prettiest couple was. Meg would undoubtedly find someone to go with her and have him running off to get punch whenever she got bored of talking to him. And I would sit at a table—probably the same table we were currently occupying—reading a book that was small enough to fit into a handbag. I could feel humiliation cropping up in my throat just thinking about it.

"It's not until the end of term," Meg said. "And we still have the harvest festival next week."

I massaged my aching head and took another sip of cola in the hope that the caffeine would work some kind of magic and turn my day around.

"I should have the costumes done by Sunday," I said. "Do you want to come by and do a fitting? We could watch the *Battlestar Galactica* miniseries again."

The girls agreed. Meg asked for advice on an essay she needed to write on *Jude the Obscure,* complaining that she couldn't even think about the title without starting to hum the Beatles. Harper sent sigh-laden glances over her shoulder at the table where Cornell pretended to not be doing the same thing. Equilibrium seemed to be restored.

But I wasn't dumb enough to expect it to last.

Harper   [9:03 PM]

It's going to be cold that night. Should I wear tights? It's not a canonized part of the costume . . .

Me   [9:05 PM]

Doesn't Supergirl normally go around with her stomach showing?

Harper   [9:06 PM]

I think Meg will be naked enough for all of us.

Me   [9:08 PM]

Then you've answered your own question. Buy tights.

Harper   [9:08 PM]

What about contacts?

Me   [9:09 PM]

You hate them and they hurt your eyes.

Harper   [9:10 PM]

But Kara Zor-El doesn't wear glasses!

Me   [9:11 PM]

Okay. Buy contacts. I'll just cut the midriff off of your top real quick . . .

Harper   [9:14 PM]

Fine. No contacts.

✴ 6 ✴

The week of the harvest festival, no one talked about anything else. During lunch, Harper, Meg, and I watched as Jack Donnelly begrudgingly climbed a ladder and strung fake cobwebs from the rafters. Mary-Anne France flounced around the quad, pinning up orange-and-black glittery signs that listed the price of admission, a herd of junior officers following behind her holding tape. Peter cheerfully greeted the lowerclassmen in the halls with his most presidential wave and fist bumps as he declared that the festival was the must-see event of the year.

I had to admit that I was excited. In exchange for using my bedroom as a sweatshop, Meg had handcrafted my headpiece. It was sleek and black with massive curved horns attached to a hood that meant I wouldn't have to worry about my hair. I'd strapped it onto my Iron Man pillow and propped it on my desk so that I could admire it while I was doing homework.

Harper and Cornell provided hours of entertainment on campus by being the most awkward noncouple of all time. They continually checked in with each other to make sure they were still meeting up at the harvest festival. Cornell would pass our table in the cafeteria and say, "See you Friday?" And Harper would try to look composed and say, "Yeah?" as though they were not literally seeing one another in the present.

"You don't understand," she groaned at me the day before the festival. "It's weird."

"Oh no," I said, giggling with Meg. "I understand that it's weird. I am ensconced in the weird. Why don't you go ask if he needs help putting up the decorations or something?"

"I could use some help," Ben West said, appearing next to our table with an armful of what appeared to be plain black trash bags. "My frosh disappeared."

"Move along, Grizzly Adams," I said without looking up.

One of the bags slipped from between his arms and fell to the floor. Harper leaned over and handed it back to him.

"Many thanks," he said, tossing the bag back onto the stack.

"You have your own frosh?" Meg asked, glancing around the caf as though she could spot a miniature West somewhere.

His mustache gave a mocking twitch as he hoisted the bags higher in his arms. "All of the officers do. We have to show them the ropes."

"What is it you do on student council anyway?" I asked. "Just haul the trash bags?"

He glared down at me. "I'm the treasurer."

"Really?" I turned to Meg and Harper. "Did we vote for him?"

"I think so," Meg said. "It was him or Mike Shepherd."

I tapped my chin thoughtfully. "Yeah, I'm sure I voted for Mike. Who knows what kind of accounting failures West could be responsible for. By the time we graduate, our budget will look like Somalia's."

West gave an unconcerned shrug and said, "Yo-ho-ho."

Before I had a chance to point out that references to Somali pirates were completely in poor taste, a small figure similarly dwarfed in trash bags streaked across the cafeteria to our table. I could barely make out the face hidden under the black polypropylene.

"Sorry, Ben," the frosh squeaked. "I dropped all of them outside and—"

Lowering the bags away from his face, I could see the frosh's stricken expression. It made him look remarkably like a Jack Russell terrier, which made it easier to recognize him.

"B. Calistero." I grinned. "You've survived another week at the Mess! Congratulations."

West looked around at us, his jaw set in such a way that I could tell he did not like that I knew his minion. Harper and Meg turned to me in surprise. I didn't often befriend the freshmen. Or anyone.

"Meg, Harper, this is the frosh I stopped Kenneth from maiming," I said, gesturing to the pile of bags in front of the frosh's face.

"Nice to meet you, froshling," piped Meg.

"I'm Brandon," said the tiny frosh. "Freshman class treasurer."

West tucked his chin back in horror, turning his body to stare down his helper. Brandon cowered slightly, taking one step of rearward retreat.

"The hot girl who saved you was Trixie Watson?" West asked, his voice heavy with disgust. "They had to take her entry out of the last D&D Monster Manual. Illustrators kept dying trying to capture her essence."

I felt myself flush in embarrassment and tried to shove the feeling aside. It was just as flattering to be referred to as a hot girl as it was horrifying to have West discredit the statement.

"Oh, suck it, West," I said, too preoccupied to think of something more clever.

"Wow, Trix." He guffawed. "That's all you've got?"

I rolled my eyes. "Suck it, you loquacious loser. Or would you prefer I think of something referring to the fact that your mother left you and started a new family on the other side of the country?"

Ah. A hit. A palpable hit.

It was Meg's comment about the treasurer race that had brought back the memory of the end of junior year. The quad had been wallpapered in campaign posters. Mike Shepherd had stood directly in the center of the *M* mosaic, screaming. It was easy to forget that Mike was a big guy. He was normally so docile, a gentle giant. Like Fezzik in *The Princess Bride,* only blond and pimply. But he'd lost it in the middle of a hot summer lunch period and started tearing down West's posters left and right. The rest of the role-playing club had tried to stop him, begging him to remember that he and West were friends.

"He's not my friend," Mike raged. "He's a loser. His own mother moved to the other side of the country to get away from him. She replaced him with a new baby. I can replace him, too."

Mike got a week's worth of detention. West had won the sympathy vote.

I wouldn't normally use the information to my advantage, but I was feeling a little stab happy after the dig at my appearance. West had set the tone of this exchange. I'd just matched him.

In stereo, Harper and Meg sucked in pained gasps. West's back straightened and his arms braced painfully against his stack of trash bags. He jerked his head to Brandon and stormed off across the cafeteria.

"Bye, B," I called after the frosh. "Don't forget to be awesome!"

Brandon stumbled and stammered, "Bye, Trixie!" before scampering after West's long strides.

Harper watched them go, a small frown appearing in the corner of her mouth. She turned back to me. "Is that the first time you've spoken since the nerd duel?"

"No," I said.

Admittedly, the nerd duel had become a kind of stalemate between us. For at least two days afterward, we had tacitly ignored each other altogether. But at some point he'd made a snide comment to me in the hall and I'd called him Benedick again.

"Don't look so tense about it," I said to Harper. "I promise not to do anything to destroy the fragile construct that is your relationship with your not-boyfriend. Even if he does have poor taste in friends."

Harper's mouth fell open. She struggled for a minute before managing to say, "I wasn't worried about—"

"Yes, you were," Meg hummed.

Harper's shoulders slumped. "Okay, maybe I was a little worried. I just want tomorrow night to be—"

"Magical?" I offered, failing at concealing a grin. "Would you like me to accidentally trap you in a supply closet?"

"No," she said firmly.

"Please give up the supply closet idea," Meg begged me. "It's really never going to work."

"Fine," I said with an exaggerated flip of my ponytail. "I'm just looking out for your future children, Cornell Jr., Cornelius, and Cornelia."

"Those are terrible names," Harper said. "Juniors are the choke chain of the patriarchy. It invalidates motherhood. I would lean more toward . . ."

She trailed off, her eyes going wide behind her glasses as Meg and I giggled. She clucked and flapped her hands at us, begging us to disregard all statements about any hypothetical children.

Meg   [5:46 AM]

I have makeup, shoes, and my crown all packed
and ready to go. What am I forgetting?

Harper   [5:52 AM]

A sweater?

Meg   [5:55 AM]

Nope. My ticket money. Oops. That would be
embarrassing.

Me   [6:07 AM]

I *shiver* to think. Ha ha ha.

✸ 7 ✸

From the outside, the Mess didn't look much different than it had when the last bell had rung. It remained stately and undecorated, blocking out most of the sunset with its looming buildings and shadowy front gate. There were people in costumes everywhere, clustered together in tight groups. I was sure anyone driving past was wondering how the genius kids had managed to get the date of Halloween wrong by almost a month. Or maybe everyone was used to us being superweird all the time.

Meg's high heels sounded like coconut shells clattering together against the pavement. It was like being followed by a *Monty Python* sketch. She and Harper clung to one another as we passed through the gate and hit a long line. We stood behind two sophomore girls I didn't recognize, both of them dressed in blatantly store-bought witch costumes.

Meg was bouncing slightly in place, although whether it was from anticipation or the rapidly cooling evening air, I wasn't entirely sure.

"Stop it," Harper hissed at her. "You're freaking me out."

"Sorry," Meg squeaked. "It's just, you know, this is our last harvest festival."

"We still have seven and a half months of school left," I said, taking a step as the line inched forward. "Don't get all nostalgic about it yet."

Mary-Anne France was sitting behind the admission table. She wore a short blond wig and a long pink satin dress. Her matching elbow-length gloves were holding possessively onto the sides of a gray metal cash box. There were freshmen on either side of her, tearing tickets.

"Ten dollars," she said to me with a bored sigh.

I surrendered my cash.

"How did you get roped into working the cash box?" I asked.

She brushed her wig with the back of her hand, showing off a fake diamond bracelet. At least I hoped it was fake.

"It was either this or get stuck for an hour in the haunted house," she said, wrinkling the little painted mole over her lip. "And there is nothing scary about Marilyn Monroe."

"Unless you're afraid of drug addicts," I said archly.

"And presidential conspiracy theories," Harper added.

"Or the smell of Chanel," said Meg.

As usual, all attempts to be clever bounced off Mary-Anne's zit-free face. She grunted a vague "uh-huh" and gestured for the three of us to take a ticket from the nearest frosh.

The entrance hall was decked out in fake spiderwebs and cardboard skeletons with hinged joints. Someone had taped a sheet of paper over the ranking's case. In dripping red paint it read: SOMETHING WICKED THIS WAY COMES. I laughed at it as we walked out into the quad.

There were lanterns strewn in the branches of the trees, casting a hazy orange glow on the festival. There were booths set up everywhere, mostly run by lowerclassmen. Dr. Mendoza, the principal, was sitting in a wet suit at a dunk tank that had a line that wrapped around the library building. There was a booth devoted to painting tiny pumpkins where a dozen people were slopping glitter onto squash. A cheery red cart popped and sizzled with an abundance of kettle corn. There was a booth of massive beverage containers that poured steaming hot cider into paper cups.

You could say a lot against the ridiculous tuition we paid to attend the Mess, but, sometimes, we used it for awesome things.

"Oh look," Meg squealed, pointing up ahead. "There are the boys."

I started to ask who "the boys" were, but glancing in the general direction of Meg's finger, I saw Cornell and Peter sitting at a table near the haunted house. Cornell was wearing what had to be Peter's old basketball uniform, with a hairy sweater underneath and a headband with pointy ears attached. Peter was decked out in a full Buzz Lightyear ensemble, his giant forehead jutting out from under a purple felt hood.

Harper staggered a little, her hand flying to the giant *S* emblazoned on her chest. I caught her by the arm, dragging her forward before she could start making excuses or trying to redirect us to the spooky bingo booth. She gave a cluck of protest, swatting at my hand until I released her. Straightening up, she led us to the boys.

As we got closer, I noticed that their table was covered in a variety of containers. There were vases and mugs and beakers, all filled with food-coloring-stained water. I glanced up at the banner over their heads and read the words *dime toss*.

Cornell all but jumped out of his chair as we approached, a twitchy smile exposing his blindingly white teeth.

"Hey," he breathed. "You made it."

"Yeah," said Harper.

She seemed to be struggling to think of something else to say, but failed repeatedly. Peter was kind enough to bail her out, waving but remaining seated.

"Excellent costumes," he said.

Meg bobbed a curtsy, her face dimpling around the tiny heart she'd painted on her cheek in eyeliner.

"So, Mr. Lightyear," I said, sweeping a hand toward the assortment of bottles and glasses. "What do I win if I get a dime into that tiny vial in the back?"

Peter turned and laughed, spotting a vial barely large enough to count as a full dram, sparkling with silver glittery water.

"A Nobel Prize in physics," he said, chuckling.

"Damn." I tried to snap my fingers, but my gloves impeded the sound. "And here I am without any change."

Peter leaned down and retrieved a cash box that looked identical to the one at the front gate. He patted it lightly.

"Oh, we have change," he said.

I dug into the pocket of my cloak, finding a dollar and handing it over. Peter counted ten dimes into the palm of my glove and I handed half of them to Meg. The dimes flew every which way, pinging off containers but refusing to make it in.

"We're waiting for our replacements to show up," Cornell said to Harper. "The lower-classmen will run the booth for the rest of the night."

"Oh," she said brightly. "Okay. Cool."

One of Meg's dimes landed with a hearty splash in the middle of a vase. She clapped her hands triumphantly. We laughed as Peter held out a wicker basket full of dollar store toys. Meg picked out a plastic kendama, brandishing it regally.

A crowd of people poured out of the farthest chem lab and wandered over to the table, edging the girls and me out of the way and thrusting money into Peter's hand. Dimes went flying again. This crowd seemed to be having about as much luck as Meg and I had.

"You guys should check out the haunted house," Peter said to us, leaning back in his chair. "It's pretty cool this year."

Meg made a face, undoubtedly trying to figure the odds of there being a clown inside the haunted house. Her coulrophobia was downright pathological.

"Is there still dancing in the cafeteria?" she asked.

"Yeah." Cornell nodded, his wolf ears sliding forward.

Meg turned to me and Harper, her hands clasped innocently behind her back.

"No," I said. "I will definitely choose the haunted house over dancing."

"But I can't go in alone," Meg said in an incredibly loud whisper. "It's pathetic."

"Why? It's not like you care who you go in with," I said. "You just want some bozo to buy you a kettle corn."

Peter frowned and glanced around the group at the table. He spotted Brad Hertz at the next booth and flagged him over. It was odd to see Brad without Jack Donnelly and Nick Conrad. Generally, they operated in the same sort of trio that Meg, Harper, and I had, except with more grunting. Brad was dressed as a generic cowboy, his curly brown hair stuffed under a Stetson.

"What's up?" he asked Peter. "I'm not tossing any dimes tonight."

"Brad, do you know Meg?" Peter asked, gesturing to Meg.

"Since the third grade," Brad said, raising an eyebrow at Meg. "How's it going?"

She twirled her kendama awkwardly. "Fine, thanks."

"Meg was heading over to the caf," Peter explained, not looking as he picked up the toy basket and extended it to the newest winner of the dime toss.

"Oh," said Brad. He looked back at Meg. "You want me to go with?"

"You don't have to," Meg said, scuffing the toe of her shoe against the pavement with excellently feigned coquettishness.

Harper shot me a look of horror. I flicked my eyebrows at her to say, *Well, at least it's working.*

"We'll catch up with you, Meg," Harper said, uncertainly. "After the haunted house."

"Uh-huh," Meg said, too busy batting her eyelashes at Brad to bother with the rest of us. She glanced up at him shyly. "Have you had any kettle corn yet?"

"Uh, no," he said. "We could grab some?"

They wandered off, leaving the rest of us to watch in stunned silence. I swung my horns to look down at Peter.

"That was impressive," I said.

He tipped back in his chair, lacing his fingers behind his head. "It's good to be king. Or president, I guess."

"Or space commander," I said.

Harper nudged me with her shoulder. "Okay, we'll go through the haunted house and then—"

"I'll catch up with you," Cornell said.

"Great," Harper said.

"Great," Cornell agreed.

Peter coughed into his fist. It sounded a lot like the word *great*. He was saved from having to cop to it by a new group of people shoving forward to throw dimes. In the split second that Cornell was distracted making change for a dollar, I shoved Harper toward the haunted house. I'd never been a huge fan of haunted houses—or typically frightening things as a whole—but I was prepared to do anything to avoid having to stand around and watch her and Cornell make monosyllabic conversation. There wasn't even a closet for me to shove them into.

I led Harper to the math and sciences building. The door was being watched by a girl dressed in medical scrubs, splattered with fake blood.

"Don't," she whispered as we passed. "Don't."

I frowned as the door slammed closed behind us. I could hear the girl whispering the same thing to the next group of suckers and immediately remembered why I hated haunted houses. The hallway that led to the computer lab and chemistry labs was almost entirely black. There were opaque tarps covering all the doorways and windows, with bloody hands stretching against the plastic. Unseen speakers piped in the sound of heavy breathing and a rapid pulse.

One of the hands concealed in the tarp brushed against my arm and I sucked in a breath, refusing to scream, even though I could hear other people screaming all around me. Harper reached out and locked her elbow with mine. Cape and cloak swishing, we moved forward.

A spotlight turned on with a thump, blinding us for a moment as a massive shape in a doctor's coat stood in our way.

"You can't," Mike Shepherd said, his eyes wild and rimmed in purple bruise makeup. He looked like a young Uncle Fester from *The Addams Family* as he waved a rubber butcher knife at us. "The infected. They're—oh, cool costume, Harper."

"Thanks, Mike," Harper said.

He nodded approvingly and then seemed to remember that he was supposed to be in character. He rocked forward again, cleared his throat, and said, "No, the infected. Don't go any farther."

We moved around the first corner. I saw spots as my eyes tried to adjust to the sudden darkness. That insistent heartbeat pulsed through the speakers, seemingly louder here. I couldn't see anyone, but I could hear whimpering and wailing. Something reached out and brushed my leg. I tightened my grip on Harper.

It's just a frosh, I told myself sharply. *Just the fingernails of a frosh trapped in the dark. Nothing scary about a frosh. They're tiny and haven't mastered chemistry yet.*

Harper screamed and I nearly leapt out of my boots, my heart slamming against my ribs in time with the faked pulse coming through the stereo.

"What the what?" I panted, clutching my chest.

"Sorry," whispered a familiar voice. "It's Cornell."

"Oh, hi," whispered Harper.

"I'll give you guys a minute," I said. "I'll be over in this creepy stretch of utter darkness."

I shuffled to the side, accidentally kicking something on the floor that whacked my leg in protest. I muttered an apology and leaned against the wall. I could hear other people padding down the hallway, screeching and running as the unseen hands reached for them. My pulse refused to slow down, even as I closed my eyes and took in a deep breath.

"Trix?" said Harper somewhere to the left of me.

"I'm right here."

Shoes scrambled against the linoleum. There was a collective intake of breath before the sound of thuds and screams as a crowd of people collided to the ground. I couldn't discern Harper's voice in the mass. A hand grabbed my skirt. I shook it off, stumbling farther away.

"Harper?" I asked in a loud whisper. "Cornell?"

"Ow," squeaked a girl's voice. "Someone is standing on my hair."

"Who is sitting on me?"

"Someone turn on the lights."

"I don't know where any of the switches are. They left us here!"

"Where's my wig? My sister will kill me."

The fallen people continued to argue with one another, grunting as they got to their feet. Someone shoved past me and I tripped over the hem of my cloak. I couldn't continue to hang out in the dark. It was too dangerous and the thudding pulse and labored breathing soundtrack was starting to get under my skin.

I moved forward, my gloved fingertips skimming the wall until I went through a doorway. Turning a corner, I found a dimly lit room full of cardboard boxes and littered with stuffed animals. A group of people were slipping through the door on the opposite end. I paused, taking in the stacks of cardboard boxes and the collection of thrift store toys sprawled on the floor. There was a giant panda in the corner. They hadn't even bothered to throw blood on it. If the rest of the haunted house was this lazy, I'd be fine.

I walked straight through toward the open door, my eyes on the panda's stitched smile. Which is exactly why I did not notice that the teddy bear on the other side of me had a person inside. It reared forward, arms outstretched, a dozen other smaller stuffed animals moving with it in a wave. I yelped and hopped out of the way, cold sweat starting to pool under my hood. I raced through the next door.

I stood alone in what I knew was actually one of the chemistry labs. The rational part of my brain took the time to dissect the room, peeling away the wash coming in from the red lightbulbs, the chain-link fence, the black sheets of plastic and hunks of cardboard streaked with fake blood. I tried to tune out the sounds of people screaming and the static screeching of the music being pumped in. A group of gleefully scared freshman girls—all dressed like farm animals in very tiny shorts—barreled past me, holding hands. My breath caught in the back of my throat as a masked Freddy Krueger popped out from behind a stack of cardboard boxes and grabbed the frosh dressed as a mouse. She wriggled and yowled until he released her, stepping back into the shadows.

I pushed myself forward, adjusting my horns as an excuse to face forward. It would have been helpful if the haunted house crew weren't all decked out in masks. One face that I clearly recognized would have been useful in calming myself down. I couldn't be afraid of my own classmates. But dozens of rubber-faced strangers leaping out and shouting unintelligibly couldn't be reasoned with. I supposed that was kind of the point.

My intestines twisted into a terrified knot as I stepped on the foot of a boy dressed in a nylon Joker costume. He passed me, laughing with his friends as he gave a trite, "Why so serious?" And then he immediately screamed as a guy in a hockey mask stepped in front of him, brandishing a long plastic knife.

Where had Harper and Cornell left me? The hall of child murderers? What kind of messed-up crap was that?

As more people swarmed around me, pushing past as they made their merry way through this nightmare, I tucked my chin to my chest. My horns were heavy and I could feel the stupid amount of makeup I was wearing weighing down my skin. I bit back the fit of hyperventilation I knew was right around the corner, but my lungs burned. The heavy velvet of my dress trapped the panicked sweat that was sliding down my back. I flexed my hands, trying to recall what I'd learned in the Chemistry of Emotions class the year before. My sensory cortex was processing the fake blood incorrectly and viewing the masked people as attackers. My hippocampus was reminding me how much I hated scary movies. I'd hidden under a blanket when the girls and I had tried to watch *The Cabin in the Woods*. I couldn't even watch *The X-Files* with my parents. My hypothalamus was begging me to scream and run in any direction, alerting my evolutionarily similar classmates to respond to my circumstances.

Knowing this didn't help. It just meant that the purveyors of the haunted house had the same information and had found a way to cut out any loopholes. Ms. Jensen, the Emotional Chem teacher, offered them extra credit for creating a truly terrifying experience.

Why had I thought that this would be better than doing the monster mash in the cafeteria?

I turned to the closest member of the haunted house crew, who was perched on top of a table in a ripped suit and a hobo-style top hat, his face hidden under a grotesque clown mask. There was a large rubber axe in his hand. Thankfully, I didn't share Meg's fear of clowns. The misshapen downward curve of the mask's mouth and the mottled blue paint over the eyes just looked like what would happen if someone stuck Mary-Anne France in a rainstorm. Which I found comforting rather than scary.

"Pardon me, homicidal clown." My voice was shaky as I forced myself to look up at him. "Any chance you could get me out of here before I have a nervous breakdown? You look like an upstanding gentleman. Not that your gender matters to me. I just require assistance."

The clown looked at me and tugged his lumpy top hat farther down, the mask puckering at the forehead. In one graceful leap, he was standing in front of me. The mask's chin wobbled, but the sealed mouth garbled any sound.

"I didn't catch that," I said. There seemed to be too much spit in my mouth and yet I felt dehydrated and dizzy. I touched a glove to my forehead. It came away slick and green tinged. "Sorry. My friends ditched me here and, well, maybe you wouldn't understand, being a murderous children's entertainer, but haunted houses really aren't fun by yourself. And I'd like to avoid being known as the evil queen who fainted in the chem lab. See"—I pushed my glove down, revealing the smear of homework notes—"I forgot to add 'don't have a panic attack' to my to-do list. A grave oversight."

The clown seemed to consider this for a second before offering me the tattered brown sleeve of his non-axe-wielding arm. I took it, too thankful to be led out to worry about cutting off his circulation. He was warm and didn't smell like fake blood.

"If it's all the same to you," I said, squeezing my eyes closed as Freddy Krueger jumped out in front of us, "I'm going to ramble until we're free. It'll help stave off the screaming and fainting thing, I think."

The clown shrugged as if to say, *By all means, Maleficent, go ahead.*

He was fairly tall for a clown. I wasn't sure why I tended to think of clowns as a shorter bunch. It would help them all pile into those tiny cars if they were small. But my axe murderer escort was nearly as tall as my horns, much too big to be a frosh. If I hadn't known that Peter was running around in a Disney sweatshirt, I would have assumed it was him. Regardless, the clown being tall and armed— even with a wobbly axe—was reassuring.

"I'm Trixie Watson, by the way," I said.

The clown saluted me with his axe. I wet my lips, coating my tongue in sweat and slimy, sweet makeup.

"First, I'd like to point out that I'm down with the consumer part of this shindig. Costumes and candy? I'm totally on board. But being trapped on campus after hours while my classmates work through their sexual frustration by making people pee themselves? Not so much. Of course, some people are working through their sexual frustration in the normal run-off-and-find-a-private-corner kind of way—did you see Teen Wolf and Supergirl come through here?"

The clown nodded while also brandishing his axe to push us through the traffic jam of giggling farm animals. They scattered, revealing the second chem lab, which was full of zombies. Groaning, drooling, claw-your-eyes-out *Walking Dead* zombies. The room stank from the solid carbon dioxide being used to roll out waves of fake fog. The music was different here, a discordant warble of distorted roaring and screaming layered under a violin being violated.

My veins tightened with another flush of adrenaline. I dug my finger-nails into the clown's sleeve as the zombies started approaching us. With a sweep of his axe, they staggered backward, a few of them glaring at him for ruining their fun.

"Supergirl is my best friend Harper," I continued loudly, jerking to keep one of the zombies from touching me. "And she's been all kinds of in love with Cornell Aaron for years. And it's about time those crazy kids went ahead and stuffed their tongues in each other's faces and all, but, you know, they could have waited until I was safely through the haunted house."

Stopping short, the clown's shoulders seized with a laugh that I couldn't hear. He lifted his axe and reached over himself to poke me in the stomach. The blade folded in on itself above my belly button. Laughing despite myself, I batted it away and gave him a grazing shove with my shoulder.

"Yeah, I know. It's stupid to get freaked out. But the rest of the crew isn't as facetious as you are. The mountain of stuffed animals that's really a person? Not a fan. I will have nightmares for weeks."

The clown wiggled his head and patted his chest proudly with his axe.

"That was your idea?" I asked.

He bobbed his head enthusiastically, the mask flapping around his neck. I was surprised at how well I could translate mime. Yet another useless skill I could put on my résumé.

"That is utterly demented," I said. "But I would expect no less from a hobo clown. Or do you prefer displaced circus entertainment professional?"

The clown held up two fingers with the hand holding the axe, in-dicating the latter option.

There were more zombies trapped behind a piece of chain-link fence, growling and spitting. One grabbed at the tail of a girl dressed as a cat and pulled her against the fence with a clatter.

I blurted out a curse and cringed into the clown's shoulder. He pulled me closer, the brim of his hat resting against my horns. We stood still for a moment. I could feel his breath rising and falling against my cheek. My arm was pinned to his side, my gloves buried deep into the fibers of his sleeve. There was an arm under that sleeve. Biceps brachii, coracobrachialis and brachialis connecting to a humerus bone. A real human arm, attached to a real human boy.

My pulse fluttered up into my throat again.

The zombies whispered "Ooo," like a studio audience. The clown and I took a step forward in tandem.

"Anyway," I said, staring firmly at my feet, "Harper and Cornell are going to be all happily ever after and the rest of us will have to deal. Which is going to be fairly sucky for me considering Cornell is now super best friends with Ben West. Do you know Ben West, homicidal clown?"

He glanced down at me, the axe going limp in his hand. From the shadowy recesses of his mask, I could barely make out confused brown eyes.

"Ben West?" I repeated. "Skinny, handlebar mustache, really lazy insults?"

The clown cocked his head and shook it side to side.

"Lucky you," I said, shivering closer to him. "You must be new. He's less of a class clown—no offense—and more of our token idiot savant. I don't know how Cornell and Peter are putting up with his jackassery. Two minutes with West is like one really obnoxious lifetime. They'll realize it eventually. Everyone does. I mean, what kind of loser do you have to be to get kicked out of the role-playing club?"

The clown yanked the elbow I was holding onto, steering me around a group heading into the next room and toward the opposite wall. He drew back a black sheet of plastic—which looked no different from the rest of the black plastic—to reveal a door that opened onto the quad. There were people prancing around with bags of kettle corn and candied apples.

"Oh, sweet merciful freedom," I said, ducking my horns under the plastic. I turned around with my hand on the doorknob. "Thank you, homicidal clown. You've been a lovely companion. If you've given up your murderous tendencies on Monday, find me in the caf. I owe you a soda for your trouble."

He tipped his top hat to me and turned on his heel, striding back through the zombies as I stepped outside. I was almost sorry to see him go, but the fresh air was such a relief that I couldn't be too troubled.

I immediately fished money out of my cloak and bought a spiced cider, drinking deep as I sat myself on a bench. With the adrenaline seeping out of my bloodstream, it was easier to focus on being happy for Harper and Cornell, as much as I would need to have a chat with them about the appropriate times to disappear together.

I sipped my cider, watching the parade of princesses and superheroes dashing over to the apple bobbing booth. I had absolutely no will to shove my face into a bucket of water after being trapped in the haunted house. I was going to keep my butt firmly planted until Meg or Harper reappeared.

I dug through the pockets of my cloak until my fingers found the worn copy of *The Hitchhiker's Guide to the Galaxy* I'd stashed inside. I pulled it out and read a few chapters, nursing my cider until it went cold and became really spicy juice.

"There's something you don't see every day."

I looked up and saw Peter standing in front of me, his hair poking out of the front of his purple hood. I adjusted my cloak to make room and he sat down heavily next to me, holding out a mostly empty bag of kettle corn.

I folded the book over my knee so that I could take some kettle corn. Like my cider, it was no longer fresh, but I ate a fistful anyway. The sugar stuck to my gloves.

"Where's your posse?" I asked in between crunching.

"Scattered."

"Same here," I said. "It looks like we're the only ones not using the costumes as an excuse to be more adventurous."

"Hey, I have been to infinity and beyond," he said, proudly displaying his costume before shaking some kettle corn into his palm. "But my knee hurts and I don't feel like dancing."

I grimaced. "Is that where everyone is?"

"Looks like it," he said. "I guess we're the only people left not paired off. Well, you, me, and Ben."

"Yikes," I said. Even with getting trapped in the haunted house, I'd been having a lovely West-free evening. "Don't lump us in with Ben West. We can't be that pathetic, right?"

Peter laughed and nudged me with his shoulder. "I guess not. I mean, we could always . . ."

He turned in slow motion, his big blue eyes asking a really stupid question. It hung in the air between us like the dry ice fog in the zombie room. It would have made sense—if I were someone else—for us to pair off because the rest of our group had. That's how things worked on TV. If there was an even number of girls and boys, you coupled up. I watched sitcoms. I got the formula. I snorted at the idea.

Peter shrank back, scalded. I hadn't meant to hurt his feelings. It was just absurd. The Donnellys had been running the Mess's student government since the school opened. Except for Jack. But I was much more suited to the sociopath than to the student council president.

"Sorry," I said, clasping my hands together in my lap. "Absolutely no offense intended. But I am so not First Lady material. I'd destroy you without even meaning to. Because I'm, you know, me. And you're—"

"A gimpy member of leadership?"

I threw up my hands. "See? You're too nice to deal with me all the time. I'm the evil queen and you save the day." I paused to consider him. He had chosen his costume well. He hadn't even needed to draw in Buzz's chin dimple. He came with one already in place. "It's not that you aren't crazy good-looking. You are. You know that. You need to find a nice Jackie Onassis."

He gave me a bemused shake of his head. "That was a lot of references in one compliment."

I cringed, thinking of West, who had said something similar about my insulting him on the first day of school. "Yeah, well. I'm off my game. I got trapped in the haunted house when Harper and Cornell went frolicking off together and I'm still a little woozy. I had to ask some dude dressed like a clown to help me escape."

Peter raised his eyebrows at me. "You asked—"

I held my hand up. "I do not want to talk about it. Apparently, I have problems with zombies up close and personal, okay?"

"Don't feel too bad about it. The drama club spent all week training them. Even Jack said they were pretty intense." He stood, peering inside the nearly empty bag of kettle corn. "Do you want another cider?"

"Please," I said. "And then can we track down our stupid newly-in-love friends? I want to get this gunk off my face."

To: Messina Academy Students
From: Administrative Services
Subject: Harvest Festival

. . . infractions against the school code will be met with the same repercussions set in place during school hours.

✺ 8 ✺

Peter and I wandered aimlessly, not spending much time at any one booth, eating through a second bag of kettle corn and drinking apple cider. Dr. Mendoza had abandoned the dunk tank, leaving damp pavement behind as the only evidence that he'd let half the student body sink him into what had to be freezing cold water.

"Even before my leg blew out, I never thought about going pro," Peter said, tossing kettle corn kernels into his mouth. "I've wanted to go to MIT since before I started kindergarten. It's the top mechanical engineering program in the country."

"Might as well aim for the best," I agreed, taking a handful of kettle corn for myself. It stuck unpleasantly to my gloves and I had to scrape the residue off with my teeth. "Are you leaning more toward Stark Industries or Skynet?"

The corners of his mouth quirked. "I don't follow."

"Nerd stuff." I shrugged. "Don't worry about it."

"Trixie! Peter!" Meg was running toward us, her legs seeming to move much faster than her shoes. Her hair had started to lose its curl. A piece stuck to her flushed cheek as she hopped in front of us. "Oh my God, tonight is the best. I danced with Brad for a little while, but then he disappeared and I ended up with Ishaan Singh. We mostly talked about cricket. He's cricket captain and fifth in the ranking, but he didn't know that J. M. Barrie started that team with Wodehouse and Kipling, if you can believe it. I thought that was common knowledge. Anyway, we had kettle corn and split a candied apple. It was very sweet."

"Confectionary even." I giggled.

"Oh," she squealed with a hop of excitement. "And I saw Harper and Cornell. They're slow dancing to the *Nightmare Before Christmas* soundtrack right now. It is so cute I could scream. I think they're officially official."

"It's about time," Peter said.

"And what about you, Meggie?" I asked. "How does Ishaan factor into your rebellion?"

She tittered absentmindedly. "Oh, I dropped a hint about the winter ball. We'll see if he picked it up. But this whole boy thing is pretty exhausting. I don't think I need an everyday boyfriend. It might be more like having a formal dress in your closet. It'd be silly to wear it in the cafeteria, but it's nice to have on hand."

Peter appeared to wrestle with this information, his forehead wrinkling as his eyes went squinty. He started to say something, choked on it, and covered his mouth with his fist.

"Don't worry about it," I said, patting him on the shoulder. "You get used to her logic eventually."

Meg propped a hand onto her hip, sinking to one leg with a huff.

"Anyway," she said loudly. "I don't think we'll be able to pry Harper and Cornell apart for a while. But I'm pretty much done here."

"Oh, me too," I said.

"Did you guys drive in together?" Peter asked.

"We walked." I groaned, thinking of dragging myself back home. My toes throbbed in protest against the stiff leather of my boots. I petulantly threw my empty cider cup into the nearest trash can.

"Do you want a ride?" Peter asked.

"Really?" Meg asked brightly. "That would be fantastic."

"We'll need to tell Harper," I said, but Meg was already prancing toward the cafeteria, her skirt swishing around her thighs.

"Don't you need to stay here and clean up?" I asked Peter. "You guys spent a week putting all of this up."

"We're cleaning everything up tomorrow morning. I have to come back to get my brother later. He's running the music in the haunted house." He leaned against the trash can, reaching up and peeling off his hood. He brushed his hair forward with the flat of his hand before stuffing the hood into his pocket. "I can't let you guys walk back. Meg looks cold."

I grinned at him. "Meg looks mostly naked."

He coughed a shocked laugh. "I mean, she looks pretty—"

"But also not entirely as clothed as usual. It's okay. It's part of her thought experiment."

Before Peter could reply, Meg reappeared in all her tiny glory, skipping toward us. If she noticed my giggle-snort or Peter's extraneous throat clearing as she approached, she didn't show it.

"Cornell is going to drive Harper home," she said with a dimpled smile. "She said she'll come get her backpack from your house tomorrow, Trix."

"Wow," I said. "She's going to part with her homework for the night? This is serious."

Peter led us out of the quad, holding the door to the main building open for us to squeeze through. After the raucous festivities, the bright fluorescent light and silent hallway was oddly jarring. All of a sudden, I remembered that we were on campus and that when we came back on Monday, the first ranking would be posted. Suddenly, the Shakespeare quote plastered to the front of the case was less amusing.

We stepped out of the front of the building. The admissions table was still set up, now run by two juniors who were whispering loudly into a walkie-talkie. Kenneth Pollack was roaring at them, his broad shoulders covered in a cheap plastic Roman-soldier chest plate.

"This is bull," he shouted. "Give me my fucking ticket."

"We can't," said a girl in bunny ears. She stabbed her finger near the cash box at a sheet of paper. "You're on the list."

Kenneth let loose another stream of obscenities as the second girl continued whisper-screaming into the walkie-talkie.

Peter strode forward, his hands open in the universal sign of jocular goodwill.

"Bro," he said, slipping seamlessly out of English and into Jock. "What's up?"

"What's up is that this bitch—"

"Language, Kenny," Meg bristled.

He ignored her entirely. "This is ridiculous, Donnelly. Tell them to let me in."

"I can't do that, Ken," Peter said softly. "You know the rules. You're on academic probation. You can't—"

"I didn't cheat," Kenneth snarled, wrenching back. His chest plate swung to the side, revealing the red T-shirt he wore underneath it.

The front door slammed open. Dr. Mendoza, now out of his wet suit and dressed in a lab coat and a stethoscope, pushed past me and Meg. Peter stepped out of his way with a deferential inclination of his head.

"Mr. Pollack," Dr. Mendoza said, his salt-and-pepper Mr. Sinister goatee gleaming in the low light. "You have already been benched for the next two games. Do you want to be pulled off the team entirely?"

"I didn't cheat," Kenneth repeated, carefully keeping his voice down. No one shouted at Dr. Mendoza. He controlled our college references.

Peter's shoulders slumped. He glanced at me and Meg and motioned for us to follow him. We did, trying to slip around Kenneth's bulk without brushing him. We walked through the front gate and into the parking lot in silence. Peter retrieved a set of keys from his pocket and let us into a silver minivan. I had to remove my horns to fit into the passenger seat.

"So," said Meg as Peter started the engine. "What in the holy hell was that?"

Peter blew out a breath, peering over his shoulder as we backed out of the parking space. I pointed him in the general direction of my house.

"Ken got caught cheating in Cline's class," he grumbled.

"Already?" Meg gasped. "We're a month in."

Carefully, I peeled my gloves off and pressed my hands to the air vents, letting the cool air roll over my fingers. "He keeps saying he didn't do it."

Meg freed her tiara from her hair and massaged her scalp. "I'm sure he did it. He's just another meathead. . . ." She shrank back in her seat, seeming to remember where we were. "Sorry, Peter."

Peter shrugged her off, steering the minivan around a corner. "No, he is a meathead. He beat the crap out of Ben last year. And he used to steal notes out of our lockers during practice. I wouldn't be surprised if he was cheating. They gave him a slap on the wrist for it, but he could have been expelled."

"He should have been," I said.

"I don't think they have enough proof yet." Peter frowned. "He kept saying the freshman class treasurer framed him."

"It wasn't B," I said. "He didn't even know he had school email."

"That's what Ben said," Peter said. "When he heard about it, he went straight to Dr. Mendoza's office and proved that Brandon hadn't accessed his account yet."

"That was nice of him." Meg yawned. "He didn't have to do that."

"No, but he wanted to make sure Brandon's name was cleared. So, now the administration is 'looking into it.' Whatever that means."

"It means Ken gets to keep playing basketball and roughing up innocent bystanders," I said, sighing. "Damn it. This is the second time this week I wished I was a detective."

Meg tilted her head at me, letting her crown flop to one side. "Do you want me to dig out my Nancy Drews for pointers?"

I tossed a glove at her.

Back in my bedroom, Meg changed into her uniform and lovingly folded her costume before stashing it in her bag. My mom offered to drive her home and I took a boiling-hot shower, clawing the green paint off my face. With half a bottle of shampoo suds sloughing the gel out of my hair, I considered what would happen if I told Harper and Meg that I had turned down Peter's offer of default dating. They probably would have forced me to commit seppuku, the only honorable death a traitor to my gender could hope for.

There had to be at least a hundred people at the Mess who stayed up late at night wishing that Peter would just look at them, much less ask them out. He was tall and good-looking and chivalrous to a fault. In the span of two hours, he'd found Meg a dance partner, stopped Kenneth Pollack from going berserk, and driven me and Meg home. He was Captain America without the emotional baggage. I knew perfect when I saw it. And Peter was the kind of perfect that girls made lists of. He was MASH-bait, if you were the kind of person who was into notebook fortune-telling games.

So maybe I was crazy. Because for all of that perfection, I couldn't force my brain to see him in *that way*—the making-out-in-a-supply-closet, think-about-him-instead-of-homework kind of way. His goofy smile had no effect on my knees. Talking to him was pleasant, but not Earth shattering. At no point while he was squiring me around the festival did I have any elaborate fantasies about holding hands or him winning me a stuffed animal at the beanbag toss.

There was no spark of interest there. I'd had more chemistry with the homicidal clown. Even mid-panic attack, I'd enjoyed the warmth of the masked boy's arm, his mute sense of humor, the faint peppery smell of his jacket.

Developing some kind of gender-swapped Cinderella scenario about a boy who could be anyone—a freakishly tall frosh or complete stranger or, worse, Jack Donnelly—was beyond the pale of pathetic. It reeked of deep-seated psychosis.

The real point was that I couldn't force myself to have the warm and fuzzies for Peter. And I got the impression that the feeling was mutual. His offer had been logical in that I was female and he was male. We were both singular and could, in fact, combine to a plural. It wasn't romantic. It was an equation. From what I could tell about relationships and love and all that noise, it needed to be more than just mathematically reasonable.

I dried my hair, aggressively rubbing a towel over my head and relishing the feeling of being clean from head to toe. I put on pajamas and flopped down on my bed, fingering the threadbare hem of the *Flash Gordon* T-shirt that had once belonged to my dad.

Sherry curled up on the edge of my mattress while I made Calculus notes. The empty Plexiglas case where the ranking would be posted swam in front of my eyes, daring me to work harder.

An hour or so into working through asymptotic and unbounded behavior of single variables—yes, I am aware how much that sounds like a metaphor for my life—my phone rang, startling both me and Sherry, who tried to sniff out the source of the whooshing TARDIS takeoff sound. With a yawn, I reached over to my nightstand and answered the phone.

"Hello?"

"Hi," said Harper. "It's me."

I rolled my eyes, knowing full well that she couldn't see me. Considering we'd been friends since kindergarten, I really didn't need her to divulge her identity to me at the beginning of a phone call.

"Harper?" I croaked, adopting a wizened tone. "Harper Leonard? Is that you? It's been a dog's age, old friend."

"Oh, shut up." She laughed. "Can we meet at the park tomorrow?"

"Of course," I said, straining to push Sherry's face away from mine as he attempted to lick my cheek. I tucked the phone under my chin and wrestled him into lying down.

"Great," Harper said. "I already texted Meg. Does ten thirty work for you?"

I could picture her sitting in her immaculate bedroom, a pen hovering over her sacred day planner. The image was much more entertaining when I remembered that she was dressed as Supergirl.

"Yes," I said. "I have no plans tomorrow other than homework."

"Great," she said again. "I'll see you then. Please don't forget to bring my backpack with—"

I sat up straight and cut her off. "Whoa, whoa, whoa. That's it? See you tomorrow and don't forget your backpack?"

"Hmm?" she said, undoubtedly distracted by writing in her planner. "Oh. Um. Did you have a good time tonight?"

"Did *I* have a good time?" I repeated. "Harper, if you think I'm going to let you hang up without telling me what happened after you left the haunted house, you have sorely underestimated me."

"But I'm going to see you in twelve hours. I'll have to repeat everything to Meg."

I shot Sherry a conspiratorial look that he did not have the cognitive functions to reciprocate.

"Are you still out with Cornell?" I asked, carefully keeping absolutely anything resembling judgment out of my voice.

"No," she said quickly. "He dropped me off about half an hour ago."

"Then you can give me bullet points now and save the epic recitation for tomorrow."

"Well," she said. "We danced. We split a candied apple. We talked."

"Just talked?" I asked, grinning madly.

"He told me that he hasn't been able to stop thinking about me. For years, I guess." She had started whispering. "He was afraid I was just being nice or something and that I didn't, you know, feel the same way."

"What clued him in? The fact that you went all klutzy when he was around or the long lingering looks in the lunch line?"

"Neither. He decided to try anyway." She gave a breathy laugh. "So, now we're together. Together-together. We're going to the library on Sunday."

"Oh, nerd love," I said, reaching over to scratch Sherry's ears. "That's really great, Harper. I'm happy for you."

"Thanks, Trix. I can't believe it, you know? It's—"

"Magical?"

"Yeah. That."

We promised to see each other in the morning. I set my phone back down and shoved aside my Calculus textbook, laying my head on Sherry's back. He idly licked my hand.

It couldn't be that difficult to track down the homicidal clown, I thought, staring at the posters on my wall. If I was going to be sitting with the student council at lunch now anyway, I could at least ask for the name of the boy who had escorted me through the haunted house. Maybe I could try to leech some of the magic of the harvest festival for myself after all.

Me   [7:43 PM]

Dad is trying to convince us to change our last
name to Cumberbatch.

Harper   [7:47 PM]

Are you guys watching the BBC Sherlock again?

Me   [7:53 PM]

Don't judge us. The Cumberbatches are a proud
people.

★ 9 ★

I strode through the cafeteria with my standard tray of salad and a can of cola. I started moving toward the table populated by the student council, but I saw Harper and Meg sitting in our usual spot and changed course.

"Does this mean we aren't relocating our meals?" I asked, setting my tray down and hopping onto the bench next to Meg. I had expected to see some sign of Harper and Cornell's newfound couple-dom in first period, but I'd only caught a glimpse of him squeezing her hand as he passed her desk. "Shouldn't we be with the student council now that you're all squishy with the VP?"

"We're sitting here today," she said simply.

"They're treating us like divorced kids," Meg announced. "One day at our table, one day at theirs. And alternating Fridays."

"You're kidding."

Harper's cheeks went red and she shoved her glasses up with her knuckle. "It was the only thing that made sense," she said to her plate. "I don't want to listen to the student council plan activities every single day, but the boys do have to check in with them. Especially now that the winter ball is coming up."

"Did you get any groping done when you went out on Sunday or did you just sit down and make a timetable?" I asked. "Excel is not sexy."

Three trays landed on the table with discordant slaps. Cornell sat down next to Harper as Peter and Jack Donnelly collapsed farther down the bench.

"I've always liked the clean lines of a spreadsheet," Cornell laughed, draping his arm over Harper's shoulders. She lifted her face to his and placed a painfully chaste kiss on his cheek.

"Hi," she whispered.

"Hello," he whispered back.

"I know," Peter said to me and Meg, shaking his head. "They're already disgusting together."

"And yet no one has answered my groping question." I took a bite of salad, grinning at Harper as I chewed.

"And I don't intend to answer it," she said.

"I could," Peter said.

Cornell glared at him. "But you won't."

"I'm on Team Let's Not Talk About It," Meg said.

"Thank you." Harper lifted her slice of pizza and took a dainty bite. Cornell leaned over and stole a pepperoni. They took a moment to giggle at each other, undoubtedly having some kind of love-born telepathic conversation about that one time he pulled that piece of meat out of her tresses in freshman year. I took another bite of my salad.

"So, what do you guys do around here?" Jack asked, wedging most of a slice of pizza into his mouth.

"Do?" Meg asked.

He bugged his eyes at her. A droplet of grease slid down the side of his chin. "Are you guys like a club or something? You're always together."

"You're always with Nick and Brad," I said. "What do you guys do?"

Other than murder small animals and try to build a Deathlok.

"Obviously I'm not always with them," he said, flapping his pizza at me. "Right now, I'm here with you people."

Peter ducked his head toward his brother, as though exposing his neck to us would make him invisible. "You wanted to come."

Something slammed into my elbow, nearly causing me to choke on my fork. I looked up in time to see Ben West snag the soda off my tray, his assault weapon of a backpack slung carelessly over one shoulder. His hair seemed even less tidy than usual, sticking out more on one side than the other.

"What the hell, West?" I snarled, reaching my hand out as I awaited the return of my drink.

He glanced down at the shining red can clenched in his hand and admired his reflection in it before he cracked the tab. He took a long drink, setting his mustache aquiver.

"Ben," Cornell said.

But West ignored him, wiping the back of his hand carelessly over his mouth to clear the cola droplets from the tips of his mustache. He looked down at me, his mouth cocked into a satisfied smile.

"Your debt is paid, Beatrice Watson," he said.

"My debt?" I gaped at him. "The only thing I owe you, West, is the fourth-place spot when the ranking comes out today. And possibly a razor so you can get that thing off your face."

"I'd love to stay and chat," he said, looking over my head at the rest of the table. "But I hate to deprive the student council of my jackassery."

The words slammed into my chest, negating all the venom I had stored up. I forced myself to look straight into his eyes. They were dark brown and did not match the smile on his face. I examined him closely. He was taller than I'd ever really thought about, easily the same height as the Donnelly twins, just thinner.

If you've given up your murderous tendencies on Monday, find me in the caf. I owe you a soda for your trouble.

Of course Ben West was the clown. Of course I had latched myself onto his arm and blathered on about how much I hated him, not knowing that I was telling him personally. Dear God, I'd devoted precious brainpower to thinking about tracking him down. . . .

I was suddenly in need of a shower and some lye to start the arduous process of trying to scrub away that particular memory. Maybe I could ask my mom to have one of her med school friends hook me up with a lobotomy.

"What are you talking about?" Peter asked. "Go grab Trixie another soda and have a seat."

"No." My lips felt numb. "It's his soda."

For the first time, I saw genuine dislike in West's eyes. Not just the usual annoyance that persisted between us, but dense and unbearable loathing. I turned back to my salad and my guts pitched.

"And my two minutes are up," he said. "See you all later."

He strode across the cafeteria toward the student council table, leaving behind a silence that seemed entirely aimed at me. Meg raised her hand patiently in the air.

"Yes, Miss Royama?" I asked weakly, not looking up from the salad I no longer intended to eat.

She lowered her hand to her lap and popped her lips. "What the eff?"

Cornell sighed, resting his elbows on either side of his tray. "At the harvest festival when Harper and I left the haunted house, Trixie ripped into Ben. He's, uh, not happy about it."

"Trixie," Harper said with a groan.

"It is not my fault," I spat. "I was having a zombie-induced panic attack. It's not like he told me that he was the one in that clown mask."

Meg shuddered beside me. "Ew. He was a clown?"

"Not the point, Meg," Harper said quietly. She glanced up at me. "What did you say to him?"

"How should I know?" I lied.

"You guys looked pretty comfortable from where I was sitting," Jack said, stealing a napkin from Peter's tray. He rubbed the grease from his chin. "Cuddling in the quarantine zone."

"There was absolutely no cuddling," I shrieked. "Again, zombie-induced panic attack. I was trying to get through without passing out."

"You were in pretty bad shape when I found you," Peter said. I wasn't sure if he was lying to cover for me or if he was being accidentally insulting.

Cornell winced. "You said something about him being an idiot savant who shouldn't have friends."

"Adding 'savant' to that should have softened the blow." Jack guffawed.

I whirled on him. "I really don't need your help, evil twin. What are you even doing here? We aren't your friends."

That plucked his laughter out of the air. He and Peter wore matching hangdog looks for a moment, but Jack's soured immediately.

"I'm sorry," I said to the ceiling. "I'm just—"

"She's deflecting," Meg said. She put her hand next to my tray. "Did you really call Ben an idiot savant?"

"Oh, come on," I said, a fraction too loud. "It's not like he hasn't said equally horrible things to me. Last week, he told me that the only difference between me and Miss Havisham was that she'd at least had one dude interested in her. And I accepted that Dickensian insult without having to whine to everyone about it like a girl."

"Gender normative and antifeminist," Harper muttered under her breath.

I grabbed my bag and threw the strap over my shoulder. "Fine. Call him back over and enjoy the absolute pleasure that is his company. Since Jack is so concerned with our lack of activities, you can start a Benedict West fan club for all I care. I'm going to the library."

"Trixie," Peter said. "You don't have to—"

I looked down at his big, imploring blue eyes. My throat tightened into a vise, making it almost impossible to shove the words out.

"I told you. You don't want to deal with me every day."

The cafeteria door slammed behind me. I was fully aware that I was being melodramatic, but a slithering guilt was creeping up the back of my polo. It was easier to be indignant rather than confront it. I'd honestly never thought I'd see the day when one of my insults to West actually cracked the surface. I didn't want to be the bad guy because I'd won the battle of wits.

And wasn't I just as injured as he was? Why couldn't he have taken off his stupid mask and said, *Hey, Trix, it's me, your archnemesis. Look at my stupid mustache. Don't go home and wonder whether or not I'm boyfriend material.*

The vinaigrette in my stomach jumped up and scorched my esophagus as I trudged into the library, passing the librarian without bothering to look at her. I threw myself down at a table, drawing my Economics notes out of my bag. My own handwriting stared up at me, meaningless.

Why had West bothered escorting me out of the haunted house? Wouldn't it have been more amusing to sit back and watch me collapse in a heap of velvet and horns while the kid dressed as Freddy Krueger called for help? Or was it all part of some master plan to get information to use against me later? If that was the case, it had obviously backfired since he was in a blind rage.

I squeezed my eyes closed. I refused to take full blame for this. If Harper, Cornell, Peter, Jack, and Meg knew everything that had happened, they wouldn't have been able to guilt me about it.

But I couldn't march back into the cafeteria after my grand exit. And I didn't particularly like the idea of announcing to the group that West and I had shared some kind of pleasant exchange before I started slandering him to his masked face. Saying it out loud would make it true.

So, I stayed in the library and highlighted important pieces of information in my Econ notes until the bell rang.

I kept my head down during Calculus and Programming Languages, taking voracious notes and avoiding raising my hand, even when Mike Shepherd started ranting about dotted-pair notation in the Lisp system in the middle of a lecture about C++.

The bell rang and I dutifully shut down my computer, packed my bag, and strode out of the computer lab, cringing as I recognized the hallway that had been the entrance to the haunted house. I shoved through the door, using my messenger bag as a shield against my classmates, and darted toward the main building. The halls were packed tight, hundreds of students all trying to make it to the administrative office.

"What's going on?" asked a frosh.

"Your first ranking is out," replied a passing junior.

I clenched my hands into fists as people crowded around me, all of us trying to press near the case. The people standing directly in front of the ranking lists ran the gamut of emotions, some laughing, some mute with shock, one girl wailing in unabashed misery.

The administrative office was hidden behind blinds. The office staff didn't want to deal with us on a ranking day. I would have bet my savings that the door was locked.

Something heavy grazed the toe of my shoe and I spotted the back of B. Calistero's head, his arm trailing his rolling backpack behind him.

"Hey, B," I said.

He turned and stared up at me in surprise. "Trixie! Hi."

"Are you ready for your first rank?"

"No." He frowned. "Not really. I didn't even know about this until ten minutes ago."

It was cruel that none of the freshman teachers bothered warning the new kids about the ranking. I remembered my own first ranking, the horror of seeing the name of everyone in my class listed next to a number. Meg had cried and Harper had tried not to gloat about already being in the top five. I wished that I could comfort B and say that eventually you got used to everyone knowing how you were doing in your classes. But you didn't.

"You'll be okay," I said consolingly. "Your rank doesn't really matter until sophomore year. That's when you have to start recording it for your college applications. This is a test run."

The crowd surged forward again as the first group of onlookers pushed their way toward the front door. B moved forward, his rolling backpack providing a clear path for me to follow. He stopped short, slamming into the back of some dude's polo.

"Sorry, I didn't mean to—Oh, hey, Ben!"

West glanced over his shoulder, his mustache leading the way for the rest of his face. He looked down at B and then up at me. His mouth curved downward.

"Brandon," West said. "Move away from the shrew."

B's shoulders twitched.

I gestured to the solid wall of shoving people around us. "There's nowhere else to go. Just turn around prepared to get slapped with the ranking."

West narrowed his eyes at me, his teeth clenched in an ugly snarl. "I should have let you faint."

My shoulders felt too tight, like I was going to start She-Hulking out of my polo. "You should have. What the hell were you thinking?"

B, trapped between us, had the horrified expression of a kid stuck between warring parents. I prayed that he had a happy home life, otherwise he might go into some kind of regressive blackout.

"I thought you were acting like a human being for once," West said. "My mistake."

"One of many mistakes. Like your personal grooming and the lack of filter between your brain and your mouth."

"You didn't have any complaints on Friday night."

The people around us had turned to watch now. Whispers rose around me and I couldn't be bothered to try and decipher them. I thought I could see Cornell out of the corner of my eye, but I didn't look away from West.

"And you did? You seemed perfectly content to squire me around, practically holding my hand. You knew who I was. What's your excuse?"

An intense flush spread across West's cheeks. He spun around, craning his neck to see the front of the crowd. Mary-Anne France had her finger pressed to the case, scanning downward.

"Mary-Anne," West shouted over the hubbub of the crowd. "Who's third and fourth?"

There were various protests shouted, but Mary-Anne moved her fingernail up the list. I held my breath, my hands still clenched into fists.

"Trixie is third," Mary-Anne called. "And you're in fourth, Ben."

I let out an audible sigh of relief, expelling every knot and tangle from my muscles. Thank Thor. I deserved something good to happen today.

West's chest puffed up and down against the Mess emblem on his polo.

"Si vis pacem, para bellum," I said with a satisfied smirk. *If you want peace, prepare for war.*

"Me mordre, chienne."

B gave a shocked gasp as West barreled his way through the crowd, throwing his elbows at anyone who stood in his way.

"You speak French?" I asked B.

He squirmed, both nodding and shaking his head at the same time, adding to his general appearance of a shivering dog.

"A little bit," he murmured. "He said 'bite me.' And then, uh, some other stuff."

"Lazy even in another language," I chuckled, ruffling B's hair with the flat of my hand. "Good luck, sport. I'm going home."

I moved around the crowd, unconcerned with trying to find my friends in the mass. If they were there—and I was sure they were—they would have undoubtedly watched the entire exchange between me and West and would be primed to make me feel like crap about it. Admittedly, having a shouting match in the middle of the entire student body wasn't the best choice, but all that really mattered was that I was well on my way to achieving my goal of beating him in the ranking come graduation. All I had to do was maintain my grades.

I danced home.

Unknown Number   [6:05 PM]

Here's the link to that NPR interview Cline
referenced this morning.

Oh, sorry. It's Cornell. Hope you don't mind Harper
gave me your number.

Me   [6:08 PM]

No problem. Thanks for the extra credit points.

✦ 10 ✦

I got to school the next morning, bone tired and hiding behind my aviators. I'd been up late working on an essay for Russian Lit and woken up much too early to edit and upload it to the homework portal on the Mess website. To my surprise—and slight annoyance—I hadn't heard from Harper or Meg after the ranking came out. I had at least expected a chastising text message from one of them. Even if they hadn't personally witnessed my blowout with West, someone would have informed them of what happened.

Meg was waiting for me at the front gate as I hit campus. She wore neon-green tights under her khaki skirt and had a bow in her hair to match, making me feel even more slapdash than I had before. She beamed at me.

"Good morning. Congrats on placing third."

I yawned, peering at her over the top of my sunglasses. "Where did you—"

"Fourteen," she sighed, flourishing an unconcerned hand. "It's the ocean of three point nines. Not all of us can surpass a four point oh in the first month of school. Did you see Kenneth's rank?"

"No." I yawned again and my jaw cracked. "Mary-Anne told me where my rank was. I haven't looked at the list."

Meg's eyes glittered deviously. "He's on the bottom. They didn't even give him a number. It just says AP. As in 'academic probation.'"

"Whoa," I said. "I've never seen anyone stripped of their rank."

"It's crazy. They should have just expelled him. It'd be less humiliating."

"I don't think Kenny Pollack cares that much about his position on the list."

I looked over her shoulder at the people walking through the front gate. The morning after the ranking was always a more somber affair than a normal day. Everyone looked as beaten down and exhausted as I felt. Except for Meg, of course, who looked like she'd woken up at the bottom of a coffee pot and drank her way to freedom. Which she probably had. Caffeine had been her thought experiment in sophomore year. We'd had to scale her back on quad shot mochas after she'd started tap dancing in first period.

"Let's go in," she breathed. "Harper is driving in with Cornell and they'll probably get distracted by loving each other."

I wondered if the real reason for us not hanging out near the gate was to keep me from seeing West again. Maybe Peter had given her pointers on how to keep the peace. I wasn't sure why the idea bothered me so much, but it did. I didn't like the notion that I was being treated like a feral animal.

"About what happened at lunch yesterday," I said. "I want to point out that the haunted house made for very unusual circumstances. I didn't seek out West on purpose to torture him."

"And he was a clown," she said pertly. "Which is terrifying. I understand."

"Right. I was having a meltdown. I didn't mention it before because . . ." *I was harboring secret fantasies about the clown being tall, dark, and nerdy?* The thought slipped into my brain without my permission and I shuddered it away. "Because I was embarrassed about it. I got an A in Chemistry of Emotions and I still got roped in by the negative stimuli."

"I get it. Why do you think I didn't go in?" She bounced her backpack against her spine and led me through the gate. "But, you know, he really isn't that bad. Ben, I mean. He made a really good *Doctor Who* reference in our Gender Roles class the other day. About that episode where the Doctor and Martha go back to that all boys' school?"

"'Human Nature' and 'The Family of Blood,'" I muttered. "It's a two-part episode."

"Right. That one." A smile cracked over her face like a gooey egg. "Anyway, you both like *Doctor Who* and you read the same comics and you have . . ." She paused and gave a shifty look around us before whispering, "The same IQ."

My Mary Janes dragged to a stop against the gleaming white pavement. "Can we forget about that? The nerd duel was a mistake."

"I'm just saying," she stressed, placing her hands on her hips defiantly. "Maybe you could try to be nicer to him? You can't spend every lunch in the library. You'll starve to death."

"I'll play nice," I said. "Just don't let him talk to me."

"I think we should go with a Russian Winter theme," Mary-Anne France announced to very little interest. "Like the ball in *Anna Karenina*. I bet Ms. Gronski would give us extra credit for it."

I stabbed my fork into my salad and Harper shot me an apologetic look. Our first lunch with the student council was off to a running start. Peter had done his best originally to keep his underlings from talking about the winter ball, but there was no stopping it. The other officers had all pushed aside whatever textbooks and novels they'd been using to distract them from the noncouncil members at their table. Mary-Anne had dug out her official secretary notebook and had her pen poised over a fresh sheet of paper.

"I could sew jewelry into the hems of everyone's dresses if we're going all Romanov with it," I offered.

"Would we have to pay extra for the firing squad?" West asked. There were six people between us, but I could still clearly see him decimating a plate of French fries.

"It's not Romanov themed," Mary-Anne corrected sharply. "It's Russian Winter. It's romantic."

Peter frowned and tapped his thumb against his tray. "Maybe we should steer clear of race-related themes."

"It's already the winter ball," Cornell said, sliding a bag of chips toward Harper. "Does it really need a second theme?"

"The theme is let's make enough money to pay for the cricket team's whites," said a boy next to Peter.

"And to keep shipping them off to other schools that play cricket," muttered one of the sophomores.

"But that isn't romantic," Mary-Anne protested, slamming her pen down and reaching for the bottle of iced tea that apparently constituted her meal.

"What about something like 'a night to remember'?" asked one of the junior officers to my right.

"We're at a school for the gifted," parried one of the sophomore girls. "We have to be able to think of something less trite than that."

I laughed, nearly inhaling a piece of lettuce. While I already missed having conversations about things that interested me—like anything other than the winter ball—it was fascinating to watch the student council snipe at each other. Sixteen politicians in training at one table was a cage match just waiting to happen. I hoped poor B would escape unharmed. He was doing his best to hide behind his scientific calculator.

"Then what about separating the caf into an Oslo party and a Stockholm party?" West asked, flourishing a fry around to gesture to the imaginary dividing line.

The rest of the table turned to him in confusion. He cocked his head to the side, his face twisted in annoyance.

"Really?" he asked. "No one got that?"

The confused silence persisted. Honestly, at a table where almost everyone could speak another language, recognize passages of ancient text, and build a functioning computer, it really was abysmal that no one could find the connection between Oslo and Stockholm.

"It's a Nobel Prize joke," I said.

"Thanks, Trix," West said.

The previous day's boiling hatred seemed to have mellowed back to the usual amount of indifference. I assumed Peter had given him the same stern talking-to that Meg had tried on me.

"There's ketchup in your 'stache," I said, turning back to my lunch as he hunted for a napkin.

Meg gave me a smile that said, *See? Isn't it fun when we're all nice to each other?*

"We can't really say that it's a Christmas dance," Peter said, blithely steering the conversation back to a safe place. "But it could be something like a Mistletoe Ball."

"Formal wear and mononucleosis?" I asked.

"Gross," said Meg.

"It's not a Christmas dance," said one of the sophomores. "It's the week after Thanksgiving. It's not even in winter."

"We've been over this," Mary-Anne said. "It's in December. It's the cultural idea of winter."

"The Cultural Idea of Winter ball." West sniffed. "No, I don't think that's going to work either. A little too on the nose."

"What about a quote or something?" asked Harper, daintily retrieving one of Cornell's chips.

The lowerclassmen threw out a bunch of terrible song quotes, which digressed into a long string of insults about everyone's musical taste. Harper and Cornell got distracted entirely and muttered sweet nothings at each other.

B's voice floated around West's shoulder. "What about From Spring Days to Winter?"

The rest of the table didn't seem to have noticed him, preoccupied with explaining to the junior secretary why they refused to use a Taylor Swift song as the quote.

"Say that again, Brandon," West said.

"From Spring Days to Winter?" B squeaked.

West's eyebrows drew together and he reached up to stroke his mustache.

"'Love whom mine eyes had never seen,'" he quoted lightly. "'O the glad dove has golden wings.'"

That pulled everyone's attention. Benedict West randomly spouting poetry was not everyday lunch behavior. I wondered if anyone else felt like they were having a stroke. Mary-Anne was certainly a little greenish, but that could have been because poetry was her deal and she should have thought of it first. She was the only person at the table with a literary agent, after all.

"We could have little gold doves everywhere," said one of the sophomores. "Like, fake ones."

"It works," said Peter, nodding in approval.

West seemed thoroughly unimpressed by his victory. "The last stanza is all about death, but the rest of it works."

"It's Oscar Wilde," I said, still staring at him in shock.

He grinned at me and inclined his head, silently thanking me for catching a second reference. The motion drudged up the memory of him proudly miming in the haunted house. I hadn't entirely reconciled myself to the fact that we'd had a pleasant moment together. I'd made excuses and denied it and avoided giving explicit detail about it, but that couldn't wipe it out of my head.

"You still have ketchup in your mustache, friend," I told him. I leaned back so that I could see B. "Good work, B."

The frosh gave me a self-conscious smile before turning back to his lunch. West glared at me, scrubbing his face with a battered napkin. Whatever insult he was trying to piece together was cut off when Brad Hertz scrambled up to the table. His polo was drenched in sweat. There was a pungent odor wafting off him that reminded me of when my mom had forgotten about a Tupperware full of curry in the back of the fridge. I promptly pushed away my salad.

"Peter," he wheezed. "Dude, did you hear?"

Peter glanced around at us before looking back at Brad. "Hear what?"

"That you ran laps around the parking lot and then passed out in a Dumpster?" West asked.

"They took down the ranking," Brad said.

There was a clattering of plastic forks and hamburgers hitting paper plates. Everyone at the table turned to Brad, who was sloughing sweat off his forehead with the back of his hand.

"All of the rankings?" asked one of the juniors.

"No, just ours," Brad said, wiping his hand on his pants. A wet stain showed dark against his khakis. "The senior list is gone."

"Why?" Cornell asked.

"Two more APs," Brad gulped.

"APs?" echoed a frosh from the other end of the table. "Advanced Placement classes? Do we even have those?"

"I took all of them in middle school," said another.

"Academic probation," I said, staring up at Brad. "Who?"

"Alex Nguyen and Ishaan Singh. They got a week's suspension each."

Meg sucked in a gasp, her hand flying to her chest. I couldn't tell if she was more horrified that Ishaan had been caught cheating or that he wouldn't be allowed to attend the winter ball.

"But Ishaan is in the top ten," Harper protested. "Why would he cheat?"

"Why is anyone cheating?" West asked. "We're a month into term. It's a little early to panic."

Peter rubbed a hand over his temple in picture perfect presidential concern. He should have been bracing his hands against the desk in the Oval Office.

"Did they pull Ishaan off the cricket team?" he asked.

Brad nodded.

"Shit," Peter muttered.

Harper gave a small cluck, obviously protesting the use of harsh language in front of his cabinet. Cornell patted her arm.

"How did you find out about this?" Mary-Anne asked, narrowing her eyes at Brad.

"I was in the admin office when they brought in the list." He looked back at Peter. "Just thought you should know, man. I need to find Jack."

"He's working in the library today," Peter said. "Thanks for the update."

Brad staggered off, pushing his way between tables. Everyone at the table slowly resumed what they'd been doing before. Books were opened, beverages were consumed. Harper leaned her head against Cornell's shoulder, chewing the inside of her cheek in thought.

"I've never seen anything like this," Cornell said. "Three people caught cheating in a week?"

Peter sighed. "It's senior year and people are starting to get nervous about their college apps. I wouldn't have expected it of Alex or Ishaan, though."

The sophomores down at the other end of the table, unaffected by the news that the senior class was lousy with cheaters, started chattering excitedly with one another. After some whispering and pointing at each other, one of the girls sat up straight and raised her voice.

"What if we do a masquerade?"

"No masks," West declared.

The sophomore officers deflated, their thought balloons all soundly pricked. Although West was looking straight at the sophomore girl, I could feel the sharp point of the words aimed at me.

"What about mandatory gags?" I asked. "That would keep the mono threat down and keep West from boring everyone to tears."

The bell rang, like the triumphant clang at the end of a boxing match. West bolted from the table without saying goodbye. I leapt off the bench and scooped up my bag, a satisfied smile on my face.

"Oh, Trixie," Meg muttered, sadly adjusting her lime-green bow as we started moving toward the doors.

"What?" I asked.

Harper and Cornell caught up to us, their hands locked together. Again, I was struck by how comfortably they fit together. They moved and spoke without any indication that a week ago they'd been orbiting around each other. Their twin looks of quiet disappointment only added to the overall effect. It wasn't entirely unlike when my parents teamed up against me.

"Come on," I said, hopping onto the defensive without waiting for an invitation. "I was perfectly nice other than that last bit. I can't control the outside stimuli of the conversation."

"That's true," Harper clucked.

"It's just . . ." Cornell furrowed his brow, which only served to make him look more distinguished. "Never mind. Don't worry about it, Trix."

Me   [7:18 PM]

I need a homework vacation. Can either of you
spare half an hour sometime for quality time with
the park? (And each other, obvs.)

✿ 11 ✿

The next two weeks passed in a sort of time loop. I stayed up late working on homework, came to school twitchy and exhausted, and clenched my teeth during lunch to keep from eviscerating Ben West while he rambled. Harper and Cornell devised yet another meticulous schedule for comic book shopping that would limit an overlap between our shopping and the boys' shopping to no more than three and a half minutes. I should have felt guilty that they were going to such extreme measures to keep me and West separated, but I was too relieved to care. It was one thing to have to deal with him at school. I didn't want to see him bogarting the Marvel shelves.

I walked to school, already daydreaming about getting a full night's sleep. I'd spent two days working on a ten-page paper for History of the American Immigrant. With it finally uploaded to the homework portal, I could sit back and relax. I had three unread comics in my bag and I had every intention of going to the park after school to truly enjoy them. The weather was in my favor—slightly too overcast for me to justify wearing my sunglasses, but no real sign of rain.

Harper and Meg were waiting for me outside the front gate as I strolled up. A jolt of annoyance straightened my shoulders as their heads popped up in unison and their mouths clamped into mannequin smiles. It had become more and more common for their conversation to halt at the sight of me. It'd be easier if they just cornered me and had whatever intervention they were dancing around. I might not like whatever they had to say, but it'd be better than their continued failed attempts at being covert.

"Good morning," Meg said, quickly jumping to attention. "How are you?"

"Exhausted, as per usual," I said. "I really should take up drinking some kind of caffeine in the morning. I don't have to worry about stunting my growth anymore."

Harper gave an anxious cluck. "Well, women don't officially stop puberty until around twenty or so, but you are tall enough as it is."

"Must be nice," said Meg with a warbling laugh. "You know, not being Lilliputian. Like me."

I peered at them. Things had been on the weirder side recently, but this was a new shade of uncomfortable. Harper seemed about ready to start flapping her arms until she took flight.

"Yeah," I said slowly. "I didn't hear back from either of you last night. Do you want to take a homework break after school? I was thinking we could go—"

"I can't," Meg interrupted. "I'm doing an extra-credit project for Gender Roles. I'm going to watch three versions of *Pride and Prejudice* back to back to point out the impact that the production date has on the gender normativeness—"

"Is that a word?" Harper asked. "Normativeness?"

"I think so," Meg said.

"Anyway," Harper continued blithely, "Cornell and I are going to the library after school. We're going to get a head start on the American Immigrant final. You're welcome to come, if you want."

I did everything possible not to roll my eyes at her. Being stuck with Harper and Cornell in their love den of a study room at the public library would definitely register as one of the lower levels of the Inferno. Even Dante would have thrown up his hands and said, *Hey Virgil, this is too much. Let's go back to the level where everyone is being stung by wasps.*

"You could come watch *Pride and Prejudice* with me," Meg offered. "I could convince my mom to make something vegetarian for dinner."

"That's okay," I said to both of them. "But, if you don't hear from me by tomorrow, make sure I didn't go all Rip Van Winkle."

Meg's mouth flopped open and her eyes shone with bright and blatant shock, which was a bit extreme in the reaction department, even for her.

"Sorry," I said. "Too early for a Washington Irving pull? I thought Sleeping Beauty would be too glamorous for the drooling-on-a-tube-slide imagery."

"No," Harper said. She jerked her chin in the general direction of my left shoulder. "That."

I turned and saw the boys walking toward us from the parking lot. Jack had extricated himself from the group, veering in a parabola toward the gate. Peter was limping next to Cornell, whose stride shortened to keep from making Peter strain his knee. They were in uniform, the same pair of pleasant smiling faces that I'd gotten used to seeing across from me at lunch. There was a third boy behind them. His hair was cropped short on the sides and twisted and teased into a messy point above his forehead made up of smaller, messier points. As he fell into step with Peter, his mouth curved to the side in a cocky smirk and I held back a squawk of alarm.

At some point between calling me a hag at lunch the day before and now, Ben West had shaved his mustache and had a haircut. He may also have grown an inch or so, if that were possible. Or maybe he was just standing up straight without his facial hair weighing him down.

"Hey," Cornell said as they reached us. He wrapped an arm around Harper's waist and bent to kiss her.

"Oh my God, Ben," Meg squeaked as West and Peter approached.

"Oh my God, Meg," West parroted, hooking his thumbs in the straps of his backpack. He hazarded a glance at me. "Morning, Trix."

I tried to remember the last time I'd seen West clean shaven. Junior year, he hadn't had the silly mustache, but he had taken to not shaving his scruffy face as some signal to the general public that he was a pubescent male.

"Well spotted. It is, in fact, morning," I said, schooling my face so that I wasn't gaping at him along with the girls. "Were you attacked by a deranged barber?"

He reached up and touched his bare upper lip with an unmistakable longing.

"Something like that."

He looked away from me quickly, as though afraid of what I'd say next. Which wasn't entirely unfounded. I could have made endless jokes about his makeover. *She's All That, The Princess Diaries, My Fair Lady*—my friendship with Meg was a continual source of chick-flick-related insults, even if they pandered to gender normativeness. But none of them seemed entirely appropriate.

"You look great, Ben," Harper said, her head pressed to Cornell's shoulder.

West grinned at her. His smile seemed broader without the mustache to impede its progress. "Don't flirt with me in front of your boyfriend. He might go all Othello on us."

Cornell laughed, folding his fingers through Harper's. "Shakespearean racism. Great job, Ben."

"Just trying to keep it classy," West said.

"I'll try not to drop a handkerchief anywhere. I'd like to avoid being strangled, if it's all the same to you two." Harper giggled and Cornell nudged her, chuckling into her hair.

"You look like the ninth Doctor," Meg said, still beaming at West.

"The tenth," West and I corrected in unison. I shot him a dirty look and continued, "The ninth was shaved head, big ears. You're thinking of David Tennant, Megs."

Peter scrunched his face. "I'm totally lost. Is this another *Star Wars* reference?"

Harper craned her neck back to look at Cornell. "How can you be best friends with someone who thinks the Doctor is from *Star Wars*?"

"He means well," Cornell said. "He was born without the geek gene. He's getting good at playing Magic, though."

"The Doctor," I explained to Peter gently, "is the main character on the long running BBC series *Doctor Who*. West's new product-heavy look is reminiscent of the tenth actor who played him."

"Oh," said Peter. "Is that good?"

"There are worse things," I said, refusing to jump on the "let's all congratulate Benedict for grooming himself" bandwagon. "Can we go in now? I have notes to take and ranking to secure."

Everyone agreed, although Meg made a derisive noise at my mention of the ranking. We moved through the gates in V formation with Harper and Cornell's clasped hands operating as the apex.

"Are we still on for this afternoon?" Cornell muttered to her.

"Definitely," she said. "How did your rough draft go?"

"Oh, I'd say it's pretty solid."

"Are you going to let me peek at your notes before I write mine?"

"That's completely unfair," I said. "You can't join forces against us."

"That's collusion," West agreed.

Harper and Cornell shared a smile while Meg swallowed a series of giggles. I goggled at them, not understanding the joke.

"Sorry," Harper said with a delighted shiver. "We're all in the same class. Our notes should be about the same, right?"

We hit the front door and Cornell held it open, motioning all of us through. Meg and Peter waved to us and joined the throng heading toward the quad. Harper and Cornell veered toward the American Immigrant classroom, whispering to each other and giggling like little children. West passed me with his head down. I sighed and followed him into class.

Me   [2:51 PM]
Hulk smash. Must eat sandwich.

Don't say I told you so.

Meg   [2:54 PM]
The Thought Experiment proved that breakfast
was fundamental to metabolic stability.

Me   [2:55 PM]
THAT MEANS I TOLD YOU SO.

✮12✮

My stomach rumbled through both of my last classes until I was positive that I could feel the vibration in my temples. I pushed through, my fingers flying over the keys of the electronic quiz Mr. Holbrook had set up.

I'd spent lunch in the library to study. Jack had also been forgoing sustenance, his wide back hunched over the keyboard of his laptop next to a pile of textbooks.

"Programming Languages sucks," he'd said as I passed him.

"Agreed." I paused. Jack had been ghosting around the cafeteria lately, appearing in line and then disappearing again. A wriggle of annoyance twanged up my vertebrae as he ducked his head behind his screen again. I didn't like Jack Donnelly, but there was only so much damage I could be responsible for. I cleared my throat. "Hey, I'm sorry about that evil twin comment from the other day."

He didn't look up. "Who wants to be the good twin?"

It was a fair point.

"You didn't come back to sit with us," I said. "I didn't want that to be my fault."

"I don't have a problem with you. But Ben West never shuts up."

He set his hands to the keyboard again and started typing. "I'm not Peter. I don't have to spend time with the student council when I don't want to."

No one would ever mistake you for Peter.

"Okay. Good talk," I said.

I'd found an empty table and rummaged for my notes. My stomach protested, but I promised it a sandwich and spent forty-five minutes trying to commit the three equality functions equations to memory. It seemed to work. I finished the quiz with seven minutes to spare and watched the clock in the corner of my screen until the bell rang.

I was the first person out the door—although I had to shove Nick Conrad for the privilege. All but running, I scampered out of the front gate, making my way to the deli between the Mess and the park near my house in record time. Sweating despite the chill hanging in the air, I darted inside the deli and purchased the largest hummus-and-sprout sandwich available. I scarfed a bag of chips on the walk to the park, washing it down with half a bottle of soda.

I really should have taken Meg's advice on the merits of breakfast. The Great Thought Experiment wasn't always wrong.

The park was deserted. Each blade of grass in the field moved eerily in the light breeze. The chains on the swings creaked. Metal and wood groaned under my feet as I climbed up to the play structure. I threw myself down and inhaled my sandwich with far less chewing than I would normally employ. I crumpled the parchment paper and flipped open my bag to retrieve my comics and a cardigan. With food in my stomach and a sweater on, I was immediately less frantic. I hopped down off the play structure, dragging my bag by the strap, and crawled through the bark under the small slide.

The cement cubby between the slide and the stairs had always struck me as some kind of design flaw. Thousands of local kids had probably hidden from their parents in it when told it was time to leave. Someday, the city would realize there was a nonplastic park still in existence and would rip the cement and splintered wood out of the ground. But, until then, I had one perfect place to go.

I wedged myself inside the cubby, pressing my back to one wall and my feet against the other. Once upon a time, I'd been able to fit here with Harper. We'd hidden during a third-grade birthday party that our parents had forced us to go to. I couldn't remember whose birthday it was, but I could vividly recall Harper and I squeezing into the cubby to avoid playing Red Rover on the green. Back then, it was our personal submarine; I'd been in my Jules Verne phase. Now, it was my personal sanctuary. Call it yet another pitfall of having no siblings, but I liked my private space.

I let out a contented sigh as I opened the first comic I'd brought with me. The cubby was protected from the breeze, keeping my pages from ruffling. I read leisurely, savoring each panel and speech bubble as though I had all the time in the world—instead of a back-pack full of new homework.

Halfway through the third comic, I heard footsteps outside of the structure. I lowered the soda from my mouth, praying that it was a jogger or someone else who wouldn't interrupt my quiet time. It was almost too cold for anyone else to be outside. I really didn't want to have some prodding child discover me hiding under the little slide.

But instead of the pitter patter of obtrusive feet, the stairs beside me shuddered with heavy footfalls.

"This is huge. No, gargantuan. This is so frakking ginormous that I have to use made-up words and possibly apply Hubble's Law to the situation."

I sat up straight, thwacking my forehead against the cement as I recognized Meg's voice. I started to slide out of my hidey-hole when Harper's voice said, "We can't tell Trixie."

With one hand pressed to the wall of the cubby—and the other pressed to my throbbing head—I froze. The concrete scraped against my palm as my arm slid down the wall into my lap. Granted, the last few weeks hadn't been the coziest our group had ever seen and I knew that they were continually having conversations that weren't for my ears, but I'd assumed that they were upset about me not getting along well enough with the student council. But this was information that I wasn't supposed to have. I stared up, as though I could will myself to have X-ray vision and see my best friends.

We didn't hide things from each other. We'd never needed to. Harper told me when my essays veered off topic. Meg told me when I was projecting. We were all in charge of making sure no one's bra straps were showing. It'd been us against the world since elementary school.

"We have to tell her," Meg shouted. I felt a swell of relief in the pit of my hummus-lined stomach. At least she was on my side. Whatever my side happened to be.

"No," Harper countered. "I swore to Cornell that I wouldn't tell her. I probably shouldn't even have told you, but I couldn't keep it a secret anymore."

In my head, I tabulated a list of secrets Harper and Cornell could be fostering. She'd been fairly mute about the physical part of their relationship. Had they moved past chicken-peck kisses?

That wouldn't be damaging to me personally. I wasn't the guardian of Harper's nether regions and I'd been the one threatening to push them into closets.

"If he was in love with me, I'd want to know," Meg said loudly. "I'd run across town, bang on his door, and throw myself into his arms."

"But you aren't Trixie," Harper protested. "She'd laugh in his face if she knew he was in love with her."

My mouth flopped open. Someone was in love with me? Beatrice Watson me? Who in the world could be in love with me? Or, more to the point, who could be in love with me and would have confided that to Cornell?

I thought about Peter at the harvest festival and his offer of a relationship by default. Had I misread that entire exchange?

Now I was sure I wasn't going to climb out of the cubby. Not until I was absolutely positive about what was going on. Or until I got the feeling back in my toes.

"We should give her that option," Meg said. She sounded frantic, her voice constantly changing volume. "She could—"

"She won't," Harper said. I felt the vibration of her stamping her foot against the play structure. "You know she won't. She'll tear him apart for this. God, you know what she's like."

What she's like? I thought, my hands crumpling my comic. *Your best friend? Loving and nerdy if a little opinionated?*

"I know," Meg said. There was a thump and her voice was suddenly closer. I guessed that she'd sat down. "But maybe she could see that he's, you know . . . perfect. I mean, no offense to Cornell—"

There was another thump and Harper's voice was closer, too. "No, I get it. Cornell is amazing, but Ben . . . Ben is geeky and smart and funny and considerate."

Ben?! I mouthed the name, trying to make it sink in. There was no way to confuse Ben with Peter. But the idea of Benedict West being in love with me was so ludicrous I almost laughed. Remembering that I was eavesdropping, I slapped my comic to my face. Obviously, someone had their wires crossed. There was absolutely no chance that Ben was in love with me. He couldn't even be in the same room with me without verbal bloodshed.

"Do you know what he did when he heard that Kenneth Pollack was trying to frame his frosh?" Harper continued. "He wrote an affidavit. He even had it notarized before he brought it to Dr. Mendoza. He said that if Brandon Calistero went on academic probation, then he would strip himself of his ranking in protest. Who else would do that? I mean, Trixie's been really nice to Brandon, but Ben went above and beyond."

"He's more mature than any other guy on campus," Meg mused. "And when he showed up today with that haircut and his mustache shaved, I almost fainted. He's legitimately hot."

I tried to picture Ben West's face, sans silly mustache. The haircut was definitely an improvement. And he did have a strong jaw, there was no denying that. The problem was the mouth attached to it.

"Did he cry?" Meg asked suddenly. "After the harvest festival? I couldn't even believe how awful she was to him."

I started to shout at them that I had no way of knowing that West was lurking under that stupid clown mask. I'd been fighting off a panic attack. I couldn't control the nonsense coming out of my mouth when I was surrounded by zombies, even if they were just the sophomores caked in makeup.

"He's devastated," Harper said. "Cornell and Peter are so worried about him. Because even after what she said—"

"The idiot savant thing or the part where all of his old friends ditched him?"

"Both. Even after that, he's still completely and utterly in love with her. I guess he always has been. Have you noticed that he's never even looked at another girl on campus? He's only ever loved Trixie. Since the first grade when the thing with the monkey bars happened."

"Is that why he pushed her?" Meg asked.

"That's the worst part," Harper wailed. "He didn't mean to. He told Cornell that he'd been trying to hold her hand and she slipped. He's been trying to make up for it for years and she's so—"

"Blind," Meg simpered.

"Exactly. She'll always hate him."

"You're right. We can't tell her," Meg said softly. "If she knew that he wasn't really fighting back because he loved her, she would eviscerate him. He deserves better than that. Can't Cornell or Peter talk him out of it?"

"They've tried," Harper said. "But it hasn't done any good. And he's been trying so hard this year. Like when he recited that Oscar Wilde poem at lunch? And she just ignored him."

Because he was trying to steal B's spotlight. But that didn't seem right. Why would he try to stomp on B's moment if he'd risked having his ranking stripped so B could walk free? Ben had been looking at me while he quoted the poem. He hadn't even noticed when the rest of the table around him had gone back to planning.

Dear God. Were they right? Was this real? Did this really span all the way back to the monkey bars?

"The boys keep trying to tell him to stop talking to her," Harper continued. "But he insists that it's better to let her tear into him because at least she's paying attention to him."

"We should tell him to stay away from her. Who knows what she'll say to him next? One wrong word and—I don't even want to say it. He'll—he'll—"

Harper's voice was barely loud enough for me to hear. "He'll kill himself."

I was starting to feel the walls of the cubby closing in. My skull felt like it was packed with fiberglass. I was trapped in this alternate universe where up was down and black was white and I was some kind of horrible demon who had never noticed that Ben West was in love with me.

Ben West was in love with me. Like telling-his-friends-and-possibly-on-the-brink-of-suicide-if-I-kept-making-fun-of-him in love with me.

Oh my God. I puffed out my cheeks to keep from hyperventilating. *The mustache. He shaved off the mustache. Because I went too far. I hurt him and I didn't even know. I thought it was all the same game.*

But it'd never been a game. Ben had been trying to silently communicate his love for me since we were six years old on top of the monkey bars. And I had been trying to make him shut up—or cry—for just as long. Every time I made a dig about his intelligence or mentioned his mother moving across the country to start a new family or anything else in my arsenal. . . .

I was a bully.

I was a monster.

Even my best friends knew that I couldn't be trusted. I was the Hulk and they were the Illuminati deciding to ship me off to a planet where I couldn't hurt anyone.

What could I do about it? I couldn't run across town and bang on his doorstep, the way that Meg would have if it had been her. First of all, I didn't even have my bike with me. Second of all, I had no idea what I would say. I was in no way prepared to deal with this.

"I need to get home," Harper said. "I still have to start my American Immigrant paper. But after lunch today, I couldn't study with Cornell. Ben looked so depressed when he realized she wasn't coming."

"But what about Monday?" Meg asked. "What do we do?"

"I'll try to get to Ben before Trixie can. I'll tell him that he should stay away from her as much as possible. Maybe he can switch to different classes next term. I bet Peter could pull some strings in the office to make sure they aren't taking anything together. That might help. Cornell said that Ben was having a hard time focusing with her in American Immigrant. He's already dropped in the ranking. You know he almost beat me for second last year."

"We have to do what's right for him," Meg said firmly. "He's such a catch. He's brilliant and funny and handsome and—"

"In love with the wrong girl," Harper finished sadly.

The structure creaked again and I felt each of the girls' retreating steps vibrating against the walls of the cubby. And then I was alone with a destroyed copy of the newest issue of *Daredevil*, shivering and close to tears.

"Trixie?"

"Beatrice Lea?"

My head snapped up and I stared at my parents, who were watching me in mirrored concern. The bowl of vegetarian chili steaming in front of me sent sleepy spirals of steam into my face.

"I'm sorry. What were you saying?"

"Oh, lots of things," said Dad. "We contemplated changing the curtains in the living room and then moved on to discussing buying a DeLorean and then we decided it would be best if we skipped dessert and played a rousing game of beer pong."

"What?" I asked on the wrong side of shrill. My brain had been the consistency of pudding for close to two hours. I felt it attempting to create thoughts through the sludge. "Beer pong?"

"We asked how your Programming Languages quiz went," Mom said. "And then Sherry ate the biscuit you dropped on the floor."

"Oh."

I glanced down and saw that Sherry's nose was covered in crumbs. Normally, I would have pointed a threatening finger at him for stealing portions of my dinner, but I wasn't hungry. There was too much hummus and anxiety pushing around inside of me, fighting each other for dominance.

"Rough day at the salt mines?" Dad asked me.

"Kind of," I said.

I wasn't comfortable with the idea of laying the Ben West situation out for my parents. I was sure they were full of the usual roundabout adult wisdom about unrequited love, things like *Let him down gently* and *Treat others the way you want to be treated.* But I was incapable of thinking of anything else at the moment. I kept replaying snippets of Harper and Meg's conversation.

You know how she is.

He's in love with the wrong girl.

"I think I'm having lady problems," I grumbled, pushing my bowl away.

Mom immediately sprung to attention, her face setting into its official Doctor Watson lines. Pursed lips, narrowed eyes. "Do you need a heating pad or some anti-inflammatory—"

Dad gargled his chili in discomfort. My hands twitched the universal sign of *No, stop now, please.*

"I'll be fine," I said. "I'll take Sherry and lie down for a bit."

I stood and snapped my fingers lightly until Sherry jumped up and followed me, probably thinking that I had a stash of biscuits for him somewhere. I grabbed a bag of his treats from the top of the fridge and retreated to my bedroom. I stuffed a Milk-Bone into his mouth before sprawling onto my bed. I curled myself around my Iron Man pillow while Sherry crunched happily on the floor.

Seventeen years of life had prepared me for a lot of things. I was a fine cricket player and I could sew a dress in two hours and I could strip down any literary text until it was just metaphor and authorial intention. But I was utterly lost when it came to this newfound issue of boys. Or boy, I guess.

On the one hand, I was horrified. Not just that the first person to fall in love with me had been Ben West, but that it'd happened a decade ago and I'd never noticed.

On the other hand, it was almost nice. I'd always assumed that I wasn't the kind of girl that anyone would stay up late thinking about. And here I was with a boy who was thinking about me. It just happened to be a boy whom I spent hours torturing.

And what did that say about Ben that he'd accept that kind of punishment from me without losing interest? Was that a sign of psychological damage?

I decided that wasn't fair. Because the constant dueling was fun. Even West wouldn't have been able to deny that. Some people played Sudoku or chess to flex their intellect. Ben and I used words. Not only with each other, but with everyone. If I changed tactics to avoid continuing to crush his soul, it wouldn't necessarily be all that different. Meg had pointed out that West and I were similar. We read the same comics and watched the same TV shows. There had to be a way to converse with him that wouldn't end in further destruction.

Somehow.

I frowned and glanced over at my phone, sitting silent on top of my covered sewing machine. The thought of undertaking this change of heart without the help of Meg and Harper was disconcerting. I wanted to call them over and have them reassure me that I wasn't the monster I thought I was. Stubborn, sure, and maybe even a little too dogmatic and crass, but not entirely without hope.

But I couldn't tell them I'd overheard their conversation. There were too many things I wasn't ready to talk to them about. I didn't have a plan of action and they had already decided to keep me away from Ben. Which wasn't the worst idea ever. If they could talk him out of his feelings for me, then I'd never have to tell anyone that I knew about it.

The idea needled at me. I rolled onto my back and stared up at the ceiling. I couldn't lie—to myself or anyone else—and say that I'd ever had a similar inclination toward Ben. Except in the haunted house.

The haunted house. Why hadn't I seen it the second I realized that Ben and the clown were the same person? He'd leapt in to rescue me, offered me his arm, made me laugh. I'd felt more in five minutes with him than I had in an hour alone with Peter. I'd come home and obsessed about it and made plans to track him down.

He'd been there the entire time, hidden behind a ghastly piece of facial hair and ten years' worth of rivalry.

If I was being honest with myself—and I was, far beyond my comfort zone—I did look forward to seeing him. Not exchanging words with Ben during the day was as disappointing as not talking to Harper or Meg. Attempting to say something nice to him would be like sparring with a foiled blade. That made it a sport instead of a bloodbath.

Monday morning, Harper and Meg intended to corner him and tell him to stay away from me. I couldn't let that happen before I had the chance to talk to him for myself. At the very least, I needed to apologize.

But more than that, I wouldn't know how I really felt about this until I was standing in front of him.

Harper [6:22 PM]

Cornell told me he loves me.

Me [6:23 PM]

Whoa! Already?

Meg [6:24 PM]

OMG OMG OMG. Yay! Tell us everything!

Harper [6:25 PM]

He had dinner with me and my dad at that new Indian place. And then he drove me home and said it. And I almost forgot to say it back; I was so surprised. But I did and we are and it's amazing. Chicken tikka masala is the food of nerd love!

Me [6:27 PM]

Congrats! (Is that antifeminist? I mean: congrats that your feelings are reciprocated not that a man has proven your worth?)

Meg [6:29 PM]

Please email me all details that you're comfortable with. I need the notes for my thought experiment.

Harper [6:30 PM]

Pylean dance of joy

✫ 13 ✫

It rained for the rest of the weekend and into Monday morning. With a Spider-Man umbrella held high over my head, I splashed to school. My plain black rubber rain boots protected my legs from most of the bigger puddles, but water soaked into my khakis, plastering them to my knees.

As I pushed through the front doors of the Mess, I closed my umbrella. A few stray raindrops splattered onto the top of my head. The hall was thick with the dusty smell of the heating vents and wet nylon taffeta from hundreds of discarded umbrellas. Stepping lightly to avoid my Wellies sending me sprawling, I made way to the American Immigrant classroom. I tugged at the hem of my cardigan, which, I realized too late, was slightly smaller than the last time I'd worn it. I never should have entrusted my laundry to my mother. Apparently, an M.D. did not qualify one to tell the difference between hot and cold wash cycles.

Most of the desks were already occupied. Harper was turned around in her seat, chatting with Cornell. Ben was staring out the window. There were drops of rain trapped in the artfully arranged spiky bits of his hair. I swallowed thickly as I walked down the aisle.

"Hey," Harper said, beaming at me.

I hadn't considered how I would feel seeing her or Meg after Friday afternoon. But something traitorous and injured reared up in me, something that wanted to scream at her for keeping secrets from me, even if they weren't her secrets to spill. She and Meg thought they were helping. I couldn't deny that they'd made a valid argument for not letting me in on their covenant.

That didn't make it suck less.

I forced a smile as I sat down.

"Hi," I said. "How was your weekend?"

"It was okay. I finished my first draft of the final. You?"

"It was all right. Watched some *Red Dwarf,* read some Gogol. The usual."

I turned away from her, setting my umbrella on the floor beside me and looping the strap of my bag over the back of my chair. Out of the corner of my eye, I could see Ben lean a fraction into the aisle.

"Nice umbrella, Trix."

I found myself holding my breath as I glanced up at him, trying to take in his appearance without considering the past. He had a perfectly serviceable nose, straight and thin. His mouth, curved into a sleepy smile, had a heavy lower lip. His eyes were large and dark brown, edged with oddly long eyelashes. They blinked at me expectantly and I realized that I hadn't spoken yet. I wet my lips self-consciously.

"Thank you," I said. "Are you keeping up with the new *Spider-Man* run? The last issue was pretty great."

He tilted his head at me, his expression quietly surprised. "Uh, yeah. Miles Morales is awesome."

I nodded in agreement and turned back around, satisfied with a decent start. It may not have been a heartfelt apology, but it was definitely better than nothing at all. I avoided acknowledging Harper's eyes boring into the side of my head and busied myself with retrieving my binder.

———

I ran out of Russian Literature the second the bell interrupted Mrs. Gronski talking about *The Overcoat*. It was even bleaker outside than it had been when I'd arrived on campus. The sky was progressively turning a more ominous shade of charcoal and leaked fat blobs of water onto the kids speeding through the quad.

Hastily closing my umbrella, I squeezed into the cafeteria. The sound of my boots against the linoleum was drowned out by the cacophony of a full house. Everyone who normally took their lunch in the shade of the trees in the quad or pressed against the side of the gym was now trapped in the same room, smooshed together on long plastic bench seats.

Balancing a bowl of vegetable soup and a handful of oyster crackers on my tray, I shoved my way across the room to the student council table. While the Mess generally avoided the high school movie trope of having the "jock" or "weirdo" tables assigned in the cafeteria, no one ever seemed to accidentally sit down on the bench where the senior class officers ate. It remained empty, awaiting Peter and Cornell's arrival.

The sophomore and junior officers were crowded together at the other end, their trays pushed aside to make room for piles of poster board. I could just make out the outline of the words WINTER BALL under the ten hands that were all shaking glitter and pouring glue. Mary-Anne France was watching them with the resignation of a foreman overseeing a troop of monkeys as she idly nibbled spinach off the end of her plastic fork.

Froshling B was hunched over a plate of meatloaf and an open graphing notebook, which he made notes in between bites. As he was a much more welcoming sight than the crafters, I set my tray down next to him and his head shot up, a piece of ground meat spilling out the side of his mouth.

"Hey, Trixie," he said, clawing under his notebook for a napkin. As he cleaned the grease from his chin, I peeked at his notebook and found a handwritten spreadsheet. Tiny cramped pencil-written numbers were squeezed between painstakingly straight black lines.

There was even a small bar chart crammed into the bottom-right corner.

"Business or pleasure?" I asked, gesturing to the notebook with my spoon.

"Just some profit-and-loss specs for the winter ball." He flushed, waving over the paper with his dirtied napkin. He stabbed a finger at a figure in the middle of the chart. "Here's what would happen if half of the upperclassmen attended. There's an eighty-three percent return and it increases steadily from there."

I took a sip of soup and recoiled as it scalded the roof of my mouth. Choking slightly, I pointed at the chart on the bottom. There were letters under each bar with a plus or minus symbol beside them. "And this?"

B's face pinched and he glanced around the table, making sure that the crafting council members were still occupied before he lowered his voice to a conspiratorial whisper.

"That's the list of academic probation students charted based on their sway with the rest of the school," he murmured with a hint of pride.

"Really?" I abandoned my spoon and scooted closer. "How'd you figure that?"

"Eavesdropping, mostly," he whispered. He tapped the bar with the letters KP underneath. "See, Kenneth Pollack's probation hasn't hit that hard—the rest of the basketball team will still buy tickets to the ball for the most part. But Ishaan Singh—" His finger slid over to a much longer bar. "Since he's—or, was—the captain of the cricket team and the dance is a cricket fundraiser, that means we'll lose about thirty-two attendees, give or take."

"Wow, B," I said, leaning back. "You're quite the boy genius."

He squirmed and closed the notebook, turning his attention back to his meatloaf. "It doesn't mean we know how to actually fix the problem."

"Step one," said Ben, dropping his tray onto the table with a clatter, "is to get people to stop cheating."

Mary-Anne yanked her elbow out of the way to avoid him touching her as he leapt onto the bench. She slid closer to the crafting lowerclassmen.

"Good luck with that," she said, fluffing her coif as though Ben's presence had mussed it. "'Corruption, like a general flood, shall deluge all.'"

The corner of Ben's mouth twitched and he shot me a sidelong look of exasperation. "That's not the full quote. You can't edit Pope."

"You get the point," she said. "People are going to cheat because people are cheating."

I took another slurp of soup, ignoring the protest of my singed taste buds. I kept my eyes on Mary-Anne. "And if all of your friends jumped off a bridge . . ."

"It isn't peer pressure, Beatrice." She sighed, as though I were a very simple creature. She leaned over the table, her chest in danger of falling into her spinach salad. "Right now, it might just be athletes and people whose antianxiety meds stopped working, but what happens when the college rejections start coming in? People who worked so hard and then got wait-listed? They'll do something desperate. And it'll be mass hysteria."

"The seniors can't deal with the competition," said one of the junior council members, holding aloft a bottle of Elmer's glue. "If you compare our top five with your top five, our percentages are—"

"Oh please. You all don't factor," Mary-Anne scoffed. She cringed a smile at the girl's injured look. "No offense."

"Do you guys have to do that here?" Ben asked, pointing accusingly at the craft supplies.

"What's the matter?" I asked. "Afraid of a little glitter in your mystery meat?"

"It's not a mystery." He lifted his fork and stabbed into the end of his meatloaf, which wept a puddle of grease. "It's beef."

"I think it's turkey," B said. "Or pork?"

Ben frowned. "Huh. Then I concede to the mystery." He jerked his chin toward my bowl. "Still avoiding anything that had a face?"

I opened my mouth to respond and paused, searching his face for signs of pining. This was the boy who was in love with me, after all. But there was no mushiness in his eyes, no radiating waves of adoration. Mostly, he seemed vaguely disappointed in his meatloaf and confused by the accidental staring contest I'd started.

"Pretty much," I said. "I'd be screwed if they found out tofu was sentient."

He smiled, displaying the effects of many years of orthodontia. "If you're worried, we could take a slab to the bio lab."

I smiled back without thinking about it. "Better not risk it."

Harper and Cornell walked up with Meg and Peter trailing behind. Harper looked from me to Ben to Cornell and seemed to think better of commenting as they sat down. With a flush of embarrassment, I shoved another spoonful of soup into my mouth.

"We thought you'd gone to the library with Jack," Meg said, throwing herself down next to me before carefully smoothing her skirt over her knees. "According to the schedule, we're supposed to be at our table today."

"We are?" I asked, mentally kicking myself. I'd been so focused on making peace with Ben, I'd completely forgotten about our lunch timetable. "I must have confused the days."

"I offered to print it out," Harper said.

"I can't contribute to your spreadsheet addiction," I said.

"Excel is the gateway software." Cornell chuckled. "Before you know it, you're freebasing Gnumeric."

Harper elbowed him in the ribs and he laughed, capturing her arm and pressing a kiss to her knuckles.

"Speaking of spreadsheets," Ben said, turning to Peter. "Brandon's pretty much done with our research on the winter ball. I think we should go ahead and start selling tickets this week. More time only works in our favor."

"You mean before the rest of the seniors get put on AP and can't buy them?" Mary-Anne asked.

Ben's lip curled. There was a small nick in his cupid's bow. He must have cut himself while shaving off the mustache. It would have been a lot of work getting rid of that much hair in one go.

"Will you let it go?" he growled. "This whole third-dance thing was your brilliant plan. You couldn't shut up about it a week ago."

"That was before," she shouted, throwing her fork down. It somersaulted and rolled to a pathetic stop against a dried cranberry. "Now we might as well cancel the whole damn thing."

All around the cafeteria, heads turned. No one was focused on whatever conversation about quantum physics or Baroque composers or which video game system had the fastest CPU they'd been engaged in before. Everyone watched in horror as Mary-Anne threw herself, snarling, to her feet.

"This was supposed to be special," she screamed, slamming her hands onto the table. She wasn't even looking at Ben anymore. She'd turned on the room at large, her indignation making her seem bigger than usual—like a kaiju rising out of the ocean in a red blazer. "And all of you are going to ruin it. Your damn petty life problems are going to ruin everything."

She snatched up her plate and chucked it, full force, at the juniors. Vinaigrette-soaked spinach and chicken and cranberries rained down on them, splashing into soup bowls and sticking in their hair. Pink dressing splattered against the wet glitter on the poster board and the crafters howled. The junior girl next to Mary-Anne got the worst of it. She clawed at her eyes, trying to get the dressing out.

Peter leapt to his feet, his hands flying to try to stop Mary-Anne from finding another projectile. She twisted and roared as Peter held her back, her pulse visible in her neck as her manicured fingers scrambled for her bottle of mineral water. The table erupted in a chorus of furious, multilingual curses. The water spilled, forcing the rest of us to get to our feet to avoid the flood. B held his notebook and graphing calculator over his head, looking around wildly for an adult to save him.

Ben and Cornell jumped off the bench and ran around to help

Peter, shoving Mary-Anne backward, away from the student council, which was about three seconds from attacking her with their
plastic forks while chanting, "*sic semper tyrannis.*"

"No one cares about you!" Mary-Anne screamed, her voice con-
strained with the force of Peter's arms wrapped around her waist.
"No one cares about any of you! You're all insignificant. Why should
we do anything for you people? It means nothing! You mean nothing! You're all going to fail and it doesn't mean anything!"

"That is enough," roared a much louder, much angrier voice
somewhere outside of the chaos. Dr. Mendoza was striding toward
our table, buttoning his suit jacket with one hand as he walked. Even
the blob of mayonnaise in the corner of his goatee couldn't diminish his overall aura of total authority.

The cafeteria hushed. I nudged B in the side and he lowered
his arms, clutching his notebook and calculator to his chest like a
security blanket.

"Release her, Mr. Donnelly," Mendoza demanded.

Peter acquiesced immediately, holding his hands up in surrender. He, Ben, and Cornell stood aside, making room as Mendoza
eyed Mary-Anne, who was panting with the effort of keeping her
mouth closed.

"Miss France," Mendoza said, his voice back to its usual quiet
gravitas. "Perhaps I should make a phone call to Vassar and submit
an addendum to your letter of reference."

Harper gasped, but Mary-Anne stared back at him with no out-
ward sign that she'd heard him at all. A piece of her perfect hair slid
out of place across her forehead. Seeing her vaguely unkempt was
even scarier than watching her flip out.

"With me, please," Mendoza said. It was not a request.

Mary-Anne yanked her backpack out from under the table. It
slammed into the shoulder of the junior girl next to her, sending the
glue bottle flying across the wet winter ball sign. As the crafters
squealed and scraped smears of glitter off the poster board, Mendoza sighed and led Mary-Anne out of the room, his hand hovering
behind her elbow, poised to grab her if she tried to run.

We all stood and surveyed the damage. I kicked my messenger bag out of the way of the river of mineral water spilling down the sides of my tray.

"I'll go get napkins," Harper announced.

Meg scurried around the boys, patting the arm of the junior girl who'd been closest to the green zone. The girl's eyes were red and streaming and there was a chunk of chicken on her polo.

"Come on, honey," Meg said sweetly. "We'll go and get you cleaned up."

She ushered the girl out the same way that Mendoza and Mary-Anne had left, a line of other salad-coated officers following behind like ducklings.

Harper passed out handfuls of napkins like relief blankets. We all worked in silence, sopping up the puddles while the remaining crafters tried to clean the worst of the damage to their poster.

"In positive news," I said, sitting down and checking to make sure nothing had landed in my soup, "she'll probably write a bitchen sonnet for the yearbook about all this."

The bell rang and everyone pushed toward the rain-soaked quad. I waved to B as he scurried off to his next class. Harper and Meg were still deep in a renewed conversation about the merits of renting a limo for the winter ball versus driving someone's mom's car. Peter and Cornell were pretending to be interested. They moved through the door and I fiddled with my umbrella. When I looked up, the group was running in separate directions and Ben was holding open the door for me.

"Thanks," I said, lifting up the umbrella as I slid into the quad. Rainwater slammed into Spider-Man's face, sliding off the sides and flecking against my shoulders.

"No problem." He released the door and stepped into the deluge with a grimace. His hair immediately started to wilt as the rain hit it, sloughing off whatever product he'd used to create the spikes. He looped his thumbs in the straps of his backpack, ready to bolt.

"What's your next class?" I asked abruptly.

"Computational Biology." He paused, brushing water out of his eyebrows. "You?"

"Multivariable Calculus," I said, holding back the urge to demand which math class he'd opted for this year. Instead, I held the umbrella high enough to cover both of us. "No point in ruining your hair."

"Thanks." He ducked under the canopy, his neck swiveling to avoid losing an eye to one of the plastic bits on the end.

We walked toward the math and sciences building like we'd accidentally entered a three-legged race and instantly regretted it. His arm brushed mine and I clutched the stem of the umbrella until the metal cut into my hand. Which was ridiculous. I'd had a full week to come to terms with the fact that Ben was the clown. I'd held onto that arm for dear life at the harvest festival. It shouldn't take a zombie hoard to make us comfortable with each other.

He looked down at me and gulped before looking away.

"Cline's getting a bit overzealous in American Immigrant, huh?" he asked.

"Today's bit of *Angela's Ashes* was all right," I said. "His Irish accent is really coming along. It was decidedly less Jamaican today. Although it was almost New Zealander. . . ."

"Well, they've got sheep there, too. He's getting closer. I've got Graham for Math in the Ancient World. He sings equations. I'd gladly listen to Cline butcher dialects for hours than hear the Euclidian algorithm jingle again. 'The GCD is A and B. They're natural, you see. . . .'"

"Wow. That's both really obnoxious and really catchy."

"Exactly. It's been in my head for weeks. I can't shake it."

We lapsed into silence, continuing to plod forward. I was intensely aware of his proximity, the hint of laundry detergent smell on his clothes, the slight swing of his arms as he moved. I couldn't stop myself from cataloging all of it, overriding the existing Ben West folder in my head.

"Look," I blurted at the same time Ben said, "So, uh."

We both stopped moving, frozen in the middle of the mosaic *M* set into the concrete at the center of the quad. Rain pelted noisily into the top of the umbrella.

"Go ahead," I said.

He shifted his weight and his right arm shot back under the umbrella, the sleeve of his jacket soggy. He wiped it pointlessly on his hip. "Are you reading *Saga*?"

"I've never heard of it," I said. "Is it a comic?"

"Better. It's a Brian K. Vaughan comic." His eyebrows went up a fraction. "You do know who Vaughan is, right?"

"I'm not a dilettante, West. I read all of *Runaways*."

"He did a run of *Buffy,* season eight, too," he said. "But you should check it out. *Saga*. It's kind of gory, kind of *Star Wars*-y."

"That sounds like my deal. I'll add it to my list," I said.

Around us, people were dashing off into buildings and the clock was ticking, each second getting us imminently closer to the fifth-period bell. I was positive that anxiety couldn't lead to anaphylaxis and yet my throat did seem to be closing up.

Ben coughed and gestured forward.

Right. Walking to class. Breathing air. Avoiding rain. Normal things. Be normal. But my heart continued to pump a little too fast.

"You were going to say something," he said, tromping through a puddle. "Before."

"Oh," I said, with a sinking feeling that was not entirely unrelated to fear. "I was just going to say that you look much better without the mustache. Less like a supervillain. More . . . not a villain."

I know, I know. *Beatrice Watson, you have a genius IQ and that's the best you could come up with?*

"I am saving a lot of money on mustache wax." He grinned. "And tiny combs."

"There was wax in it?" I laughed. "That can't be hygienic."

"Probably not, but it was cool while it lasted." He glanced at me sidelong. "My mom didn't want it in my graduation pictures."

My first impulse was to express my surprise that he still spoke to his mother. I'd never really thought about the current state of their relationship. I didn't even know if he'd met his half sibling.

"Ben." It was weird using his first name. I didn't know the last time I'd attempted it aloud. I was fairly sure that I hadn't been calling him by his last name when we were in first grade. Then again, my parents had always maintained that I'd been overly precocious from the word go.

"I—" I faltered again. I'd spent all weekend trying to craft the perfect apology, but in practice, I couldn't seem to find the right sequence of words. "About the harvest festiv—"

"Don't worry about it," he interrupted as we reached the front of the math and sciences building, the most imposing of the Mess's various brick structures. Its spire stabbed into the blackening sky. "You were having a panic attack. No big deal."

"No," I insisted, stepping in front of him before he could reach for the door. The umbrella slipped and a raindrop hit me in the eye. Partially blinded, I could only vaguely make out the downward turn his lips had taken. "You were really nice to me and I was—" *Abhorrent. Reprehensible. A demon from a Hell dimension that only makes really mean people.* "Awful to you for no reason. Thank you for helping me."

"Don't worry about it," he said. "Thanks for sharing your umbrella. We're square."

He reached around me and opened the door. I looked up at him, from the damp droop of his hair to his earnest brown eyes to his toothy grin and thought, *Oh hell. I don't think we are.*

To: West, B.
From: Watson, B.
Subject: A Request

If I concede that Saga is amazing, will you bring the rest of the series to school tomorrow? Because it's crazy amazing and I'd rather not rob Busby to get the rest of the books.

Can of soda for your trouble.

Trixie

To: Watson, B.
From: West, B.
Subject: Re: A Request

Don't rob Busby over Saga. Over the Who figurines, maybe. I'd help with that heist. Dibs on the Cyberman.

A can of soda and the newest Buffy. Deal?

Ben

✲ 14 ✲

No eating, spitting, or smoking within six feet of them," Ben said, holding the plastic-wrapped comics reverentially between us as people shoved their way past into the computer lab for fifth period.

"I don't smoke," I said with a sigh of impatience. "I didn't make you work this hard for your soda."

Strictly speaking, that wasn't entirely true. I had purchased the soda and left it—with the *Buffy* issue—underneath Ben's usual seat at the student council table before everyone else had sat down. There was no point in alerting the world to this exchange of goods. B had seen me do it, but, being a good frosh, he'd kept his mouth shut as Ben had slipped the comic into his backpack. Everyone else had been too busy stressing the newest ranking coming out to notice.

"You lack my foresight." Ben smiled, propping one Mess-regulation dress shoe against the wall. A haphazard amount of shoe polish had been slathered across the toe, highlighting the scuffs and divots rather than masking them. "For all you know, I could read *Buffy* in a bathtub filled with barbeque sauce and a handful of lit matches."

"Whatever keeps you bathing regularly," I said, laughing. "I need to know what happens to Alana and Marko. They're like Wash and Zoe from *Firefly* but they've also got the whole star-crossed warring alien species thing going. And Lying Cat! Have I mentioned how much I want a gigantic cat who can tell when people are lying?"

"You could try to train Meg to do it," he said. "She's about the same size as Lying Cat."

"I'll work on that. But first—"

I reached out and snatched the comics out of his hand. He released them easily, chuckling as I tucked them into my messenger bag. As I redid the clasps on the bag, Ben's wide smile shifted into a rigid blankness. I followed his glance over my shoulder and saw Mike Shepherd lumbering down the hallway toward us. He was impossible to miss, a colossus of acne stuffed into a drenched polo.

"Hey, Mike," I said, ignoring the silencing look Ben was shooting at me.

Mike blinked at me before raising a meaty hand in a loose wave. "Oh. Hi, Trixie." He and Ben eyed each other in a moment of profound and unbearable silence, as though every second of their former friendship was being replayed in real time. Mike broke first and said simply, "Greythorn."

Ben gave an upward jerk of his chin. "Shep."

I watched as Mike continued down the hall and disappeared into one of the labs. Ben grabbed his backpack from the floor and swung it heavily over his shoulders.

"How long were you two chums?" I asked lightly.

"Eighth grade," Ben bit off, looking at the door Mike had disappeared into.

"Didn't you found the role-playing club together?"

He turned to me sharply, a familiar wall of hostility starting to rise up between us. "Do not start calling me Greythorn."

"Wouldn't dream of it." I pressed my lips together to prove that I could easily resist the impulse to mock him. He relaxed a fraction and I continued, "I was wondering what you thought about Alex

Nguyen getting put on the AP list. He played Dungeons & Dragons with you and Mike, didn't he?"

He rubbed his hand over the back of his neck. "Yeah. But there's not much to think about. I don't talk to any of those guys anymore. Shep didn't like losing the student council election to me."

I stopped myself from pointing out that the student council treasurer position was a dumb reason to end a friendship. It wouldn't help and I wasn't going to risk reigniting the battle of Watson versus West. If we went back to openly hating each other, I'd have to give back the *Saga* volumes currently poised inside my bag. And there was no way I was going to do that. They were my preciouses.

"But do you think he did it?" I asked.

"Why not? He was pretty far down in the ranking. I never saw him copying anyone's homework, but we didn't talk about classes much. It was all just the game. D&D is pretty involved."

I held back a derisive snort. Again, mocking him would accomplish nothing. But it was almost adorable how much weight he'd given that last sentence. "Meg said that Mike got heated about it."

"Yeah, well. Mike expects a lot from people." He tugged on the straps of his backpack. "The bell's gonna ring soon. Tell me how you like the books."

"Sure," I said. "Would you like that essay in MLA or APA?"

"MLA. I like a good parenthetical." He smiled and I watched the freckle next to his eye wrinkle out of existence. "Or just text me."

I felt my eyebrows fly up toward my hairline. Exchanging emails through the Mess site had felt safe. It wasn't unusual to get emails from people who'd missed a lecture or wanted confirmation on a due date. Texting felt personal, unregulated. It was completely outside of our lives inside school, where cell phones were strictly forbidden.

"I don't . . ." I paused and cleared my throat like I could somehow regulate my heartbeat through my esophagus. "I don't have your number."

"Oh. Right." He swung his backpack around and unzipped the

front pocket, retrieving a small notebook and a mechanical pencil from inside. His hand flew across the paper. He tore it out and handed it to me, his fingertips brushing mine for a split second.

I opened my mouth to say something—not that I had a witty line prepared—and the bell rang.

"Oh, hell." I shoved the paper into my pocket and started running toward the Calculus classroom.

It wasn't until after I was seated and Dr. Kapoor had started her lecture that I slipped the note out of my pocket and saw that, above the scrawl of numbers, he'd written *Ben "West" West.* Stifling a laugh, I put the paper in my binder.

The student body crowded into the halls of the administration building at exactly 2:50. It took about fifteen seconds before the screaming started.

The Plexiglas case was empty. The pushpins that had held October's ranking lists were still sunk into the corkboard, but there wasn't a scrap of paper left behind.

"No ranking today," Mr. Cline called, using his briefcase to push through the crowd as people hurled questions at him. "You don't have to go home, but you can't stay here."

At 2:53, the office staff had entered the fray, a legion of administrative assistants refusing questions and trying to push all of us toward the front doors. Mrs. Landry, the head secretary, was holding a stack of hall passes and using them to wave everyone away from the office.

There was a buzz of static through the speakers hidden in the ceiling. After a moment of muttering and paper ruffling, Dr. Mendoza's voice cut through the noise in the hall.

"Messina Academy students," he boomed. "I apologize for the lack of warning, but there will be no class ranking posted today. You will be notified by your first-period teacher when the list will be available to you. For now, we ask that you leave the campus. Any student remaining on campus after three p.m. will be dealt swift disciplinary repercussions." There was a pause. "Have a good afternoon."

The front doors burst open and I was swept up in the tide of vacating students. As I walked into the bracing cold of the front steps, I could hear a hundred different theories being bandied about. A junior girl was loudly declaring that Mary-Anne France was to blame for the ranking being pulled. Another was openly crying about needing her current ranking for her college applications.

"It has to be another probation," Harper said as she drove me and Meg off campus. "There's no other logical explanation."

"I'm texting Peter," Meg said from the backseat. "I tried to find him when Mendoza was talking, but I didn't see him."

"Why would Peter know anything?" Harper asked.

"He's student council president," Meg said, as though this should have explained everything. When Harper and I turned to her, she tossed her cell phone into her open backpack. "He's the liaison between the students and the administration. If they were going to tell anyone what's going on, it'd be him, right?"

"I don't think he even gets his own parking space," Harper said.

"Well, he should," Meg said, sulking. "And we deserve to know what's going on. They've never withheld the numbers from us before. It's an academic apocalypse."

"We'll survive," I said. "It's not forever. It's just not today."

With it being freezing cold out and periodically pouring rain, the girls and I had forgone our last few post-Busby trips to the park. Considering the last time I'd sat in my cubby, I'd overheard the girls casting—accurate, but hurtful—aspersions on my character, I was more than happy to spend time in Harper's bedroom instead.

To say that Harper was spoiled would be both an understatement and a skosh unfair. Nothing in Harper's personality reflected her state-of-the-art Apple products, her king-sized bed, or her custom-made comic book shelving. In talking to her, you couldn't see that her bedroom could have easily held mine and Meg's and still had some extra space for her walk-in closet.

Of course, Mr. Leonard, for all of his generosity, did prohibit her from having a television in her room, which was why my house was used for movie nights. But, still. The three of us could have lived in Harper's room for days without ever seeing each other.

With mugs of instant hot chocolate and bags full of new comics, the three of us settled into a comfortable silence. Thoughts of the ranking and the Mess disappeared as I turned the pages of *Uncanny X-Men* and *Scarlet Spider.* I curled up on the floor as I finished my hot chocolate and retrieved the first of Ben's *Saga* comics from my messenger bag.

"What is that?" Meg asked from her position on the gray loveseat in the corner.

It took me a moment to see that she was pointing at the comic I'd laid in front of me. I propped myself up on my elbows to see Meg's face clearly from over the bed between us.

"Oh, it's a Brian K. Vaughan series. Star-crossed lovers in space, intergalactic war. It's like if Joss Whedon wrote a *Futurama* episode." I paused, glancing down at the next panel. "A really R-rated episode."

Harper scooted down the bed and peered over the edge, squinting behind her specs to try to discern the page I was open to.

"Cool," she breathed, tilting her head to examine the artwork. "Where'd you hear about that? You never read indies."

"It's not that indie," I said, quickly closing the book. I knew that I could have told the girls that Ben West had been the one who'd mentioned it to me, but I didn't want to deal with whatever the reaction would be. As far as everyone was concerned, the last couple of weeks had been pleasantly incident-free. I couldn't explain that Ben and I had made a concerted effort to make small talk between classes without also explaining that I knew that he was in love with me.

And if the girls knew that I knew, they'd ask a lot more questions. Like what I intended to do about that particular problem. Or if I was encouraging him by playing nice. Or if I'd noticed the freckle next to his left eye that wrinkled when he smiled.

Yeah, I didn't want to talk about any of that. It was easier to keep quiet.

Lucky for me, there was a knock on the door and Harper's dad popped his head in. "Good afternoon, ladies."

"Hi, Daddy," Harper said.

Mr. Leonard stepped into the room. He was still in his work suit, his tie firmly knotted at his throat. His steel-gray hair was parted at the side. He folded his hands and eyed us over his knuckles.

"I received an email from Dr. Mendoza on the subject of academic honesty," he said. "It was addressed to all the parents of the senior class."

Meg's face fell and she closed the comic in her lap. "Oh crap."

I glanced at her. "You didn't tell your parents about the probations?"

"I didn't want them to worry about it."

"I'm sure," Mr. Leonard continued soberly, "that none of you is involved in any kind of unsavory behavior. But I implore you to be on alert for those around you. The scent of a scandal could severely damage your futures. College acceptance letters have yet to be issued and if any of the admissions boards hear that there is anything untoward happening at the Messina—"

"I told you," Harper interrupted, waving him off. "The three boys who were put on academic probation have nothing to do with us."

"Two athletes and the vice president of the role-playing club," Meg agreed. "Nowhere near our circle."

"Regardless," Mr. Leonard said, "be on alert. There is no point in jeopardizing your futures. If you are aware of someone passing off someone else's work as their own, report it to the administration office immediately. Even if that person is someone you hold in, ahem, high esteem."

Meg shot me a look of dry amusement. Any curiosity we'd harbored about Mr. Leonard's feelings about his only daughter announcing that she was in mad-crazy love with Cornell Aaron was assuaged by him straightening his tie—supportive, if uncomfortable.

I wished I could pat him on the shoulder and tell him we were all in the same boat on that front, but I doubted it would go over well. I wasn't even comfortable calling him Greg. I certainly wasn't going to attempt jocularity.

"Of course, Daddy," Harper said with a placating bow of her head. "Do you want me to make dinner tonight? I only have a short take-home quiz to do."

He smiled at her warmly. "No, you enjoy yourself, sweet pea." He nodded to Meg and me. "You girls are welcome to stay, of course."

"No." Meg sighed, stuffing her comic back into the blue plastic bag at her feet. "I'm going to have to go home and deal with my mother. Ugh. This is gonna suck."

"And I've got an essay to finish," I said. "No rest for the nerd girls."

"Better busy than bored," Mr. Leonard said. "Idle nerds become supervillains."

"Maybe that should be the new school motto," I said, grinning at Harper.

"It's catchier than 'truth and loyalty,'" she agreed. "I'll get started on the Latin translation after I drop you guys off."

Me [9:03 PM]
Saga is giving me all the feels. This is your fault.

Ben [9:04 PM]
It does that. How far are you?

Me [9:07 PM]
Marko's parents.

Ben [9:07 PM]
It gets worse.

Me [9:09 PM]
That is not comforting.

Ben [9:10 PM]
There, there. *pat pat* (It gets so much worse.)

Me [10:14 PM]
OMG WHAT JUST HAPPENED TO ME

Ben [10:15 PM]
I told you so. Vaughan will murder everyone you love.

Me   [10:16 PM]

He should join the Joss Whedon/Steven Moffat club of nerd torturers.

Ben   [10:18 PM]

The League of Extraordinary Character Killing Gentlemen

Me   [10:19 PM]

Ugh. I hate Alan Moore.

Ben   [10:20 PM]

WHAT. Watchmen!

Me   [10:21 PM]

Snore.

Ben   [10:22 PM]

V For Vendetta!

Me   [10:23 PM]

The movie was better.

Ben   [10:24 PM]

Turn in your geek card, Watson.

Me   [10:26 PM]

You can pry it from my cold, dead hands.

Me   [11:47 PM]

Quicksilver. Obviously.

Ben   [11:48 PM]

Obviously because he's cute?

Me   [11:49 PM]

You think Quicksilver's good-looking, Mr. West?

Ben   [11:52 PM]

I'm comfortably heterosexual. I'm not blind. I thought Rogue was your favorite?

Me   [11:53 PM]

I love her, but she's mostly useless.

Ben   [11:55 PM]

That's how I feel about Toad.

Me   [11:57 PM]

Oh! Did you read Marvel 1602?

Ben   [12:00 AM]

Yes. All hail Neil Gaiman.

Me   [12:01 AM]

The Doctor's Wife. Best Doctor Who episode of all time.

Ben   [12:03 AM]

Great episode. Best episode? Nightmare in Silver.

Me   [12:04 AM]

You like cybermen too much.

Ben   [12:07 AM]

They Are CYBER MEN. What's not to like?

Me   [12:10 AM]

You really like Asimov, don't you?

Ben   [12:11 AM]

Does anyone not like Asimov?

Me   [12:14 AM]

I respect what he did for the genre . . .

Ben   [12:16 AM]

TURN IN YOUR GEEK CARD.

✷ 15 ✷

"Where are we so far, Brandon?" Peter asked, clasping his hands behind his head.

Another rainy day, another crowded lunch. B struggled to open his binder without toppling over the drink of the girl next to him. He flicked through the color-coordinated tabs in the corners, the sounds of turning pages drowned out by the chewing, laughing, and general chatter of the student council table.

"As of yesterday," he announced, planting his finger at the bottom of a column of handwritten numbers, "we've sold forty-seven tickets."

Peter's hands flopped back into his lap. "Seriously?"

B cringed and shot a pleading look at Ben, who was yawning widely. I wasn't sure of the exact time stamp of the last text he'd sent me the night before, but it was definitely past both of our normal bedtimes. I'd stolen some of my mother's heavy-duty concealer to hide the bags under my eyes before I'd dragged my tired butt to school. Ben, on the other hand, had shown up late to American Immigrant with bed head and a splotch of toothpaste on his chin.

The toothpaste was, thankfully, gone now.

"Well," he said at the tail end of the yawn. "That doesn't include whatever they've sold today."

We all looked across the cafeteria, where the junior officers were sulking at a card table beneath one of their spangled winter ball signs. A blotch of salad dressing remained on one corner. The cash box had been shoved aside in favor of the secretary's physics textbook.

"Not that business seems to be booming," Ben finished, reaching for his soda.

"It would be if we'd opened up to the lowerclassmen," said the girl next to B, whose name I didn't know but who appeared to be the sophomore class treasurer. "With the rate of senior suspensions, you'll be lucky to have anyone left to go to the dance."

"Yeah," said the freshman president from behind a copy of *Beowulf.* "Do you guys even have a ranking list yet?"

I considered how lucky the table was that Mary-Anne had started avoiding the cafeteria. I'd spotted her and Jack Donnelly arguing near the library as I'd marched across the quad. If she'd been present, there was no doubt that it would have turned into a screaming match between her and the younger officers.

"The Messina handbook expressly says that formal events are for the junior and senior classes," Peter said with uncharacteristic force. He dragged the heels of his hands over his eyes. "It's too late to put in for a request to amend the policy."

"Well, I already bought tickets for me and Harper," Cornell said, loud enough to drown out the mutinous murmurs from the lowerclassmen.

"I could have bought my own ticket," Harper said.

"You can pay for prom." He chuckled. "It's more expensive."

"And I bought mine," Peter said. "What about you guys?"

I attempted to look engrossed in my grilled cheese, which was difficult as it was leaking oil at an alarming rate. I took an overlarge bite anyway and chewed painstakingly through the gush of rubbery bread and waxy orange cheese.

"I bought one for myself," Meg said pertly. She sighed, adding a soupçon of eyelash fluttering for extra innocence. "And Trixie is boycotting."

I rage-chewed at her, using my tongue to pry cheese off my molars instead of telling her to shut up.

Peter's jaw dropped. "No way. You have to go, Trix."

"I really don't," I said thickly as I started ticking off reasons on my fingers. "No date, no dress, no will, no way."

"Oh, bull," Ben said into his soda can. The sound echoed like a hundred scathing voices. "We're all going stag, except Corny and the Harpsichord—"

"Terrible nicknames," Cornell said.

"I kind of like them," Harper said, snickering. "Corny."

Ben ignored this, leaning back imperiously in his seat. "What's one big cliché high school experience?"

"Yeah, Trix," Meg cheered, reaching out and shaking my forearm until I thought I could hear my brain rattling. "It'll be a stag party!"

"That does not mean what you think it means," I grunted.

"We could all chip in and buy your ticket," Peter said.

My brain scanned tirelessly for a loophole. The winter ball was a fundraiser for a pointless and esoteric sports team. It was two weeks before finals. It was a slippery slope from winter ball to prom. I was too tall to wear high heels. I wanted to watch all of *Battlestar Galactica* again. I needed to ace my finals and win third place in the ranking. If we ever got the ranking back.

"Hell, I'll buy the ticket," Ben said, slamming his soda down on the table. Underneath the bravado and the lack of sleep was a stunning sincerity. The rest of the room disappeared for a second and I could clearly see that I was the only thing that Ben was looking at. It was the same look I'd envied between Harper and Cornell, a spotlight of love that only I could feel the scorch of.

He smiled, a slow unveiling of teeth. "Nut up, Watson. All the cool kids are doing it."

My heart rabbit-punched me in the teeth. "I will consider it. Everyone shut up about it for a while, okay?"

"Fair enough," Harper said, her lips stretched white with the effort of holding back a grin. "Terrible weather we're having, huh?"

Friday night was officially take-out night in the Watson household. With the kitchen table covered in white oyster pails, my parents and I took our plates to the living room. Mom and I had vetoed Dad's plan of watching both versions of *Dune,* arguing that seeing Sting in a metal diaper would put us off our spicy eggplant. So, instead, we settled in for Chinese food and *Fawlty Towers*. Classic BBC comedies paired well with all meals.

After I took my empty plate back to the kitchen, I curled up on the loveseat, wrapping myself in an afghan GG Bea had knitted. Sherry hopped up beside me, resting his chin heavily on my hip and licking garlic sauce from the tips of my fingers. I scratched his ears absently.

"You know," Dad said, setting his chopsticks down on the coffee table. "You really should have applied to a college in the UK. There's a ton of shows that we never get over here. It'd be nice to have a BBC supplier."

"The Internet exists," I said. "If we bought a region-free DVD player, you wouldn't have to ship me to another country."

"True," he said. "But think of all the *Doctor Who* swag we never get in the States."

"Oh, Scotty." Mom sighed, resting her head against his shoulder. "Don't say 'swag.'"

He furrowed his brow and tapped her arm in thought. "Merch? Nifty crap?"

I laughed, raising my index finger in the air. "I vote nifty crap."

"Nifty crap for the win! Boom!" He punched the air victoriously and Mom sighed again, resettling herself against his side.

"And this is why we had to stop having game night," she murmured.

Dad took her hand, entwining their fingers together before craning his neck down to kiss the top of her head. "P is for pwned."

I giggled. "And people let you teach their children."

He winked at me. "I know, right?"

The pocket of my pajama pants buzzed. Sherry leapt back against the opposite arm of the loveseat, woofing indignantly as I retrieved my cell phone. I glanced at the screen and took in a shaky breath as I saw Ben's name pop up.

Checking to make sure that my parents were focused on John Cleese shouting in fake German on the television, I opened the text message.

Come to winter ball.

The phone trembled in my hands as I covertly typed a response. Technically, the no-electronics' rule of a Watson movie night only applied to watching something for the first time and I had definitely seen every episode of *Fawlty Towers* at least a hundred times. Still, I didn't need my parents noticing what I was doing.

Why?

I squeezed my eyes closed and slid the phone under the afghan. I jumped when it buzzed again.

Because it's going to be lame as frak.

I held back a laugh as my brain shouted, *He watches Battlestar Galactica!* I had to stop myself from immediately asking him what he thought about the ending of the series. Making a mental note to badger him about it later, I typed quickly under the cover of the blanket.

I know. That's why I didn't want to go. I can sit alone in the cafeteria any day of the week. Why add formal wear?

He responded immediately. Why would you be alone if i'm asking you to go?

I reread the message until the letters went fuzzy. When I'd first thought of what would happen if I went to the dance, I'd imagined sitting alone and drinking punch, wondering how everyone else's night was going. But I wouldn't be alone. Ben wouldn't let me stare at a wall. He'd sit with me, equally uncomfortable with the surroundings, and pick a fight about the best Marvel superhero or which teacher on campus was the most likely to have a criminal past. We wouldn't bother discussing corsages or posed pictures snapped by our parents. We might get into a shouting match about the literary allusions in *Doctor Who,* but that would be worth leaving the house for.

And if I stayed home, I would miss spending time with my friends. I wanted to see who Meg tricked into escorting her around. I wanted to see Harper cluck and blush when Cornell asked her to slow dance. I wanted to make sure that Peter didn't use his knee as an excuse not to talk to girls.

I also wasn't opposed to the idea of seeing Ben in a suit.

I flexed my hands and typed slowly. Throw in a soda and you've got a deal.

Ben responded with a smiley-face emoticon. Diet or regular?

I sat up straight. "Hey, parentals? Do you think it would be at all possible for me to get an advance on my allowance?"

They exchanged a frown. Mom's mouth rounded into the disapproving O of "no."

"How much of an advance?" Dad asked tentatively.

"I don't know." I slipped my phone back into my pocket and pulled the afghan up around my armpits. "How much does a prom dress cost?"

The force of their surprise bordered on offensive. Mom's mouth flopped open and Dad's hands flew up to his cheeks like he was afraid they were going to fly off his skull. It was like seeing what happened when they shut the power off on the Hall of Presidents at Disney World. I cringed away from them.

"Uh, guys?"

"We could certainly pay for a prom dress for you," Dad said quickly. I wasn't sure but I thought I could see the image of his camera flashing in his pupils. He shot a sidelong glance at Mom. "Jeanie?"

"Yes," she said, seemingly shaking herself out of her stunned fog. "Of course. When do you need it, Trix?"

"Winter ball is in two weeks, so sometime before then. I think Harper and Meg wanted to go shopping this weekend, but I could hold off—"

"Do you have a date?" Dad asked.

I peeled back the afghan and got to my feet. "That's enough questions. I'm going to call Harper and see when they're going to the mall."

As I walked down the hall to my bedroom, Mom said, "I think that means she does."

"Okay, we can stop talking about it now," I called over my shoulder.

"Oh, she definitely does," Dad whispered loudly. "P is for pining."

"God, I wish I had siblings." I slammed my bedroom door.

Meg   [9:42 PM]
Omg! Yes! STAG PARTY!

Me   [9:45 PM]
Okay, I really need you to google that phrase.

Meg   [9:47 PM]
STAG PARTY EXCEPT NOT WITH STRIPPERS!

Me   [9:47 PM]
See you in the morning.

Meg   [9:48 PM]
!!!!!!!!!!!!!!!!!!!!!!

or the last time," I said with my head in my hands, "that is a wedding dress."

Meg sashayed side to side, letting ten pounds of lace flounce and ripple around her knees. "But it's a very short wedding dress."

"That does not negate the fact that it is intended for matrimony." I sighed, flopping over in the plush chair I'd been stuck in for the last twenty minutes.

My regret of agreeing to go dress shopping with Meg and Harper had started somewhere between Orange Julius and the first department store when Harper announced that she'd set aside four hours for this excursion. The regret had intensified at the second department store when Meg launched into a tangent on open-toed shoes. And now, in store number three, I was keeping myself occupied by plotting to eat enough sequins to have to be rushed to the emergency room but not so many sequins that I actually died. Which ruled out ingesting the last dress Meg had tried on.

"It is a very nice dress, Meg," Harper said, appearing out of the dressing room in a cupcake-dress the same shade of pink as her glasses. "But didn't you want something in purple?"

"I guess you're right," Meg said, stroking the skirt with an unmistakable longing. "I'll go try on the next one."

She skipped past Harper and disappeared into the dressing room in a blur of white satin.

"That's pretty," I said, gesturing to Harper's ensemble.

"Oh, please. I look like Glinda the Good Witch." She tossed herself down in the chair next to me, the toes of her sneakers peeking out from under the shimmering hem of her gown. "This might be more enjoyable for you if you actually tried something on. There has to be something here that you won't hate."

"I suppose," I grumbled.

She turned in her chair, the volume of her skirts making it difficult. She squirmed her way into a more comfortable position. "I know that this isn't your deal. But I am really excited that you're here. Most people go dress shopping with their moms. . . ." She trailed off and rolled her eyes at her own slip of emotion. "I'm happy I get to do this with my best friends."

"Of course," I said, feeling guilty about how impatient I'd been all day. I'd waved off my parents' offers to accompany me shopping without even considering how much it would have meant to Harper to have that option. Mr. Leonard had just handed her his credit card and an itemized budget for her spending.

I wondered, not for the first time, what Harper's life would have looked like if her mom had been alive. Would Mrs. Leonard have driven all three of us to the mall? All I could remember about her was her waist-length blond hair. The first time I'd seen her, I'd told Harper she looked like Carol Danvers, the original Ms. Marvel.

"No," Harper had said, her pale eyebrows drawn together over the big owl glasses she'd worn in kindergarten. "My dad says that she's a grown-up Supergirl."

I thought of Harper's harvest festival costume and trained my eyes on the floor.

"You always have us, Harper."

"I know." She smiled. "And the dance wouldn't be the same without you. You could even go in jeans, if you wanted."

"No," I said, patting the armrest between us and climbing out of the chair. "I came to find a dress. I guess I will attempt to track down something not awful."

She scrunched her nose at me. "Me too. This thing is crazy itchy."

I wandered out of the dressing area and into the fluorescent-lit and overly perfumed racks of formal dresses. Hangers clattered together as I smashed past a rainbow of sequins and lace. I wasn't a frilly dress kind of gal. No rhinestones, no straps made of flowers, no puckered skirts. Nothing that could get me confused with a dessert or a disco ball or an overgrown contestant on *Toddlers and Tiaras*.

I found a rack of black dresses. Black seemed safe. It didn't immediately scream, "Look at me!" and it wouldn't require the additional purchase of color-coordinated shoes. I looped a few over my arm at random and marched back to the dressing room to an empty stall.

Stripping out of my T-shirt and jeans, I shimmied in and out of the first three dresses to no avail. I threw each of them back onto their hangers with mounting frustration. As I reached for the next one, my phone buzzed somewhere from the depths of my pile of discarded clothes. I fumbled for it and found a text from Ben:

Found out who the new ap is.

Who? I sent, tapping my heel furiously into the carpet. After two days of no new information, I had let go of my theory that the ranking had been taken down due to a new cheater. If someone had been stuck on probation, word would have traveled fast.

Jack Donnelly, Ben replied.

"What?" I said to the screen as I started typing. Sure, Jack Donnelly was a sinister miscreant, but he was still a Donnelly. Donnellys didn't cheat. They didn't need to.

Of course, that could be said for most of the Mess's student body.

I tried to remember if I'd seen Jack since the ranking came down. He'd been consistently skipping lunch for weeks. I assumed he was sneaking food into the library with him while he crammed over his computer and avoided the rest of us. It had certainly looked like he was studying when I'd run into him.

But maybe cheating and studying were equally taxing.

Peter told me and Cornell, Ben continued. We're not supposed to know. His parents are contesting the charges.

Can they do that? I asked.

They're Donnellys. They can do whatever they want.

Apparently, I replied. Thanks for the info.

I tossed my phone back onto my clothes and started to run out of the dressing room before remembering I was still in my underpants. I snatched the nearest dress off its hanger and threw the mass of satin over my head.

"Meg? Harper?" I called, zipping up the back as I tumbled out of the stall.

Two doors opened and the girls popped into the hallway. Meg was back in her regular clothes, clutching a lump of purple tulle.

"Oh, Trixie," she cried. "You look beautiful!"

"Huh?" I looked down at myself. The black strapless dress that I'd flung on actually fit. And I didn't resemble a pastry. "Oh. Cool. No, Jack Donnelly is the reason the ranking got taken down. He's the new probation."

Harper stumbled forward, tripping over her skirt. She fisted her hands in the fabric and lifted it above her sneakers. "Jack?"

Meg stamped her foot, her cheeks turning an indignant shade of pink. "So, Peter did know what was happening!"

"They'll have to investigate it if a Donnelly is involved," Harper said. She paused, clucking so rapidly under her breath that she sounded like a tiny motorboat. "The Donnelly family contributes a lot of money to the school. Peter and Jack's parents went to the Mess. They were the third or fourth graduating class."

"But it's not like Jack didn't do it," Meg said. "He's, you know . . . Jack."

Harper frowned. "Being unpleasant doesn't necessarily make him a cheater."

"Maybe being a cheater makes him unpleasant," I said.

Meg hugged her dress closer to her. I spotted a rhinestone

hiding under the tulle. "Poor Peter. Did he seem upset when he told you?"

I stared at her in confusion before realizing that neither of the girls would assume that I would have received this information from anyone other than Peter. Harper saved me the trouble of lying.

"Of course he's upset. His brother could be expelled for this."

"Cornell and Ben are with him," I added quickly. "So, at least he's not dealing with the news alone."

Harper narrowed her eyes in thought, her tongue making contemplative *tsk*s. "I promised my dad that I would make some cookies for him to take to his office on Monday. I'll make some extra for Peter, too. I'll ask Cornell if he knows what kind would be best. Maybe peanut butter." She nodded through a series of unspoken items on her mental to-do list. Shaking herself back to normal, she looked me up and down imperiously. "You are buying that dress, aren't you?"

"I guess so." I smoothed the skirt, running my thumb down the seam on the side. "I think I could probably add a panel of something here. Make it a little wider, give it some personality. When we were buying stuff for the harvest festival, I saw some cool *Star Wars* fabric."

Meg's eyes widened. "You're going to cut it?"

I gave the skirt a tentative swish. It skimmed against my unpainted toenails like dark water. "Should I not?"

"No, no," she breathed. "It's just—that's going to be so frakking cool."

"It's like adding a T-shirt to your formal wear. It's very Trixie," Harper agreed. She ran her hands through her hair, letting it fall back into place in fractions. "I think that I'm going to go back for that first pink dress. Do you guys want to stop in the food court?"

"Oh! We can get funnel cake!" Meg squealed.

"And lemonade." Harper grinned.

"Best plan ever," I said, laughing. "Someone unzip me so I can be normal again."

Unknown Number [6:33 PM]

Hey, it's Peter. Did you hear that my brother got suspended? I told Cornell he could tell you, Harper, and Meg. My parents don't want a bunch of people to know.

Me [6:35 PM]

I heard. Sorry.

Peter [6:42 PM]

It's okay. I'm trying to get all of his homework together from 5th and 6th yesterday. Can I get the Programming Languages notes from you?

Me [6:43 PM]

No problem. Give me an hour or so to type them up?

Peter [6:48 PM]

Thanks x 10^100

Me [6:51 PM]

You're welcome a googolplex.

✪ 17 ✪

And thus," Mr. Cline said from behind his steepled fingers, "I must beseech all of you, on behalf of the Messina faculty and staff, to protect yourselves. If you are having difficulty in your classes or are contemplating some extreme end, please seek the assistance of a tutor or school counselor."

There was a contemptuous sound behind me. I looked up from the note I was tracing on my wrist and turned around, catching Ben attempting to hide his scoff in the sleeve of his shirt. He cocked his head to the side and rolled his eyes back until all I could see were glossy whites.

"There is no shame in asking for help," Cline continued, raising his voice to its usual theatrical echo. I faced forward again, choking down a laugh. "And there is no quick fix for falling behind. A grade you had to steal is a personal failure, whether or not it has been reflected in the letter red-penned to the top-left corner. *Fide et veritate,* kids. Truth and loyalty. Both will out in the end.

"And with that," he said, dusting off his hands as though their serious position had tainted them, "my duty is done. Please remember to read the McCune essay, making particular note of the idea of assimilation. There may or may not be something in the family tree of a quiz tomorrow."

The bell rang on cue and everyone launched to their feet, grabbing backpacks and coats in a flurry of activity.

"All of that because Jack stole an essay off the Internet," Ben grumbled, pushing his way over to me, Harper, and Cornell.

"Ben," Harper said in a scathing whisper, searching around us for obvious eavesdroppers. She dropped her voice to an almost inaudible murmur through clenched teeth. "You know that Peter doesn't want it to spread."

"What Peter wants and what Jack wants are unrelated," Ben said, adjusting his backpack and following as Harper and Cornell led us out of the room.

We stepped into a throng of passing students. Cornell inclined his shaved head toward the end of the hall where Brad Hertz and Nick Conrad were shoving their way into the quad. "Brad and Nick are already telling people that Jack's suspended for the week. They were talking to Mary-Anne when I got here."

"Are they hoping to turn him into a slacker Che Guevara?" I asked. "I would not wear *that* T-shirt."

Harper snatched the headband off her head and replaced it aggressively as she walked. "It does not matter if other people are talking about it. We do not need to assist the rumor."

"It's not a rumor," I pointed out, carefully skirting around the fact that gossiping about Jack Donnelly was how most of the senior class spent their lunch hour. "It's a fact. He is, in fact, suspended."

Ignoring me, she tilted her chin at Cornell. "I made chocolate chip cookies for Peter. He'll like them, right? I know you said that he liked oatmeal, but my dad—"

"God, Harpo." Ben groaned. "It's not like Jack has cancer. He just cracked under the pressure of being a Donnelly."

"Being a sullen jerk takes its toll," I added. "He's the Loki to Peter's Thor."

"Minus the costumes," Ben said.

"And the dead sexiness of Tom Hiddleston," I said.

Ben scoffed. "Man, I wish Peter would rock a winged helmet."

"You could get him a hammer as a hint," I suggested.

Harper stopped short. If she could have whipped off her specs and shot us with ocular laser beams, she would have. "You two are completely impossible. It was so much easier when you just went at each other."

I raised my eyebrows at her in patient quizzicality. "As you wish." Without waiting for her to respond, I turned to Ben. "Benedict, you have all the tact and intellectual capacity of an unmanned Muppet."

The corners of his mouth twitched. "We can't all be Skeksis. It must be hard since the Gelflings wiped out the rest of you." He looked back at Harper. "Better?"

I laughed. "We could bring up the monkey bars, but I think it'd feel forced."

Harper glared back, seemingly unaware that Cornell was straining with the effort of not laughing. She raised a threatening finger at us.

"If I'm late to second period because of that, neither of you gets cookies at lunch."

Turning on her heel, she strode off.

"Tough, but fair," Cornell said. "I'd better catch up to her before she starts ranting at innocents."

He jogged up the hall, following Harper out into the quad. Ben and I trailed behind at a safe distance, still giggling.

"A Dark Crystal pull?" I asked. "Old school. Very solid."

"I just took your lead. I hope we still get cookies."

"Me too. She made them with M&Ms. Meg will sneak some to us. She appreciates humor. Well, except for pretending to be a Lying Cat. She still refuses to say 'lying' on cue." I nudged him with my elbow as we came to the doors to the quad. I gestured to the left. "I'm off to Econ. Yay, Third World politics."

He twitched his head to the right, indicating the opposite hall. "I've got Gender Roles. I'll start hinting to Meg about the cookies. See you."

Without pausing, he reached down and took my hand, squeezing gently. My breath caught in my throat and I managed a choked "Later" before he released me and darted down the hall.

I stuffed my hands in my pockets, trapping the foreign warmth as I hustled toward second period.

"This," said Cornell, raising half a cookie over his head, "is a fine cookie."

"Mighty fine," Ben agreed, dusting crumbs off his shirt.

"You really didn't have to bring me cookies," Peter said, unironically shoving another one into his mouth and chewing with relish. "I'm not the one who got suspended."

Adhering to the seating schedule, we were tucked away at our old table in the cafeteria, away from the prying ears of the student council. As much as I felt guilty for abandoning B to the claws of his political peers, it was nice to have some semblance of privacy.

Harper turned up her nose with all the poise and profile of a monarch. "That doesn't mean you aren't also under stress."

Peter nodded in concession and swallowed with some effort. "It's been tense. It's not just my parents who are pissed. My whole family went here. So, half of the family is pissed that Jack is ruining the legacy and the other half is pissed that the Mess thinks that a Donnelly would cheat."

My ankle exploded in white-hot pain as Meg's heel slammed into it. I jerked my head to glare at her, but she just batted her makeup-enhanced lashes at me in slow, pointed blinks. She slid a cookie across her lunch tray, leaving it hovering on the rim. Her eyebrows waggled a fraction.

"Well," I said, picking up the bribe cookie begrudgingly, "did he do it?"

As Harper narrowed her eyes at me, Peter leaned forward, resting his elbows on the table. He spun his cookie between his fingers, examining the cracked candy shells of the M&Ms.

"I don't know," he said. "He keeps saying 'it'll work out.' I don't know if that means he's expecting the family to buy his way out of it or if he's actually innocent. They're saying that one of his essays is a copy of something that was turned in last year. But I've never even heard of the kid who wrote the first one. Just some girl who went here last year. She's a frosh at Brown now." He took another bite, wincing sheepishly. "I looked her up to make sure."

"I'm sure that Jack is right," Harper said, not even slowing down to acknowledge that it was definitely the first time anyone had ever said that. "It will work itself out. If he didn't know the person who wrote the original essay, then how could he possibly have cheated? It's not like there are copies of old essays floating around the school."

"Not unless there's a black market on campus we don't know about," Ben said affably.

"Do not make me take away your cookies," she snapped.

"No, he has a point," Meg said, scooting forward on the bench and dropping her voice to a conspiratorial whisper. "The Mess is a school for geniuses. You can't rule out malicious mischief."

"Idle nerds turn into supervillains," I said.

Ben grinned at me from across the table. "I like that. 'Idle nerds.'"

"I can't take the credit. Harper's dad said it."

"It's a flub," Harper said, her breathing coming in short bursts. "A mistake. There's no reason to start making up conspiracies—"

"What about Ishaan and Alex?" Cornell asked her. "And Ken Pollack? They all said they didn't do it, too."

"Then maybe they didn't. They weren't expelled, were they?" She pointed across the cafeteria in three different directions, pointing out all three of the AP boys at their respective tables. Alex was sitting with Mike Shepherd and the rest of the role-playing club. Ken was throwing something at Brad Hertz while one of the other guys from the basketball team held his phone under the table, secretly taking a picture. Ishaan was reading an extracurricular paperback book with a robot on the cover.

Cornell gave an incredulous laugh. "What do you think happened?

There were four random clerical errors that only hit the senior class?"

"Why do you want to believe the worst?" Harper countered hotly, swinging around on the bench to face him. She pushed her glasses up her nose as patches of pink indignation spread under her freckles. "Everyone assumes that the APs are guilty, but there's no evidence. It could be a glitch or the teachers being too quick to start calling plagiarism. We're all getting the same lectures and taking the same notes and reading the same books. It isn't out of the realm of possibility that some people use similar phrasing in their essays."

"But that isn't logical!" Cornell exclaimed.

Harper's jaw shifted, pushing out her lower lip, the tips of her teeth showing like the edge of a buzz saw. "Excuse me?"

Meg shot me a look and I knew that she was also hearing the ominous music that preceded Harper going berserk. Soon, her hands would curl into talons and her shoulders would shake and the freckled and bespectacled blond girl we loved would turn into a towering inferno of telekinetic rage.

"It isn't logical," she repeated menacingly. "You mean to tell me that there is no reality where Jack happened to use the same angle for an essay as a girl he never met and the administration decided to make an example of him?"

Peter drummed his fingers on the table and I thought I recognized the Morse code for SOS in the patter. "Guys, we really don't need to—"

"Here," Harper snarled, shoving the Tupperware container of cookies toward him without taking her eyes off Cornell. "You really think that if there was any evidence whatsoever they wouldn't immediately expel all four of the boys who were supposedly caught?"

Cornell reached for her hands. "Harper, I love you and I love that you want to believe the best of everyone but—"

"Don't," she bit off, rapping his knuckles as she shoved herself away from him. "Don't you pander to me, Cornell Aaron. Answer the fucking question."

Ben's eyes went wide at me and he mouthed, *An F Bomb?* I sighed, mentally retracting all of my previous delight at not sitting with the student council. Harper never would have lost her temper in front of the froshlings. Next time, I'd make sure B was with us.

"I think they gave Ken a slap on the wrist so he could keep playing basketball. They did the same thing last year when he beat up Ben," Cornell said flatly.

"Ah, memories," Ben said, grabbing another cookie. "I didn't know people gave swirlies in real life."

"What's a swirly?" Meg asked.

"Ken shoved Ben's head in the toilet," Peter said.

"And flushed," Ben added.

Meg cringed. "That's disgusting."

"Not expelling Kenneth for cheating set a bad precedent," Cornell continued, raising his voice over the others. "So the most Mendoza could do was suspend the others. That doesn't make anyone innocent. It means that the administration took a soft route and it paved the way for more bad behavior."

Harper clucked, swishing her hair over her shoulder. "The obvious parallels to McCarthyism are nonsensical? Everyone's guilty because they look guilty?"

"Yeah, I'm going to go ahead and use the dictionary definition of a coincidence. It's not something that happens over and over again," Cornell said. "People don't just happen to write essays that look like other people's work." His cheeks inflated with a breath that he slowly exhaled in a low hiss. "I'm sorry, Peter. I don't mean to say that your brother deserves to be expelled."

"No, I get it," Peter said. "If he did cheat, then he shouldn't get to stay. I don't want it to be—"

"Why?" Harper exploded. "Why should he be expelled?"

Peter twitched in alarm and looked around the table for assistance. Cornell squeezed his eyes closed, tapping out of the battle.

"Because," I said, with all the care and delicacy of passing a land mine, "academic dishonesty is the number-one no-no of the Mess? Or any school."

Harper bent forward like a predator ready to strike. Meg shivered closer to me as though I could stop Harper from diving across the table.

"Has anyone else considered the insane amount of pressure they put on us here?" Harper hissed, a wild glint behind her specs. "Do you know what other seniors are doing right now? They're reading Jane Austen—for the first time. They're taking pre-calc and getting a full night's sleep every night. When was the last time any of you got eight hours of sleep?"

A longing silence passed over the table. I distantly remembered waking up at noon sometime in July.

"But we're not normal seniors," Meg said softly. "We're here because we're different."

"There are geniuses everywhere," Harper said. "Other schools don't push them to the breaking point. Everyone who has been caught cheating went from Aragon Prep to the Mess. Thirteen years of never being cut a break. It's not healthy. I mean, if it weren't for the ranking, Ben and Trixie wouldn't have spent four years trying to kill each other. Now that it's been taken down, it doesn't matter who's number three."

Ben coughed, throwing me a horrified look. "It's not that it doesn't matter. . . ."

"Not knowing isn't the worst thing," I conceded. "Not that I have any doubt about where I placed."

Harper folded her arms over her chest. "But you don't know and so you can't flip out about it. If—and I'm not saying that I think he did it—if Jack cheated, it wouldn't be because he wasn't capable of writing an essay himself. Any one of us could have gotten into college years ago. There are genius kids all over the country who aren't stuck in a holding pattern. They leave middle school and go to college.

"If anyone cheated it'd be because of their ranking. Because we've been told since we got here that we aren't worth anything unless we're properly ranked. So, whether or not anyone is actually cheating, it's the school's fault for making us all feel like crap to start with." She whipped her head to look at Cornell. "Is that logical enough for you?"

"Remind me not to get on Harper's bad side anytime soon," Ben murmured in my ear as we watched a shell-shocked Peter make his way toward the main building with Meg beside him. Harper and Cornell had disappeared in separate directions the second the bell rang announcing the end of the longest lunch ever. "That was gruesome. Like watching Cinderella hack apart an army of teddy bears with a machete."

"Imagine how much worse it would have been without cookies," I said. "Cornell really shouldn't have told her that she wasn't being logical. He flipped her kill switch. She's a blond Spock. You never question her reasoning."

Ben shifted his backpack as we walked. "Do you think she'll still want to go to the dance next week?"

"You mean, do I think she and Cornell are going to break up?" I asked. He made a noncommittal grunt and I shook my head. "No, I think they'll be fine as long as he lets this drop. And we bought dresses this weekend. There's no way out now."

His mouth twisted into half of a smile. "Sound less excited, please. Your enthusiasm is embarrassing. It's like you got bribed into going."

I laughed, nudging him with my shoulder. "I did get bribed into going, you doofus. You all lambasted me. If I opted out now, I'd have to take my lunches in the library with Mary-Anne."

"Which would be much worse than putting on a dress and dancing." He grinned as we reached the front of the math and sciences building. He grabbed the door as it started to close behind the group ahead of us.

I made a face at him as I passed into the building. "I did not agree to dancing. Dress, yes. Dancing, not so much."

He followed me inside and down the hallway that stood between our fifth-period classes. I'd grown accustomed to this stretch of wall. It was ever so slightly closer to my Calculus classroom than to Ben's Computational Biology class because Dr. Kapoor would eviscerate me with questions if I got stuck in the front row. Mike Shepherd passed us with a half wave and Ben didn't even twitch.

"You agreed to go to a dance. Obviously, there is dancing involved," he said.

I leaned against the wall and looked him over. While my feelings about him had warmed over the last few weeks, he was the same gangly scarecrow he'd always been. He was just a scarecrow with excellent hair now.

"You dance?" I asked dubiously.

"Does the chicken dance count?"

"Are you a thousand years old? Why would they play the chicken dance at the winter ball?"

He bent close to me, his eyes shining with mock seriousness. "There are some perks that come with the weight of my elected office. In case you hadn't noticed, I'm a very important member of student council. I'm in charge of choosing and paying the band."

It was increasingly difficult to breathe with him standing so close. I caught a whiff of something that reminded me of apple cider. "And you're going to use this grand power of yours to request the chicken dance?"

"Unless you'd prefer the Macarena."

I wet my lips and took a small step to the side, just to maintain a modicum of my sanity. "I can't say that I know how to chicken dance or Macarena. We did learn the Electric Slide at Aragon in PE."

"I remember that. You complained the whole time." He reached into his back pocket and pulled out a click-top pen. Before I could stop him, he took my left arm and pushed back the sleeve of my cardigan until it bunched around my elbow.

I squirmed. "Those are my personal notes."

"Then you shouldn't have left them out where I can add to them. Haven't you heard of paper?" he said, holding my wrist in place with one hand as he wielded the pen with the other. The ballpoint pressed lightly against my skin as he scrawled. I tilted my head, taking the free moment to examine the points of his hair. There was a spike askew near his right temple. He straightened suddenly and announced, "There."

I pulled my eyes away from his fingertips still pressed into my wrist. Underneath my Russian Literature reading assignment, he'd written LEARN CHICKEN DANCE.

I laughed loud enough to draw the attention of the people passing us in the hallway. Clamping my mouth shut, I tugged my sleeve back down.

"Harper's wrong, you know," I said, glancing up at him as I fiddled with my sleeve.

He chuckled. "You don't think the Mess is working us like dogs? Because your wrist says otherwise."

"No, about us being . . ." I choked on the word *friends*. I hadn't stopped to consider whether or not Ben and I were friends now. It wasn't completely ridiculous. But it didn't feel like the right word— not that anything else sprang to mind as an easy replacement for it. I tried again. "About us being okay with each other now. I didn't hate you before the ranking was taken down."

"Ditto." He smiled before adding, "Not that either of us have stopped thinking about the ranking."

"Oh, of course not." I smiled back. "I will destroy you."

"And I'll buy you a soda when you graduate fourth in the class." He swung his backpack off one shoulder and unzipped the front pocket, pulling a white sliver of card stock from its depths. He handed it to me and I saw the words *Winter Ball, Admit One* printed on the front in a flowery font. "But first, you will learn to chicken dance."

Me   [8:49 PM]

Stop emailing me dance videos. I am not going to
learn Thriller. I have homework.

Ben   [8:49 PM]

First day of vacation, Trix. Can't you write essays
and listen to Michael Jackson at the same time?

Me   [8:51 PM]

You know I hate zombies.

Ben   [8:52 PM]

Do you want to borrow my rubber axe?

Meg   [6:02 AM]

Happy Thanksgiving, friends!

Harper   [6:04 AM]

Happy Thanksgiving!

Me   [7:05 AM]

Enjoy your turkey, meat eaters. It smells like burnt
tofurky in the Watson house.

Harper   [7:08 AM]

Trixie, you can come have squash with my family, if
you want.

Me   [7:11 AM]

I have resigned myself to eating an entire pumpkin
pie. That's the same thing, right?

Peter   [7:17 AM]

I support you, Trixie!

Ben   [7:20 AM]

Why are you all up so early? It is a holiday.

Cornell   [7:22 AM]

Dude. Parade.

Meg   [7:24 AM]

There's a Sonic The Hedgehog float!

Ben   [7:25 AM]

God bless us, everyone.

✸ 18 ✸

It seemed unfair to make the lowerclassmen decorate for a dance that they wouldn't be allowed to set foot in, but no one else seemed to question the mandate—probably because it came from Peter. The week back from vacation, the student council table was overrun by arts and crafts. Even Mary-Anne came back to the cafeteria to supervise the giant butcher paper scroll where the juniors were inscribing Wilde's "From Spring Days to Winter." Peter sat with us in three-minute stretches, wolfing down whatever was on his tray in between glad-handing the juniors and seniors into buying tickets.

"It's a shame he can't run for reelection," Harper said the Monday before the dance, watching as Peter sat down with some of the drama club girls. "This is easily twice as much work as he put into actually campaigning last year."

"That's because his campaign was, 'Hey guys, I'm a Donnelly; look at my family's name on all these plaques,'" I said. "Speaking of, did Jack actually come back to school today?"

"He's here. Peter's got him selling dance tickets in the library," Cornell said, stealing a French fry off Harper's tray. After their lunchroom spat the week before vacation, Harper had insisted that they'd "agreed to disagree." But she bristled as Cornell ate the fry.

"It'll be a miracle if the cricket team actually gets their uniforms out of this," Ben grumbled, fussing over a scientific calculator and making notes in the small notebook he kept in the front pocket of his backpack. B was stuck with the other frosh officers at the ticket table next to the door and he'd left Ben with a pile of price estimates.

Cornell elbowed him, grinning. "Remember in DC, when we told the other interns that our school had a cricket team? They wouldn't even believe us when we pulled up the website. They swore it was a prank."

Ben gave a vague laugh as he continued punching the numbers on his calculator. "When, in fact, it's just one of many dumb things our tuition pays for."

"What are you doing?" Mary-Anne shouted at one of the boys hovering over the butcher paper poem. She reached over and snatched the paintbrush out of his hand, waving it over her head like a dueling wizard. "It's a calligraphy brush, Marcus, not a crayon. Clean strokes! Clean!" She thrust the brush at the nearest underling. "Fix it before it dries."

"You guys actually have council meetings, right?" I asked Cornell.

"Every Tuesday," he said.

I motioned around the table, from the butcher paper to the piles of paper lanterns and pots of paint and glitter. "What do you guys do at meetings if you bring all of this here?"

"More of this," he said. "No one wants to sacrifice too much homework time, so it spills over into lunch."

Ben laughed under his breath, his head still bent over his notebook as he scribbled. "Believe it or not, there's more arguing."

"Lying Cat says, 'lying,'" I muttered. He glanced up at me and smiled.

"Have we officially given up on the idea of a limo for Friday night?" Harper asked, scooting forward on the bench. "It does seem kind of unnecessary to pitch in money just to get driven here."

"It seems like it because it is," I said. "I was anti-limo from the start."

"You were anti-everything at the start," Meg said, scrunching her nose at me. I stuck my tongue out at her in response and ducked as her hand shot out, poised to yank said appendage out of my mouth.

Peter reappeared at the center of the table. He leapt onto the bench and reached for what I assumed was a very cold hamburger, which he took three bites of in rapid succession. He threw a hand up to keep from showing us the massacre in his mouth. "What'd I miss?"

"Mostly crafting," I said.

"And transportation plans for Friday night," Harper said. "Will you have your parents' minivan?"

He nodded emphatically, mostly to distract from him taking another massive bite of his lunch. "Definitely. Since my brother can't go, I'll have five empty seats."

"Great," Harper said. "Then you can take Trixie and Meg so they don't have to ask their parents. Or walk."

"What?" I asked. I looked at Ben, waiting for him to announce that, obviously, my transportation situation was under control. If I was going to get tricked into doing the chicken dance, he was absolutely going to have to borrow his dad's car. That just made good sense. But he continued plugging data into his calculator, seemingly deaf to the surrounding conversation.

"I learned from the harvest festival that I no longer walk long distances in heels," Meg said pertly. "And it's going to be way colder than it was two months ago."

"Cornell and I are going to drive in together," Harper continued. "But we're both on the opposite side of town. So, we'll meet you guys here."

"Are you gonna need a ride, Ben?" Peter asked.

"Nope," Ben said, still somehow not reading the look I was throwing him. "I'm set. I'm not going to risk getting stranded here like I did during the harvest festival."

"I did apologize for that." Cornell frowned.

Ben looked up just long enough to throw him a lopsided smile. "It's no big. I've got wheels."

"Then we're set," I said, each word sharpened down to a knife-point. "Harper and Cornell are going to drive in together. Peter is going to drive me and Meg. And Ben is going to go solo."

Harper reached over and clapped her hand on Peter's forearm, momentarily putting a halt to him stuffing his face. "See, you were worried about not having a date and now you have two."

"I'm a lucky guy." Peter beamed at us. "Although, I guess I'll have to buy two corsages now."

"I'm cool without, thanks," I said, inwardly cringing at the thought of spending an evening with a flower strapped to my wrist. I didn't even wear normal bracelets, much less ones made of flora. It sounded cumbersome. And itchy.

"What about you, Megs?" Peter asked, cocking his head at her.

Out of the corner of my eye, I saw Meg turn an interesting shade of fuchsia. There was a chance that her limbic system was finally winning against her thought experiment.

"She's going to be wearing purple," Harper said.

"Cool," Peter said. He polished off his burger and stood, throwing his backpack over his shoulders. "Duty calls. See you guys later."

He limped across the cafeteria again, planting himself at a table full of juniors. I could feel Meg's leg trembling next to mine. I knocked her foot with mine and she let out a long breath.

Harper folded her hands neatly on the table. "Well, that all worked out quite nicely."

"Quite," Meg squeaked.

Ben continued writing silently in his notebook.

Ben   [6:31 PM]

I think Cline used google translate on this essay.
Have you been able to track down the original
German article?

Ben   [7:09 PM]

I emailed you the link to a better translation. I
should send it to Harpo and Corny.

                                                 [7:10 PM]

I'm not going to send it to them. Now we can fight
to the death for valedictorian. Ha ha!

Ben   [8:51 PM]

Earth to Beatrice.

                                                 [8:51 PM]

West to Watson.

                                                 [9:02 PM]

Trix?

✦ 19 ✦

The music pouring through my headphones drowned out the whir of the sewing machine as I fed satin under the needle. I'd long ago learned to lock Sherry out of my room when I was sewing, as he had a habit of leaping up on the desk to see what was making all the racket and getting his paws tangled in the thread. My headphones blocked the sound of him scratching at my door, too.

I squinted against the glare of my desk lamp, watching as the machine serged the crisp *Star Wars* fabric to the slit I'd cut in the side of the black dress. I pinched the fabric until my fingertips went white with the effort of keeping the slippery satin from sliding away from me.

I didn't really have time to waste on an extracurricular project. I could have been asleep already, like my parents. I could have been listening to an audio version of one of my schoolbooks—like the recording of *The Cherry Orchard* I'd downloaded from the library— instead of a loop of *Doctor Who* scores.

But, no. I was awake in the middle of the night, attempting to be my own fairy godmother and put some personality into a lifeless sack of black satin that—had I not cut open the side—could have easily paid for months' worth of comics, Slurpees, and hummus-and-sprout sandwiches.

It was stupid—and pointless—to be disappointed by what had happened at lunch. For whatever reason, I had deluded myself into thinking that Ben West had asked me to the winter ball the way normal people got asked to fancy events. Like it was a real date. Like he was validating everything I'd overheard Meg and Harper talking about a month ago. But that wasn't what had happened. He'd asked me to go because, like me, he didn't actually want to have to go to this ridiculous showcase. I was moral support to keep him from being the fifth wheel on everyone else's double date. Because we were friends.

Gritting my teeth, I yanked the dress more aggressively under the machine's presser foot. After years of having only Harper and Meg, it was actually kind of nice that we'd branched out. I enjoyed spending time with the boys. I liked that Peter didn't understand all of our references—and vice versa—and that Cornell always had an interesting insight into our homework. It was nice having more real friends, instead of just classmates to nod to between classes.

But being friends with Ben bugged me. Walking to class together, murmuring comments in the cafeteria, the buzzing of texts pouring into my phone—it was false advertising. It looked like friendship, but it didn't feel like friendship. It felt like something else, like I'd been ramping up to something huge and found out that it was flat ground.

It was worse because it wasn't even his fault. He hadn't cornered me and professed his undying love. I'd heard about it third hand from two people who didn't even know that I knew. And who was to say that Harper and Meg were right? For all of their musing about Ben being absolutely gaga for me, there'd been no sure sign of anything other than him being a fairly likeable dude—once you got past the rambling.

The problem was me. In the crushing guilt of realizing that I'd been hurting Ben's feelings for years, I had opened myself up too much. I'd tried too hard. I'd gone from insulting him in the hallway to texting him from the second I got home until the moment before I fell asleep. I'd hunted for his good qualities and found them—he made me laugh and he pushed me to work harder and he always smelled like apples—Fujis, not Granny Smith. He was nice to Meg and Harper and didn't abuse the froshlings. He'd returned my copy of *Buffy* clean and with the packaging taped so the comic wouldn't bend.

The problem was that I actually liked him quite a bit. And the idea of him not returning that feeling in the same way was a new kind of awful.

I shut off the sewing machine and shook out the dress, which gave a crack of stiff fabric loud enough that I could hear it over the BBC orchestra in my ears. The added panel flared out of the mass of black satin, a pop of loud color and Lucasfilm intellectual property. It was everything I'd imagined it to be. I threw it on my bed as my phone bleeped, interrupting my music.

Pulling the phone out of the pocket of my pajama pants, I braced myself for another text that I wouldn't answer. Instead, there was an email from the Mess administrative office waiting in my inbox. There was no chance that the office secretaries were sending out emails after eleven to announce Free Ice Cream and Puppy day. I'd unsubscribed to emails regarding sports, orchestral concerts, and drama club performances. This would not be good news.

To: Messina Academy Students
From: Administrative Services
Subject: Urgent Student Information

Due to a networking error on the part of the Messina Academy's homework portal, the administration asks that all students turn in any and all assignments in hard copy. Deadlines for Tuesday's assignments will be extended to

Wednesday. The library and computer labs are available to those in need of printers. Please avoid use of your school email accounts until further notice.

Regards,
Dr. S. Mendoza, Ph.D., Ed.D.

I popped out my headphones. "Frak."

Ben   [8:32 PM]

Two days and still no website.

Ben   [9:47 PM]

Thanks for bringing me those Daredevil back issues today.

Three days and no website. You'd think they'd change up the error code message.

Ben   [7:22 AM]

Four days and no website. What are you guys even doing in Programming Languages?

Me   [7:23 AM]

Worksheets. Why are you texting me when we're standing across from each other?

Ben   [7:23 AM]

Testing a hypothesis.

Meg   [7:24 AM]

Who are you texting this early?

Me   [7:25 AM]

Will you do my makeup before the dance tonight?

Meg   [7:26 AM]

Of course. Like I trust you with your own face.

Me   [7:26 AM]

Thanks?

Harper   [7:26 AM]

You guys look crazy right now.

Me   [7:27 AM]

I needed to point out to West that it's rude to hold
secret conversations in front of your friends.

Cornell   [7:28 AM]

Did I miss a memo? When did we all take a vow of
silence?

Peter   [7:29 AM]

Are you guys having a secret nerd conversation
that I won't understand? I learn best through
immersion.

Meg   [7:31 AM]

Peter, will you pick us up at 6:45 tonight at Trixie's?
I don't want to give my parents the chance to
analyze you.

Peter   [7:32 AM]

No problem.

Harper   [7:33 AM]

This is a flagrant misuse of technology.

Ben   [7:33 AM]

I'm going inside.

✿ 20 ✿

The sunlight was fading into shadows, leaving the sky stretched out like a bruised eggplant. The tulle of Meg's skirt floated like one of the lavender clouds as she teetered in impressively tall sequined shoes, holding firmly to Peter's arm. Walking behind them, I examined the elaborate up-do Meg had crafted in my bedroom with the assistance of a dozen unintelligible diagrams and Internet videos.

I had narrowly avoided cauterizing my neck with a curling iron. My hair looked pretty much the same as it had when I'd taken it out of my ponytail. I pulled the mass of it over my shoulders for warmth and held my tiny purse a little harder as we followed the twinkling white lights in the sycamore trees toward the cafeteria.

"Now that is a wedding dress," Meg said under her breath as we approached the ticket table.

The masses of white foofaraw that composed Mary-Anne's skirt took up all of the space under the ticket table. A silver tiara shone from the top of her dark hair as she stretched her hand toward Peter for his ticket. Her upper lip arched into a perfectly calculated sneer, just low enough to keep the tip of her nose safe from being stained rosy pink.

"Peter, your brother was looking for you guys," she said. "He went to change."

"Change for the dance?" Meg asked. Even in her towering shoes, she had to tip her neck like a Pez dispenser to see Peter. "Isn't he still banned from school events?"

Mary-Anne ripped through their tickets and flourished them back to Peter. "Apparently not."

"He and my parents had another meeting with Mendoza earlier," Peter said.

Meg whacked him with the massive white corsage he'd attached to her wrist in the parking lot. "How could you not tell us? Does this mean he's cleared?"

"I don't know. I haven't heard anything since they left the house."

"Well, if you go inside, you'll see him soon enough," Mary-Anne growled. "Let's keep the line moving, shall we?"

I handed her my ticket.

"You look nice," I said.

Her scowl dimmed as she returned my ticket stub. "So do you. That eye shadow makes your eyes look less dreary. You should reapply your lip gloss, though."

I wasn't wearing lip gloss. I'd swatted Meg's hand away when she'd come at me with the goopy wand.

"Good talk," I said and moved with Peter and Meg through the doors of the caf.

The froshlings had been busy in the hours since the sixth-period bell rang. The cafeteria was transformed by bolts of white and gold fabric that hung from the ceiling and washed the room in a dim glow. The long utilitarian bench tables where we ate lunch had been replaced by small clusters of round tables covered in white lace and sprigs of evergreen branches. The butcher paper poem hung at the far end of the room, spilling onto the floor underneath a balloon arch. A line of people stood in front of it, waiting their turn to use their phones to take posed pictures.

Everything kind of smelled like stale grease and Pine-Sol, but I had to give the student council kudos for aesthetic.

The band was set up in the corner where our lunch table usually resided. They wore white blazers and thin ties that seemed at odds with their battered instruments and scruffy facial hair. As the guitarist played a static-laden riff, I felt myself start to grin. The student council had entrusted band selection to Ben West and Ben West had delivered a band that would re-create the dance setlist from *Back to the Future.*

The dance floor was packed with people clapping and capering. I doubted whether anyone else was jazzed to be listening to "Johnny B. Goode." Everyone seemed to be giddy not to be studying. Even the teachers positioned around the room were less disgruntled than usual. Mr. Cline appeared to be singing along while Dr. Kapoor and Ms. Jensen cringed in secondhand embarrassment.

Meg, Peter, and I skirted around the tables. Peter kept pausing to thank passersby for coming. Meg said something to me that was entirely drowned out by the music and I had to lean in close for her to shout in my ear.

"Do you see Harper and Cornell?"

"They're probably dancing."

"Then let's go find them!"

Peter gave me a *"Well, what can you do?"* shrug as Meg dragged him into the throng. I hung back. I suddenly felt extremely exposed in a strapless dress. I'd left my coat in the minivan. The band started playing a Michael Jackson song and I watched as Brad Hertz attempted to moonwalk, knocking into bystanders as he went.

A hand grabbed my elbow and I stumbled over my heels, nearly slamming into the nearest table.

"Careful," Ben said in my ear. "If you break your leg, I'll never live it down."

I turned, straightening my skirt with my shaking hands. He cleaned up surprisingly well. Not a wrinkle or scuff in sight. He had opted for a navy-blue suit and maroon tie with a crisp white oxford shirt. A pair of red high-tops peeked out from under his pant cuffs. They matched his tenth-Doctor hairstyle to a T.

You're friends, I reminded myself. *Be friendly. Not* friendly-*friendly.*

"Cool band," I said with an airiness that didn't quite match the frog in my throat.

"How long until everyone realizes they don't know anything written in the last thirty years?" He grinned at me, leaning in close to keep the shouting to a minimum. "Where are Meg and Peter?"

I pointed toward the dance floor, where Meg was spinning in circles around Peter, her skirt flapping around her legs in a purple blur. Peter had his fists up, rocking from side to side in true white-guy-dancing form. Ben laughed loudly.

"Have you seen Harper and Cornell?" I asked.

"They're around somewhere. I saw them drive in while I was helping the band unload." He paused, fidgeting with his sleeves. "Do you want some punch?"

I clasped a hand to my chest in mock indignation. "Punch? I believe I was promised a soda."

"I left my backpack in the chem lab." He flapped his hands, as though magicking me to the spot. "Wait here?"

I nodded and watched him run out of the room. Pressing my lips together to keep from grinning like an idiot, I made my way to an unoccupied table. I opened my purse, pulling my book out of its depths. With one more cursory glance to see if I could spot Harper and Cornell, I turned my attention fully to *The Restaurant at the End of the Universe,* using my cell phone to light the pages. It wouldn't hurt to read for a minute or two.

The evergreen branch centerpiece knocked into the cover of my book as the table jostled. I looked up and saw Mike Shepherd trying to push his way between empty chairs. A too-snug sport coat partially covered his school polo. His hair had been parted severely to one side.

"Hey, Mike," I called.

He paused, craning his neck around to see me, like Bigfoot caught on film. "Oh, hi, Trixie. I was just, um, walking. Somewhere.

I don't know what to do here. I really don't want to dance, in noun or verb form."

"Me either," I said. I gestured at the empty chair he'd collided with. "Do you want to sit down?"

I wasn't sure how Ben would react to coming back to the table and seeing his ex–best friend, but I also didn't want Mike to have to wander in circles for hours. Even at a school for nerds, the weirdest of the weirdoes needed to be able to stick together.

Mike collapsed into the chair and pulled his cell phone out of the pocket of his blazer. The NASA logo peeked out between his fingers as the screen lit up.

"Two hours and seven minutes to go," he said. The phone disappeared into his pocket again.

"I know exactly how you feel. I'm also here under duress." I smiled. "Harper and Meg guilted me into coming. And then they disappeared. I haven't ruled out the chance that this is all an elaborate prank and everyone's actually drinking Slurpees without me."

"I saw Harper and Cornell driving past my house. They were too dressed up for a trip to 7-Eleven," he said, mirroring my smile. He reached out and righted the evergreen branch between us. "I don't understand the point of things like this. It's obvious that the student council will never make enough money to buy the cricket team's whites."

"Ben's projections say otherwise."

Mike seemed to digest this letter by letter. It could have been a mistake to mention Ben's name. Maybe their feud was festering more than I assumed. I wasn't sure how ending a friendship worked. Was there grieving along with all of the awkward nodding in the hallway?

"I saw you guys talking," he said suddenly. "You and, um, Ben. Are you guys friends now?"

"Yes," I said, carefully and tonelessly. "We're friends now."

He flashed me a toothy smile. "Cool. He always felt bad about breaking your arm. Oh. Uh, don't tell him I told you that."

"I-I won't," I stuttered.

The band ended a song and there was a muffled tapping on the microphone.

"If I could have your attention, please."

Mike and I turned to see Mr. Cline shooing the band away from the stage as he fussed with the microphone stand. The dancers transformed back into the pupils of a rigorous school for the gifted, standing at attention like they were about to be ordered to do recitations.

"As you all are aware," Cline boomed into the microphone, "this has been a period of upset in the storied history of this establishment. I would like to take this moment to formally apologize on behalf of the administration of the Messina Academy to four of our students who were wrongly accused of misdoings." He paused, sneaking a glimpse at a piece of paper hidden in his palm. "Kenneth Pollack, Ishaan Singh, Alex Nguyen, and Jack Donnelly are exemplary young men, who, when faced with strife, did not waver in their studies."

I snorted as the rest of the room gave a lukewarm round of applause. The Mess wrongly accused four boys of cheating and all the administration had to say about it was that their grades didn't take a hit. Mike also made a contemptuous sound.

"In fact," Cline said, "I have been told that without the tireless efforts of Jack Donnelly, we would not have been able to find the source of the issue. We owe him a great debt of thanks."

The crowd applauded again, this time with more enthusiasm. Someone on the dance floor called, "A hundred points to Slytherin!"

"Yes, quite." Cline squirmed. "The homework portal will be back online tomorrow morning and the ranking list will be updated and returned to the case at the sound of the last bell on Monday. Please enjoy the rest of your festivities. I know that I will. Play on, maestro!"

"Trixie."

I popped my head up, startled to hear my name coming out of

Jack Donnelly's mouth. His black shirt was open at the collar and his hair was slick with sweat around his ears.

"You need to come with me," he said darkly.

"Uh . . ." I looked at Mike, who was tacitly avoiding all eye contact. "Thanks, but no thanks. I'm not here to dance. Hence, the reading material."

I wiggled my book at Jack for emphasis and his face contorted into something like disgust. He bent low over the table, his large hands pressing into the lace tablecloth. I felt like a rat waiting to be dissected.

"I found out who hacked into all of the probations' files," he said.

"Um, congratulations," I said. "Did Mendoza give you a medal?"

"Trixie," he said, staring at me with fathomless blue eyes. "It's Harper. They expelled her. She's leaving now."

"What?" Mike shouted over the sound of the drums kicking back up. "Harper wouldn't do that."

He was right. Harper didn't even like playing Jenga because she couldn't abide ruining someone's work. There was no way that she had framed four people for cheating. Jack had to be messing with me, getting his jollies by making me freak out.

Knowing that didn't stop me from hiking up my skirt and running.

Blood pounded in my ears, turning everything around me into static. I was distantly aware of Mike calling my name, the slap of Jack's shoes behind me, of people leaping out of my way as I sprinted through the quad, of the sound of my heels scratching up the brick stairs. I ricocheted down the hall in the main building, skittering against the waxed floor.

"Miss Watson," Mrs. Landry shouted at me as I tumbled into the admin office.

"Harper," I panted, catching sight of Dr. Mendoza's open office door. His desk was unoccupied, although the chairs were all pushed out. "Where is Harper?"

Mrs. Landry frowned at me, sitting down heavily in her desk chair. She zipped her purse with a decisive swoop.

"She has been removed from campus. Now, if you and Mr. Donnelly would please return to—"

I didn't stay to listen to the lecture. I shoved Jack out of the doorway and ran out of the building toward the parking lot. I could just make out Cornell standing between two men that, as I approached, I realized were Dr. Mendoza and Harper's dad.

Mr. Leonard took a backward step toward his car. He was wearing his shirt and tie from work, but his jacket was missing. He glared at Dr. Mendoza. "Stuart, really. The campus is crawling with my daughter's peers."

Mendoza turned to me and Jack stiffly. "Miss Watson, I must ask you to return to the dance. Jack, you were just removed from probation. Please don't make me reconsider that decision."

"Sorry, Trixie," Jack grumbled, bowing out. He saluted Mendoza before retreating back through the front gate.

Behind Mr. Leonard, I could see Harper tucked into the front seat of their black town car. She was ghostly pale, her hair piled on top of her head in a wide bun held in place with a glittering band that looked like a collection of delicate snowflakes. She stared straight ahead, holding her father's jacket over her chest. A glint of pink chiffon peeked out at her shoulder, a whisper of the night she'd thought she was going to have.

"This is ridiculous," I said, pushing my hair out of my face. I could feel a trickle of cold sweat between my shoulder blades. "There's no way that Harper could or would mastermind this kind of crap. She would never go out of her way to hurt people." I looked at Cornell, who stared pointedly at his shoes. "Tell them, Cornell. You know that she would never—"

"Not that it is any of your concern, Miss Watson," Mendoza said, "but Mr. Aaron has already provided his deposition."

"His deposition?" I gaped around at three impassive faces. "This is a federal case now?"

Cornell's shoulders tensed. He raised his head for the first time. This was not the laughing face that sat across from me at lunch or the lovesick boy who held Harper's hand when he thought no one was paying attention. He was severe with his mouth drawn into a haughty frown.

"Before the network went down, someone got into my account," he said steadily. His eyes slid to the side, but he seemed to think better of looking directly at Harper. He flattened his hands over his suit jacket, smoothing the buttons. "All of my grades were changed. Not a lot. Enough to make sure that I wasn't first place in the ranking. Enough to make sure that Harper was."

I threw up my hands. "That's it? Just because someone didn't want you to be valedictorian doesn't mean that Harper did anything wrong."

"Jack proved that the IP address matches, Trixie," he said. "And you heard her on Monday. Talking about how the school has been too hard on us, how we were all being pushed too far—"

"Enough," Mr. Leonard said. "We're leaving."

"Mr. Leonard," I blurted. If he took Harper, then her expulsion would be real. If she could get out of the car, she could explain that she was innocent and all of this would go away. Harper could explain anything away. That was her superpower. "You don't believe this. You know that this is wrong, don't you?"

His lips were flat and bloodless against his ashen face. "I know that this is wrong, Beatrice. But I don't know that I don't believe it." He moved around the car, nodding to Dr. Mendoza. "Stuart, we will be in touch."

He slid into the driver's seat and the slam of the car door echoed into the night. As the car's engine roared to life, Harper turned her face a fraction. Tears spilled down her cheeks, leaking out from under the edge of her glasses and into her open, sobbing mouth. She locked eyes with me. For a moment she was just glitter and tears, both blinding in the light from the street lamps. And then the car wheeled around the corner. There were brake lights and then there was nothing but dark road and an empty street.

Dr. Mendoza straightened and cast a wary glance at me and

Cornell. "I would appreciate it if the two of you would use the utmost discretion about this."

Cornell stiffened. "I don't plan on telling the world that my girlfriend is a cheater."

Mendoza gave a curt nod and walked briskly toward the front gate.

I couldn't force myself to move or speak. The universe seemed to have condensed down to the head of a pin, crushing and compacting in on itself, smashing me down with it until there was only one word left in the vacuum. *No.* No, no, no.

Cornell shoved his hands in his pockets, his head tilted toward the starless sky.

"There was too much evidence," he muttered. "There wasn't anything I could do."

I couldn't think of anything to say.

I walked away, leaving him and the Mess behind.

✦ 21 ✦

Hobbled and overheated, I made it to the park and decided to take a breather. Crawling under the tube slide in my dress didn't seem feasible. I wobbled through the bark and ascended the stairs. I sat down heavily in the center of the play structure, high above the expanse of green lawn and empty benches.

Eventually, I would need to make it all the way home. I'd have to explain to my parents that Harper had been expelled and that I'd left the dance without even consuming a glass of punch.

I rested my head against the wall, feeling the rough wood hold fast to my hair. The light sheen of sweat that had been protecting my bare shoulders was evaporating fast in the night's breeze. I squeezed my eyes closed, wishing I'd thought to gather my things before I'd run out of the cafeteria. My coat was draped over the center seat in Peter's van. My purse was sitting under my book at the table where Jack had found me.

I should have gone back for them. I should have taken Meg aside and explained everything that had happened. She would have come with me to the park. She would have a plan.

But the idea of seeing Cornell again kept me in place. Anger twisted my stomach into knots and boiled up in my throat. If he had tried to give any evidence in Harper's favor, things could have been different. He could have tried. He could have told Mendoza that Harper was way too busy doing her own work to interfere with anyone else's. How could she possibly have hacked into the system and rigged five different accounts when she was doing extra-credit projects in all of her classes? Between picking up her dad's dry cleaning and making dinner and reading comics, when would she have found the time to also make sure Kenneth Pollack couldn't go to the harvest festival? And why would she target four boys that she never even spoke to? It was illogical. Harper wasn't illogical.

Wheels crunched on gravel. A boy on a bicycle was slowing down in front of the park. He passed under a street lamp and I could make out the exclamation point of his hair through the slats of the play structure.

Ben leapt down off his bike and pulled his phone out of his pocket. As he stepped into the bark, he murmured, "Yeah, I've got her. It's cool. Okay." He slipped the phone back into his pocket and climbed the stairs.

"You know," he said, depositing his backpack on the landing as he strode toward me, "when Shep came and told me that you'd run off with Jack, I was pretty offended. If you were going to choose between the two guys who hate me most on campus, I'd vote for Shep, personally. In a rank of guys you could spend winter ball with, it should be me, Shep, and then—dead last with a gun to your head—Jack Donnelly. I mean, I'm not the best guy at the Mess, but I have to be better than Jack."

I tipped my neck back to look at him. "You are better than Jack."

"Good. I just wanted to get that clear. I asked Mary-Anne and she didn't agree." He hopped down and sat an arm's length away from me, his legs extending nearly to the entrance of the tube slide. His head lolled to face me. "Cornell said you'd left. Jack Not-As-Good-As-Me Donnelly filled us in on the rest."

So, Cornell had gone back to the dance. I pictured him wearing that patronizing sneer as he sought out our friends, keeping his word to Mendoza, afraid that telling anyone what had happened would reflect poorly on him. My hands started trembling again and I bunched them in my skirt, hoping Ben wouldn't notice.

"How'd you find me?" I asked.

"Peter and Meg took the van toward Harper's, in case you followed her. Meg told me how to get to your house, but she said that I should stop here and check under the tube slide." He paused, looking around at the surrounding green. "You hid under there at my eighth birthday party."

Red rover, red rover, send Benedict right over. Harper and I had fought over what to name the giant squid from our cubby submarine. It was the only year we hadn't had someone to force us to play with the other kids. Before, there'd been her mom. After, there was Meg.

"I couldn't fit under the slide in this dress," I said, plucking at the *Star Wars* panel.

"It's a very cool dress. Did you make it?"

"I just added the panel."

He ran his hand over the raggedy wood planks, tracing the grain. He jerked as he caught a splinter and stuck the pad of his thumb into his mouth. His jaw worked and he examined the damage in the sliver of light coming through the slats. "So, what'd I do wrong?"

"You ran your hand against the grain instead of with it. Don't you remember when we made that block plane when we studied Roman engineering? When was that? Fifth grade? Sixth?"

He cut his eyes at me. Millennia of disappointment bloomed there with a couple of days of annoyance lurking underneath. "You stopped answering my texts."

"Oh," I said. "That."

He scuffed the heel of his shoe between two planks. "I know I'm not good at this."

"This?"

"This." He brandished his injured hand, gesticulating wildly between us. "There's probably supposed to be something other than school and comics. But I'm just school and comics. It's all I have. You don't get D&D references."

"You could teach me D&D references," I said.

"I could if you answered my texts."

We both stared at his hand, still hovering in the half-light. There was a spot of blood stuck between the grooves of his fingerprint. I imagined what it would be like to fold my fingers with his. It looked so easy when other people did it.

"You didn't do anything wrong," I said. "I was projecting, I think. Normally Meg clarifies that for me, but I didn't want to . . ." *Admit that she was wrong about you being in love with me and that I was having a fit about it.* "I'm not good at making new friends. Obviously. Before this year, I only had two friends. But I like being friends with you."

"I like being friends with you, too," he said flatly.

"Good," I said, stressing it until I could almost believe it. "Meg's stupid thought experiment got under my skin. Everyone kept hyping up the dance and the dressing up and the corsages and the driving places together. It got very datelike. Date-y."

"Date-esque," he said in the same wafer tone.

"Right. I'm sorry I took it out on you. It's not your fault. That's where the projecting comes in. You did me a favor buying my ticket. A friendly favor. Like Peter getting suckered into driving me and Meg. I get it now. I'm caught up. It won't happen again."

He squinted at me as though I'd spewed a stream of gobbledygook at him. "I thought you wanted to ride in with Peter. You went on and on about how he was going to take you and I was going to go solo. So, he drove you and I went solo. I figured you wanted to go with him. And then, I don't know, stay with him?" His nose twitched and I could have sworn he turned a little green as he muttered, "I mean, he is better than Jack and Shep."

"You thought that I wanted to go to the dance with Peter? For dating purposes?" It was wrong to be excited that he'd been just as nervous as I was, but I couldn't help but smile. "Have you considered that being equally smart makes us equally dumb?"

"No, but it's starting to make a lot of sense."

"For the record, I have zero designs on Peter," I said. "Dateish or otherwise."

"Me either." He rubbed down the line of his jaw. "And I don't have my driver's license. I didn't take my test before I went to DC and since I've been back—well, you know, the Mess." He motioned to his bike overturned in the bark. "Thus, the two wheels. It's not great for motives related to dating."

"Unlike the Donnelly family minivan?" I asked.

"Hey, the van has TV screens in the headrests."

"And smells like Fritos and socks," I said. "So, if you had your license, would this week have gone differently? I've seen the Yahtzee episode of *Community*. I know alternate time lines are tricky and all."

He laughed. "I would have offered to be your ride. If, in this time line, I was a decent driver who wouldn't possibly maim you. At least I would have gotten to spend more than five seconds with you." A blush crept out of his collar and continued up to his cheeks. "You left so fast, I didn't even get to tell you that you look beautiful. In the alternate time line, I would have monologued about that."

I averted my eyes, my face warming in tandem with his. "I'm wearing makeup. It's performance enhancer for my face."

"I see you every day. It's not the makeup." He reached over tentatively and lifted my chin. His fingers shook, just a little. "Your eyes really are gray, aren't they? I thought they were blue, but they're almost silver."

"Very low melanin levels," I said, faltering.

"You gorgeous mutant." A smile wobbled across his face. "That would have been a pretty good line to use to kiss you. If you . . . I wouldn't—not without asking."

My thoughts fluttered back in time. I remembered the amazement as realization after realization had come crushing down on me in the cement cubby we were now sitting above. But my limbic system had known since the harvest festival.

This was the risk that I wanted.

I swallowed and found the process more arduous than normal. "Did you really write a sworn affidavit to keep B from getting expelled?"

"What?" He frowned. "Who told you about that?"

"It doesn't matter." My pulse was slamming in my ears now, shushing everything else. "Did you do that?"

"Well, yeah. It wasn't a huge deal. He obviously didn't hack into Ken's account. He hadn't even set up his password—"

"Say it again," I interrupted. "The mutant thing."

His eyes widened, but he bobbed his head and shook out his shoulders. "Okay. Ahem. You—"

His voice broke.

I inched closer to him and set my hand against the back of his neck. Under a short rustle of hair, his skin burned. "My eyes have very low melanin levels."

"You're perfect," he stammered. His eyes flickered up to mine and held. "Don't ever stop being you."

"I'm just school and comics, too," I breathed. "I don't know how to be anything else."

"Don't be anything else. Be Trixie."

He lowered his mouth to mine, catching more of my bottom lip than the top. His nose brushed mine, a hinting nudge. My mouth opened to mirror his. There was a pattern to kissing. It was a chain of individual kisses of varying sizes strung together to make the verb. I'd never considered that before. But, for once, my body seemed to know something that my brain didn't.

The pattern wasn't a pattern. It was a parabolic wave. It was chaos falling into rhythm and forgetting it again. It was hot breath and my hands in his hair and the taste of cola. I strained into it and he was pulling me closer until I couldn't tell whether I was in his lap or he was in mine. He laughed, the sound echoing off my teeth like a triumphant yodel, like we'd found the cure for something together and both realized it in the exact same moment. *Eureka!* Archimedes may have coined the phrase, but Ben and I were revolutionizing it. *We have found it.*

Suddenly, everything I'd ever read made sense. All of the clichés about electricity and drowning and falling and other sinister metaphors for a kiss all swept over me. It was nuclear fusion. It was the door to Narnia. It was a cacophonic wibbly-wobbly-timey-wimey symphony regenerating us into a spectacular and overwhelming new form.

I broke away from him, out of breath and shivering. Half of me wanted to throw myself back at him, to lose myself entirely in the feeling until I could pinpoint exactly why it was so entrancing.

But Harper's face exploded into my head, the quaver of her chin as she cried in the front seat of her dad's car. Guilty tears boiled up in my eyes. Mortified, I shoved my face into my hands.

"Oh, hell," I said. "I'm sorry."

He pried my fingers off my cheeks and held them firmly between his. It was easy. Fingers folding together like they belonged there. Tears started to leak down my lashes. I blinked fast, trying to keep them from spilling.

"I don't have a ton of experience here," he said with a bashful cough. "But, generally, I'd assume that crying after making out to be a, uh, bad sign."

"It's not that." The embarrassment seemed to be acting like a steroid to my tear ducts. Saline poured in earnest down my face, undoubtedly ruining the makeup Meg had applied. "That was fine. Great, even. If I had a gold star in my purse, I'd put it on your lapel. If I had my purse."

"I have your purse. It's in my backpack with your soda," he said, with a beam of pride that dissipated as he seemed to remember that now was definitely not the time for it. With his free hand, he swept away some of the deluge from my cheek. "You're still crying," he murmured. "Which makes me feel bad because that was kind of the best thing ever."

I let my head fall forward, resting it on his shoulder. His arms came up automatically and wrapped around me. I continued crying on his neck, wishing that my nose weren't stuffed so I could enjoy the smell of him or at least not drip mucus onto his suit. I hoped it wasn't a rental.

"That's the problem," I gasped. "I can't be happy now, Ben. I can't. Not after—not with—"

"Harper. You're worried about her," he said into the top of my head, his hands combing through the ends of my hair.

"Of course I am," I said to his Adam's apple. "She would never cheat and she would never set other people up to fail. It's completely absurd. And now she's expelled and humiliated and she didn't do it."

"If she didn't—"

I reared back, disentangling myself from him. Strands of hair stuck to my face, glued in a combination of hairspray and saline. I shoved them out of the way. "She didn't."

He loosened the knot of his tie. "Okay, since, beyond a shadow of a doubt, she did not do it, then she's safe. They'll look into it and find out it was all a misunderstanding."

"And if they don't? Her own boyfriend, the vice president of the student council, said that he believed it was her." I struggled to stand and paced the play structure like a cage. "God, I could kill him. He's supposed to love her. And he turned on her the second they accused her, because he thought it might hurt his reputation. That worthless piece of—"

Ben leapt to his feet, the rubber of his sneakers shining white in the darkness. "That's not fair. He just said what he saw."

"Then he should have lied," I shouted. "I hope whoever set up Harper goes for Cornell next. If I could do it, I would. I would destroy him. I would watch him cry about his future going out the window and I would drink his tears. And it still wouldn't be enough. Nothing would be enough to make up for him hurting Harper. She loved him more than anything and he abandoned her. He took her future and took a steaming dump on it."

I choked down a lungful of air. My hands were shaking violently. I closed them into fists, feeling the futility washing over me. There was a tiny tilde of a wrinkle between Ben's eyebrows.

"What can I do?" he asked, taking a brave step toward me. He ran his hands over my bare shoulders, at once warming them and keeping me in place. "Do you want me to help you find who framed Harper? Do you want me to egg Dr. Mendoza's house? Tell me how to help because I'm at a loss here."

"Punish Cornell." The words slipped out of my mouth with no assistance from my brain. But after I said it, it made sense. "Make him hurt the way Harper hurts."

His arms flopped back to his sides and he shook his head until a spike flopped over his eyebrow. "No. Trixie, no."

"Yes," I said, a spark of hope flaring inside of me. Plans started locking into place in my head, clear as crystal. "You're his best friend. No one else would have the dirt that you have. You could do it. You must know something. Something that happened in DC over the summer or if he's a bed wetter or—"

"It won't help, Harper. It's petty. It's beneath you. Hell, it's beneath me and that should tell you something. Look, I'm not saying what he did was right—"

"That's exactly what you're saying. You can't sit back and let him get away with this. 'Men should be either treated generously or destroyed.'"

He scrubbed his face with his hands. "Not that quoting Machiavelli doesn't make you crazy hot, but it's also the normal kind of crazy."

"Fine," I snarled, marching toward the stairs. I stepped on the fabric of my dress as I went, no longer caring if I tore out the extra panel. "Do whatever you're going to do. I don't care. I am going to do what it takes to help my best friend."

"You're asking me to turn my back on mine!"

I charged down the stairs. "You've been friends for less than a school year. You stopped talking to Mike Shepherd without any remorse. All he did was tear down your campaign posters and tell everyone that your mom left."

His footsteps stopped. I paused and turned on my heel, grasping the railing to keep from tumbling down into the bark. Ben was frozen at the top of the stairs, his mouth set into a hard line.

"I'm sorry," I said. "That was too far."

"Yes," he said tightly. "It was. I know that you've been friends with Meg and Harper since forever and that's great. But I don't have that, Trixie. You can't ask me to give up my only fucking friends for you."

"I'm not!" In a small voice I added, "You can keep Peter."

He narrowed his eyes at me and took the stairs slowly, closing the distance between us. "I don't agree with what Cornell did. That's established. And I will help you and Harper and Meg and whomever else to make this right. But I will not humiliate my best friend. We will leave him out of this."

"I . . ." I could feel a fresh wave of tears starting. I clenched my teeth. It took a lot of effort to talk, but I forced myself to try. "I've never seen her like that, Ben. I've never seen her crumble. She's so strong and she tries so hard. Even when her mom died, she didn't . . ."

He stepped down to share my stair. "We'll make it right."

We. A plural possessive pronoun. Beatrice Watson and Ben West. We.

He nudged the hem of my skirt away with the toe of his shoe. "No Machiavelli, no Shan Yu, no Spanish Inquisition. No war or torture of any kind. Cool?"

I pressed my lips together and nodded. Shame was already welling up inside of me. I couldn't hurt Cornell out of spite. Ben was right. It wouldn't help Harper and she'd never forgive me if she knew that I'd suggested it.

"It's a bad sign when you're the voice of reason," I whispered.

"Don't make me do it again. It makes my head hurt." Eyes sparkling, he reached out and tucked a lock of hair behind my ear. "Can I walk you home? You could try to ride on my handlebars if you want. Dateishly."

I smiled at him, feeling a flutter in my chest that could have been happiness or stress-induced aortic arrhythmia. It was probably closer to the former than the latter. "I think I'll walk, if it's all the same to you. I'd rather not break my arm again. It'd be hell to have to explain on Monday."

He laughed. "Do you want your soda now?"

"Sure. But . . ."

"But?"

My lungs were starting to go into overdrive again and I struggled to take one deep breath. It took a couple of tries, but I managed.

"When I get home, I'm going to have to explain everything to my parents," I said. "I kind of don't want to add anything else to the list of big things that happened tonight. And if you walk me to my front porch, the natural conclusion for an evening of this nature, especially with the heightened response relating to stress and—"

"Trix," he interrupted. "That got beyond convoluted."

"Will you kiss me again?" I blurted. "Here? Before we get to a place where people—"

He covered my lips with his. It was nice to stop talking.

Me [9:44 PM]

My parents are already freaking out. Harper's dad called before I got home.

Ben [9:45 PM]

Frak. What'd he say?

Me [9:47 PM]

He wanted them to "be aware" in case any more "evidence" presents itself. He called Meg's folks, too. They're having an emergency counseling session to see if Meg is also "overworked."

Ben [9:52 PM]

We're ALL overworked. Did they not read the welcome packet?

Me [9:52 PM]

Apparently not.

Me [10:15 PM]

Did you see the email? "Class ranking will be reevaluated before posting"?

Ben   [10:27 PM]

Yes. Now my dad is also freaking the frak out. He
called my mom and everything.

Me   [10:30 PM]

He called your mom? (Where is your mom?)

Ben   [10:32 PM]

Yes. They're both worried that Berkeley will throw
out my application. (She's in DC. Cornell and I
stayed with her last summer.)

Me   [10:35 PM]

Why would Berkeley throw out your app?

Ben   [10:37 PM]

The Mess's security has been compromised?
Maybe we're all cheaters? The singularity is
approaching? I don't know.

Me   [11:18 PM]

Harper won't answer her phone.

Me   [11:22 PM]

I hate this.

Ben   [1:17 AM]

Goodnight.

Me   [1:17 AM]
You already said that.

Ben   [1:18 AM]
But I'm still awake.

Me   [1:19 AM]
Goodnight, Ben.

Ben   [1:20 AM]
Goodnight, mutant.

Me   [1:21 AM]
Goodnight, Greythorn.

Ben   [1:21 AM]
NO. Dislike.

Me   [1:22 AM]
You called me a mutant.

Ben   [1:23 AM]
The intention was nice.

Me   [1:23 AM]
Try again.

Ben   [1:24 AM]
Night, Trix.

Me   [1: 25 AM]
Night, Ben.

———

Me   [1:40 AM]

I still can't sleep. Do you want to watch an episode of Who at the same time?

Ben   [1:41 AM]

Yes.

Me   [1:42 AM]

I don't think I can keep typing.

"Hi."

"Hello."

"What episode do you want to watch?"

"Something happy."

"'The Lodger'? Matt Smith plays football for no reason. James Corden is brilliant."

"You get very British when you talk about *Doctor Who*."

"Maybe I'm just British on the phone. You don't know."

"I know now."

✸ 22 ✸

T his is easily the most reckless plan you've ever come up with," Meg said, stepping out of the coffee shop's bathroom in a fuzzy sweater and jeans. Her backpack was bulging. The edge of her Mess polo stuck out from the zipper. I hadn't been a hundred percent behind her idea to change out of our uniforms, but I had to admit that we were a lot less conspicuous in regular clothes.

"I told you that you didn't have to come," I said, slinging the strap of my messenger bag across my chest. "In fact, I told you that under no circumstances should you come with me. Your mother will murder me if she finds out this was my idea."

"Ditching school is a societal norm. I'll explain that the mental stress of Harper's expulsion made me do it," she said, leading the way to the parking lot. The sky was a misty white, a blank page where the sun should have been. "Being sneaky is a worthy addition to my thought experiment. My research on boys has been wildly inconclusive."

"Has it?" I patted down the pockets of my jeans, hunting for the key to my bike lock. My fingers were starting to go numb. "I thought you and Peter had a good time at the winter ball."

"We did. It went exactly as hypothesized, until the end." She set her backpack on the ground next to the bike rack and started rummaging around inside. A thousand pens clicked together. "But Cornell and Harper were my control group. From the depth of their affection, stress should have solidified them, but they cracked. I don't understand why."

"Because they aren't semicrystalline polymers," I said. "You can't heat them up and hope they turn into a milk jug."

She stuck her key into her bike lock and gave it a firm twist. "There are more similarities between people and plastics than you think."

"Please don't say that to Harper."

"Duh. We're supposed to make her feel better, not worse. No one wants to hear that they failed at crystallization."

We walked our bikes down to the intersection before climbing onto the seats. Gripping my handlebars hard, I glanced over at Meg, who had scrunched her nose in mute distaste as the wind whipped her hair around her cheeks. Her front tire was low. Since Harper had become the first licensed driver of the three of us—and the only one to own a car—we hadn't had much of a reason to take our bikes anywhere. I'd had to scrape a year's worth of cobwebs off mine before I could ride it to school.

I had decided—and Meg had agreed—to make an appearance at the Mess. But it had been next to impossible to focus in American Immigrant. Cornell had sat behind Harper's empty seat, pretending not to notice the whispers that kicked up around him. Any hope I'd had of him offering some kind of apology or explanation for what had happened on Friday night had gone out the window when the bell rang and he'd rushed out of the classroom without a backward glance.

Ben had walked with me to second period. When I'd warned him that Meg and I would be missing from the cafeteria, he'd squeezed my hand and said, "Don't get caught."

I would be lying if I said I hadn't considered pushing him into a closet and kissing him senseless just then. It'd been three days since winter ball and kissing Ben was starting to feel a bit like a half-remembered dream.

But reason won out and I'd decided not to be late to Third World Econ. I'd waited until fifteen minutes into the lecture before asking to be sent to the office. After inventing a breakfast that could have led to extreme food poisoning—a sketchy container of yogurt and runny scrambled eggs—and doing my best to look pained, the nurse excused me for the rest of the day.

After ten minutes of riding, my fingers started to thaw and my stomach clenched. I appreciated that Meg was keeping on a brave face, but I really should have calculated food into my truancy plans. I hadn't even eaten a granola bar on my way out of the house because I'd been so focused on fitting my regular clothes into my school bag and double-checking the route I'd chosen to get us away from the Mess unseen. At this point, I would have accepted the poison break-fast I'd told the nurse about.

We skirted around the main streets, cruising through neighbor-hoods I hadn't seen since we'd stopped trick-or-treating. We pedaled faster, following the curve in the road until we were under a famil-iar thicket of maple trees. In the middle of the block, Harper's cheer-fully red car sat alone in the driveway. Meg and I hid our bikes behind the hedges next to the garage. I checked twice to make sure that the glint of a handlebar or spoke wouldn't give us away before following Meg to the front door.

The doorbell boomed inside, the sound bouncing off the high ceilings and picture windows. There was a scuffling of feet, the clat-ter of a deadbolt being thrown, and Harper stood in the doorway. She was in flannel pajamas, her hair pulled back in a long yellow braid.

"This is easily the dumbest thing you've ever done," she clucked, stepping back into the foyer. "Come on in. I was just about to make lunch."

250 ★ LILY ANDERSON

With three bowls of tomato soup and three grilled cheese sandwiches fresh off the panini press, we congregated around the round
table in the breakfast nook.

"What else were we supposed to do?" Meg asked, blowing
delicately across the seam of her sandwich. "You didn't respond to
any of our texts or emails."

"Yes, and getting yourselves suspended will help," Harper said
with a sigh, settling cross-legged onto her chair and reaching for
her mug of tea—Earl Grey; hot. She held it under her nose. Steam
collected at the base of her lenses. "I'm on lockdown. Daddy even
got rid of the Wi-Fi. He's doing all his work at the office now, just in
case I decide to hack into something else."

"Harper," I said. "We know you didn't do it."

She took a long sip of tea and set her mug down with a clatter.
"That doesn't mean I'm not expelled. I have an interview at Marist
High on Friday."

"The Catholic school?" I asked.

"You don't even go to church for Christmas," Meg gasped.

Harper's face was impassive as she went back to folding her soup
with her spoon. She seemed hypnotized by the bits of basil disappearing under the tide of tomato. "I've been brushing up on my biblical
apocrypha all weekend. I think I can make a decent go of it. Maybe
they'll let me in if I do enough Hail Marys to account for being a
cheater."

"You can't go to Marist," I said. "You need to come back to the
Mess. It's where you belong."

"Someone made sure that I couldn't ever go back to the Mess,"
she shot back, pointing her red-stained spoon at me. "You guys
don't understand. When Dr. Mendoza laid out the switched tests,
the HTML code, the tracking software with my IP address im-
bedded in it—it was so clearly my fault." She stabbed her spoon
back into the bowl and swirled it aggressively. "It's like Hermi-
one Granger seeing a failed test as her Boggart. Smart girls
clearly can't care about anything other than being smart. If I'd

wanted to break into the homework portal, I would have been able to figure out how. It's easier for everyone to believe it and move on."

"Not everyone believes that it was you," Meg said. "We know that it's a lie. And Ben and Peter . . ."

She trailed off and we all resumed our lunch. The clink of spoons on ceramic and the crunch of perfectly toasted bread only underscored the rising discomfort in the room. Harper kept her eyes on her food as she whispered, "It's really not Cornell's fault. Have either of you heard from him?"

I wanted to tell her to forget about Cornell entirely, that he had proved turncoat and wasn't worth the breath it'd take to discuss him. But it wasn't my place to make her decisions.

"He was in class this morning," I said begrudgingly. "I didn't say anything to him and he didn't try to talk to me either."

"I haven't heard from him since Peter and I went looking for Trixie on Friday," Meg added.

Harper frowned, looking from me to Meg. "You guys left the dance?"

"Of course we did," I said, tossing my sandwich down on the plate. "What were we going to do? Hang out and drink punch and pretend nothing happened? If it'd been one of us, would you have stayed?"

"I guess not," she murmured. "What a waste. You looked so pretty, Trix. And I didn't even get to see your dress, Meg. Did you take pictures?"

"We'll show them to you later," Meg said. "First, we need to talk about what we're going to do now."

"Do?" Harper echoed. "I can't even leave the house. My dad took my car keys and I don't own a bike anymore."

"We aren't going anywhere," I said. "We need to figure out who put your IP address into that code."

The dry glare she gave me was magnified through her lenses. "You know that you guys have finals next week, right?"

"We're aware," Meg said. She waved her spoon over her head with a flourish. "But first, we have a case to crack!"

Harper put her face in her hands. "I love you both, but you are completely insane."

Ben   [1:47 PM]
Study Room C.

✦ 23 ✦

Meg and I parted ways at one of the major intersections. Neither of us had liked leaving Harper, but she'd shooed us out to make sure that her dad didn't come home and find us. She also made us promise not to ditch more school.

My body ached from pedaling and the weight of my messenger bag as I chained up my bike in front of the public library. There was no avoiding my sweaty, windblown reflection in the many opaque windows that broke up the building's brick face. I tried to smooth my ponytail as I made my way through the doors and into the familiar aisles that smelled like dust jackets and book glue and worn paper. It smelled like answers. Every knowable thing in the Western world was here.

Ben sat alone at the long conference table in the farthest study room, half-hidden behind a copy of *Lady Audley's Secret*. The woman's face on the cover was turned away, as though she was examining Ben as his eyes scanned the pages.

"Well," I said, tossing my messenger bag down on the chair across from him, "at least one of us got some studying done today. Unless you just had a hankering for a Victorian potboiler."

He smiled up at me and set the book down on the table, its pages splayed. "It's for Gender Roles. This is the study room. I figured I'd give it its due. I've got today's notes for Meg, too." He drummed his fingertips against the edge of the table. "How's Harper?"

"She's Harper. She lectured us about finals for a while and looked through the pictures we had from the dance," I said, gripping the back of the nearest chair. "But she's not actually okay. She's locked up in the house all day, studying for an interview at the Catholic school. Her dad's so convinced that she did this that he threw out their Wi-Fi router. He didn't change the password or unplug it. He literally threw it in the trash."

Saying it all out loud swayed me a little. It was too much. It was an unsolvable problem. I held onto the chair harder and bit the inside of my cheek. I didn't have time to panic now.

Ben got to his feet, sweeping around the table in two long strides. He didn't wait for my permission before he wrapped his arms around my shoulders. I pressed my face to his cheek and closed my eyes. As much as I felt silly accepting a hug when Harper was the one in trouble, I could almost block that out by focusing on the Fuji apple smell of him. It had to be part of the potion that made his hair stand up. Or pheromones.

"Did you guys make the list?" he asked in my ear.

I nodded. "I don't know if it'll help."

"That's why we're here," he said, tilting his head to look me in the eye. The little cut above his upper lip was almost completely gone. There was a shadow of a scar there now, a shade off from the rest of the curve of his cupid's bow. It wiggled as he spoke. "The list?"

I took a deep breath and pulled the list we'd made at Harper's out of my back pocket. I set it on the table and sat down. Ben hesitated before sitting next to me. His leg bounced idly next to mine as I smoothed the lined paper against the table.

Meg's neatly rounded letters covered the page, which she'd succinctly titled: SUSPECTS.

"There are about three hundred and seventy students currently enrolled at the Mess," I stated, matter-of-factly. "First, we divided the school into groups. Student council, drama club, cricket, basketball, et cetera. Whoever framed Harper didn't do it by accident. It wasn't a random outlier picking her name off the list. They went to the trouble of accessing her IP address and—" His leg brushed against mine and paused there before his foot snaked around my ankle and drew my leg under his chair. "Ben, this is important."

"I'm a genius. I can multitask. Can't you?"

"Fine," I grumbled, turning back to the list. "As I was saying, we dismissed anyone who Harper hadn't had a class with and, cross-referencing the list of probation students—"

"Say 'cross-referencing' again."

"Hush it, you."

"You could make me."

Heat spread across my cheeks and my brain spluttered to a stop. Sitting down, we were almost the same height, but the playing field didn't feel quite even. I checked over my shoulder at the open door. "We can't start necking in a study room."

He gestured around at the bare walls. "I don't see a 'no necking' sign, do you? I'm sure if we pulled up the official rules of our reservation, we could argue that we were not informed. I don't know if I'm going to be able to focus now that necking is on the table. We've made out, but there weren't necks involved before."

I reached out tentatively and patted his arm. "You're right."

He brightened, his eyes wide and sparkly. "I am? I mean, I am, but you know that I am?"

"We were never going to be able to focus if there was the prospect of . . ." I faltered as my brain filled with images of Ben kissing me in the park and the vertigo-inducing excitement that went along with it. "Being alone. I arranged for a hormonal bulwark."

The light went out of his eyes. "What kind of bulwark?"

B. Calistero seemed very perplexed to be sitting between us, but he flipped open his laptop anyway. Ben shot me a disgruntled look.

"Sorry I'm so late," B said for the third time, his hands shaking slightly as he connected to the library's Wi-Fi. "I forgot to pack my laptop, so my dad had to drive me home first. I told him that I shouldn't be more than an hour. Is that okay?"

"That's perfectly fine," I said, setting my school binder on the table. With B in the study room, there seemed to be more air to breathe. "So, what did you find out at lunch today?"

"Well," B said, smoothing the hair out of his face. It fell back into his eyes like two black curtains. "I don't think the basketball team is involved—"

"Wait a minute," Ben interrupted, holding up a hand. He leaned forward to look at me from around B's open computer. "You had my frosh spy for you?"

"He's a free agent," I said, making a check mark next to the names under the BASKETBALL header on Meg's list. "It's not like I had him doing sneaky treasurer stuff. That's your special thing together. I'd never infringe."

Ben narrowed his eyes at B. "So, you didn't actually lose your calculator?"

B shifted in his seat, avoiding eye contact with either of us. "She told me not to tell anyone what I was doing. I was supposed to tell people that Harper had borrowed my calculator and then see what they said."

"If you'd been involved," I added, with a conciliatory smile at Ben, "everyone would have known that B knew she'd been expelled."

Ben folded his arms and sat back in his chair, his mouth twisted downward. "Go ahead, Double-Oh Seven."

B drew my list closer to his computer, scanning it carefully. "The drama club seemed like they were actually upset about Harper. The girl with the blue wig did a monologue about it."

"Which one?" Ben asked.

"*Winter's Tale*?"

"Patricia." I laughed as Ben opened his mouth to clarify. I made a check next to her name on the list. "Good, I was hoping it wasn't any of them. Harper helped make their props last year."

"I have a question," B said. "You're both presupposing that the motive for framing Harper was personal, right? You made the list of suspects from the perspective of her friend." He planted a finger on the top of the SUSPECTS page. "But that means that the data is emotionally skewed. Statistically, Harper is well liked. But most people I talked to today also knew that she was highly ranked. When I was studying the effect of the academic probations on the profit margins of winter ball, rank was the biggest influence. Kenneth had the support of more people—"

"Even though he's a douchebag," Ben said.

B went on. "But Ishaan Singh affected more decisions. More people were staying home to study because there was an open slot in the top ten."

He minimized the list on his screen and pulled open a folder, double-clicking on an image. A photo of the senior ranking list filled the screen, today's date printed across the top. The quality was grainy, but the top ten was discernable.

1. Aaron, Cornell
2. Watson, Beatrice
3. West, Benedict
4. Donnelly, John
5. Donnelly, Peter
6. France, Mary-Anne
7. Royama, Margaret
8. Hertz, Bradley
9. Conrad, Nicholas
10. Singh, Ishaan

"Mathematically speaking," B said. "If I were looking for a motive, I'd start here. Cornell maintained his position, not gaining or losing anything numerically. But the rest of the list . . ."

Goose bumps trailed down my arms. "The rest of the list are our friends."

"But if they weren't," Ben said quietly. "They'd be people who leapt up in rank. Wasn't Meg stuck in the three point nine slump before?"

Harper and Cornell were my control group.

No, I thought. That wasn't reasonable. Meg would never risk Harper's future for the sake of the Great Thought Experiment.

Would she?

What had she said about adding sneakiness to her list of risks?

"Jack gained the most," B said. "He went from the brink of expulsion to fourth place."

"He got extra credit in Programming Languages for finding the IP address," Ben said. "Peter mentioned it at lunch."

I nodded dazedly, trying to push Meg out of my head. "He's been avoiding the cafeteria for weeks. It just seems so obvious."

"That doesn't mean it isn't true," Ben said. "He is a 'watch the world burn' kind of guy. He could have done it just to enjoy the chaos."

I rubbed my eyes. I didn't have the constitution for private detecting. The idea of anyone framing Harper made me feel sick. Putting faces to the villainy made it worse. But someone had gone out of their way to do this and letting them get away with it wouldn't get Harper back. I tried to focus on the end result. Harper with her computer and cell phone returned, going with us to Busby on Wednesday, drinking a hot cocoa as she drove. Harper smiling again and having it reach all the way to her glasses.

I needed it to not be Meg.

"There's also Mary-Anne. She's been pretty vocal about how this was destined to happen. She disappeared for a while after her meltdown. She could have been breaking into the system." I expelled a long breath. "We'll start with her and Jack. B, email me the whole list at my regular address, not through the school. I'll have Meg and Peter talk to the rest of the suspects."

I need it to not be Peter either.

Our belongings were shoved into backpacks and messenger

bags. Coats were put on. I thanked B for his superior espionage skills before he dashed out to meet his dad in the parking lot, his computer hugged to his chest.

"It's going to be okay, right?" I asked Ben, wringing my hands as B disappeared into the stacks.

He sat on the edge of the table. "Sure."

I looked at him over my shoulder. "That didn't sound very convincing."

"Sorry." He smiled, opening his arms wide to embrace the emptiness of the room. "Distracted again."

As it turned out, there was a "no necking" policy at the public library. We were hustled out of the room by an appalled librarian. It was worth it, although it would be difficult to explain to Meg and Harper that I was banned from reserving study rooms. That, I decided, was a problem for another day.

Missed call from: Dad, Work

Missed call from: Mom, Cell

Missed call from: Dad, Cell

Missed call from: Home

Missed call from: Home

Missed call from: Home

✴ 24 ✴

Even with the curtains open, it was dark in the living room with the TV off. Both of my parents were sitting on the couch. Their cell phones were side by side on the coffee table next to a half-eaten bowl of dry cereal. Mom always started snacking when dinner was running behind schedule. She must have ruined whatever was in the crockpot again. I hoped that we weren't waiting for another delivery from the vegan pizzeria. I would have preferred continuing to inch toward starvation rather than muscle through faux cheese and nutritional yeast. Meat was murder but nutritional yeast was torture.

My muscles burned in protest as I unwound the strap of my messenger bag from my shoulders and let it fall to the ground next to the front door. When I'd left the house that morning, I hadn't expected to come home feeling worse. Ben had ridden with me as far as the coffee shop, but even our long-winded and wordless goodbye hadn't been able to stop the day from catching up with me. The inside of my head went muggy as I'd tugged my school uniform back on in the espresso-scented bathroom.

I had to get the review notes for Econ and Programming Languages. I had to study for finals.

I had to find out who had plugged Harper's IP address into that tracking software.

"Where have you been?" Dad asked.

I unzipped my sweater and pried it off my arms. I blotted the sweat off my face with one of the sleeves before tossing it on top of my bag. "I texted you guys that I was going to the library after school."

"After school," Dad rumbled, gripping the arm of the couch. "Not in the middle of the day. I got a call at work that the nurse sent you home early with food poisoning. Your mother raced home to check on you."

"Lo and behold," Mom said unsteadily. "No Trixie. No bicycle. No returned phone calls."

"I had my phone on silent," I said, moving toward the kitchen. There had to be a granola bar or something to scavenge out of the pantry. "I was in the library. It's common courtesy."

"Don't walk away when we are talking to you, Beatrice."

My Mary Janes squeaked against the floor as I pivoted toward Mom's shout. I couldn't remember the last time either of them had raised their voice at me. They didn't even yell at Sherry.

"I'm sorry," I said, carefully enunciating each word to cover for the lack of sincerity. "Next time, I will make sure that I check my phone consistently when I'm studying."

"There won't be a next time," Dad said. "You are not allowed to go gallivanting around town whenever you want."

"What is on your neck?" Mom asked.

My hand itched, wanting to fly up and cover the side of my neck, even though I knew there wasn't anything there. I'd checked thoroughly in the bathroom at the coffee shop.

"I singed myself with a curling iron before winter ball. You guys took ten thousand pictures of me on Friday night. You can check the evidence." I hooked my thumbs in the pockets of my khakis. "Can I go get a drink of water now? It's a long ride from the library and I'm tired."

"Save it," Dad said. "When we couldn't find you, we called the Royamas. Meg was honest with her parents. Sit down."

Impotent rebellion welled up inside of me. I'd never refused a direct order from my parents before. There hadn't been many to disobey. Meg's dad had once told me that I had "pathologically permissive parents." Despite the poppy alliteration, it hadn't been a compliment.

I sat delicately on the edge of the loveseat. If we were going to do this, I would face them like an adult, not a sulking child. And then I would go back to my bedroom and ask Meg why she'd tattled on me.

Tags jingling, Sherry padded in from the kitchen. He lay down on my feet and mockingly crunched on a dehydrated pig's ear. My stomach contracted. The Internet had been telling me for years that bacon was the perfect food. I'd never been curious about it before now.

"What were you thinking?" Mom asked, pulling my attention away from Sherry and his porcine treat. "Leaving campus in the middle of the day, riding across town—"

"My best friend got expelled. I needed to see her."

Dad leaned forward, his hands clasped between his knees. There was glitter on his knuckles. "We know that you're upset. But that's no reason to start shirking your responsibilities. This situation that Harper has put herself in is—"

"She didn't put herself in to anything!" I protested. "You know Harper. She wouldn't do something like this. Someone framed her."

"Trixie," Mom said. I recognized the bait and switch tone she used to trick toddlers into calming down before she stabbed them with a hypodermic needle. "It isn't unusual for children who've survived a traumatic loss to act out against their surviving parent. You know that Greg has been very hard on Harper over the years. If she thought that this was her only way out . . ."

"You're all still young," Dad added, twiddling his thumbs. Years of teaching kindergarten meant that he couldn't help but give everything a bit of sign language. *This is the church, this is the steeple, open it up and see your parents' lack of faith in you.* "Your brains are still developing."

"Don't try to tell me about how my brain is developing," I snapped. "I took three years of advanced psychology and you majored in art history."

Mom leapt to her feet, scaring Sherry, who dropped his pig's ear. "Apologize. Now," she demanded.

"No," I said, nudging Sherry off my feet so I could stand, too. Why did the Mess even bother issuing the welcome packets every year if no one was going to read them? There was a whole section called YOU AND YOUR GIFTED TEEN that clearly outlined how to have a reasonable conversation without resorting to infantilizing. "I'm tired of this. You and Mr. Leonard and the Doctors Royama all sent your kids to the Messina. You wanted us to get the most out of our education and we got it. We've all worked so hard for so many years. And the first time that anything goes wrong, we're just kids. So, which is it? Are we geniuses who are allowed to interact with the adult world or are we children to be kept in our place?"

"No one is questioning your intellect," Mom said curtly. "It's your choices that we're taking exception to."

"I didn't get drunk or go swimming without a buddy," I exclaimed. "I went to see Harper because she needed me. Because she's alone. When her mom was alone in the hospital, you went to see her, didn't you? You didn't say that she'd put herself into a coma. You went to hold her hand, even though she didn't even know you were there." The color drained out of Mom's face, but I couldn't slow down now. Hunger and fury burned through the fog that had collected in my head. "Harper didn't ask me to go to her, but I went because that's what I needed to do. She didn't hack into anyone's account to spite her dad because that doesn't make any sense. Any one of us could just go to the public high school and test out."

Then why hack into four accounts? my brain asked. *Why frame Harper?*

Mathematical reactions to a personal issue. It's not one or the other. It has to be statistically and emotionally reasonable.

"I'm sorry that I abused your trust," I continued, keeping my feet planted and my head up. "I'm sorry that I was a jerk. But I won't apologize for trying to help Harper. She doesn't deserve having another person give up on her. Her dad locked her up. Her boyfriend dumped her. If it were me, wouldn't you want someone trying to find out who set me up? Nine people moved up in the top ten when Harper got expelled. I took her spot as salutatorian. If this is about statistics, then, logically, I would be the next target."

My parents exchanged a glance. Mom sat down again and Sherry came sniffing around her slippers.

"You're suggesting there's a mass conspiracy at your school?" she asked scornfully.

I threw up my hands. "It's a school for geniuses. It only takes one Mess student to run a conspiracy."

"You're tilting at windmills," Dad said. "It's not that we don't understand that this is a difficult time for you. The Royamas said that Meg has been deeply affected, too. But you can't let one bad situation ruin your future."

"Why not?" I asked. "One bad situation is ruining Harper's."

He pretended not to hear me. "Your mother and I agreed that it would be best if you took a week or two to calm down. No distractions. No cell phone. You need to focus on your finals. Starting now." He held out his hand. "Your phone will be returned to you at the beginning of winter break. We won't go digging through your search history. You can even keep your SIM card, if you're storing state secrets on it."

I stared at his open palm. An errant piece of glitter winked at me. "You're not serious. You're mad that I didn't call you back, so you're going to take the one way I have to contact you?"

"You won't be needing it," Dad said. "I will drop you off at school on my way to work and your mother will drive you home."

The translation finally clicked into place. *Your mother and I agreed,* indicative past tense. A preordained statement. They'd sealed my fate over a bowl of cinnamon rice cereal before I'd even made it out of the library.

The phrase was strange as it built up on my tongue, like some long-dead language that I'd only ever heard rumors of.

"I'm grounded?"

This website has been flagged as 'NOT SCHOOLWORK, TRIXIE'
Please enter administrative password for access.

Password incorrect.
Password incorrect.
Password incorrect.
An alert has been sent to your administrative email account.

"Go to bed, Trixie!"

My parents installed a firewall," I said, watching as my breath hung in the fog. "I can't even read my school email without one of them punching in a password. I could break through it, but that would just prove them right, wouldn't it?"

Meg shivered beside me. Her hair had lost some of its shine in the last twenty-four hours. It swung straight and loose in the frigid morning breeze.

"I knew something was wrong when I didn't hear from you," she said, kicking her feet against the planter box. "I begged my parents not to say anything to yours, but they wouldn't listen. They're afraid that this is going to turn into some kind of collective hysteria."

I hugged my jacket closer to my chest. "Like a *War of the Worlds* hysteria?"

"More like the Salem witch trials," she said. "My mom made me read a bunch of articles on conversion disorder. She's afraid that our stress is going to start manifesting in physical symptoms."

I snorted. "I'll be sure to let you know if I feel like I'm being pinched by a specter."

"I'm really sorry. I know it's stupid." She scuffed her heels against the planter again before hazarding a glance up at me. "Your parents didn't call Harper's dad, did they?"

"No." After I'd surrendered my phone, my parents had tried to make small talk over bowls of crockpot curry, but it was all too little, too late. "They're pissed at me, but they're smart enough to know that Harper would be in way more trouble if her dad found out she'd had guests over."

"That's something, at least. I couldn't stand the idea of us making things worse for her."

Thinking of the fight with my parents, it dawned on me that I'd wanted to talk to Meg about more than ratting me out.

"Why haven't you ever tested out of high school?"

She blinked up at me. "Leave the Mess?"

"Yeah. Harper said that it was a useless holding pattern. Any one of us could take a proficiency test and go off to college."

"I'd never want to leave you and Harper. I don't even like knowing that it's going to happen next fall." Her face fell as she remembered that Harper was already gone. She turned to watch the line of people marching their way through the front gate. It was hard to discern one from the next from under the masses of knitwear that everyone was wrapped in.

"Did you get the suspect notes from your frosh before the firewall went up?" she asked.

"Yeah." I bit my lip. It wasn't a lie, but it felt like one. I hadn't been able to access B's typed notes, but I did have the hard copy in my binder from my clandestine trip to the library. "I mean, he's not my frosh. He's Ben's frosh. But he actually made a really good point about how the ranking could work as a motive."

I searched her face for signs of affectation or chagrin, but she only nodded. Her eyes went glassy as she looked over my shoulder. She sat up straight and waved her arms over her head and called, "Peter!"

Peter was marching across the grass toward us. The collar of his polo stuck out from the neck of a faded MIT sweatshirt. A black beanie was pulled down over his eyebrows. "What are you guys doing out here? It's freezing!"

"Trixie's grounded," Meg said, sticking out her lower lip in a calculated pout. "We need to soak up all the quality time we can with her."

I forced a smile. "Frostbite is the truest form of friendship."

"If you say so," Peter said. He clapped his hands and rubbed them as though hoping to spark a flame. "What'd you do to get grounded? Your parents seemed really cool when we saw them before winter ball."

"It doesn't matter," I said quickly, just in case Meg decided to announce that we'd ditched the day before. Rule breaking was not the way to Peter Donnelly's heart. "Hey, do you know if Jack kept a copy of the code he gave to Mendoza?"

Peter's beanie rose an inch up his forehead. "Probably. He had to submit a copy to Dr. Kapoor for his extra credit."

"Do you think I could get a copy?" I asked. "Through my school email. I can't access my regular account until after finals."

Peter looked from me to Meg and back again. "Why?"

These are your friends, I thought. Peter and Meg were innocent until I proved them otherwise, which meant that I had to tell them exactly as much as I would have if I didn't know how much they'd gained from Harper getting expelled.

"Someone put Harper's IP address into that code," I said. "I want to see if they left any bread crumbs behind that Jack might have missed."

Peter huffed a laugh. It hung in the air and slid toward the front gate on the wind. "You think someone set Harper up to be expelled?"

I didn't like how jovial he sounded, but I held my face in a deadpan. "It's kind of convenient, isn't it? Jack was about to be expelled and then he happened to stumble onto the code that saved him?"

That wiped the laugh out of his voice. He tugged his beanie

farther down his ears. "So, now, it's not just that you think that someone set up Harper. You think it was my brother?"

Meg hopped down off the planter. "No! It's just not out of the realm of possibility—"

"Yes, it is. He's my brother. I think I'd know if he was a criminal mastermind."

"Did you know when he was drinking cough syrup for sport?" I asked. It'd never been a secret that Jack had been caught with recreational dextromethorphan in his backpack. Aragon Prep had a much sunnier approach to rule breaking than the Mess. Our entire eighth-grade class had been stuck in a two-hour-long "feelings circle" where we were all forced to tell Jack how much we cared about him.

Peter winced like I'd backhanded him. "I don't believe this. I'm going inside."

"Peter," Meg called as Peter's loping step fell in with the other people going through the gate. She kicked a hole in the grass as he went through the front doors. "That didn't go very well at all."

I ran my fingers through the end of my ponytail. Trying to get the code from Peter was always going to be a long shot. It didn't necessarily mean anything. Jack's story lined up with Cornell's. It was exactly what Harper had said would happen: it was easier for everyone to believe it and move on.

But hurting Peter's feelings hadn't been part of the plan.

"I'm sorry," I said to Meg as she bent down to scoop up her backpack. "I should have left you out of it. I didn't mean to ruin your—you know . . ."

"My what?" She hoisted her bag onto her back with a laugh of realization. "Oh God. Peter and I are not a couple, Trix. We went to a dance together. We're just friends. You know, how you two are just friends?"

Surprise crested on me in waves. I realized that I had never asked Meg if she and Peter were together. After he'd put the corsage on her wrist at the winter ball, my brain had filed them away in a folder labeled COUPLE.

Truly thinking about it, this assumption seemed grossly anti-feminist. Of course they could just be friends. With everything else that was going on, I'd been too distracted to think about it logically.

"Oh," I blurted. "Sorry. I assumed that he was the treatment group of your thought experiment. You said that Harper and Cornell were your control group—"

"I really didn't expect him to take that so poorly." She frowned and handed me my messenger bag. "He'll come around eventually. He needs to cool off. He's under a lot of stress with this student council situation."

I looped the messenger bag's strap over my chest. It wasn't actually lighter without my cell phone in it, but I could sense the void. I followed Meg's short stride through the grass. "What student council situation?"

She stopped short and smacked her forehead. "You didn't get any of my texts. Cornell resigned from student council."

Hiding in a storage closet looked a lot easier in movies. I must have looked ridiculous scarpering up and down the hall of the main building, tugging on locked doors. The third door I tried opened into a cramped closet that stunk from the various bottles and tubs that covered the metal shelves and dusty floor. Not wanting to be a choosey beggar, I tossed my messenger bag on top of a cobwebby gallon of floor polish.

I pressed my eye to the crack I'd left in the door. Everyone was moving slower in the week before finals started, a constant trudge toward the next class. There was no point in hurrying when you were just going to keep reviewing a semester's worth of work.

I spotted the back of Cornell's head gliding past the closet door. Mary-Anne was beside him, her mouth moving in a frantic whisper. Holding my breath, I opened the door a fraction and grabbed the second I saw spikes.

I pulled, staggered, and skidded hard to the right to keep from slamming into the shelving. The door clicked shut.

"This is new," Ben said, glancing up at the bare lightbulb screwed into the ceiling. He adjusted his backpack as he glanced down at me. "Passing period is still only six minutes, right?"

"Yes," I whispered. "You're going to have to talk fast."

"Talk?" He tilted his head, letting a smile unravel at the corner of his lips. "Do you need help picking a solvent? For windows, you really want something with at least four percent isopropyl—"

I stretched slightly on the balls of my feet and pressed my hands to the sides of his jaw. The zipper of his backpack clinked against the door as I crushed my lips over his. There wasn't time for a series of decent kisses. One wallop was going to have to do, no matter what my limbic system said.

"Good morning," he said as his eyelids reopened.

"Good morning." I retracted my hands and took as much of a step away from him as I could without knocking anything over. "Sorry for the radio silence last night. Quick recap: Meg's parents squealed on me, so my parents took my phone and my email access. What do you know about Cornell leaving student council?"

"Whoa." He started to put his hands up, but seemed to do the math on our limited square footage and let them swing by his sides. "Can you take that from the top? Meg's parents squealed on you? Are we mobsters now? Because I thought we were doing okay at this gumshoe thing—"

"Passing period, ticking away. Please focus," I said, groaning. I could hear people's footsteps and rolling backpacks moving on the other side of the door. There was still time before the bell rang, but I couldn't be sure how much. "Cornell left student council? That is a very big deal."

"It's not official," he said, shifting his shoulders under the weight of his backpack straps. "I've been trying to talk him out of it. He's been less than receptive."

"What does that mean?"

"He texted me a bunch of words I didn't think he knew." He shrugged. "He might have installed some kind of swearing widget. I think some of it was in Dothraki. It was impressive."

I rested my temple against the closest shelf. "But why would he quit? Student council doesn't have anything to do with Harper or the academic probations."

"No," he said slowly. "But from my prior experience, leaving a club is the quickest way to point out that you aren't friends with people anymore. It'll cost him a letter grade, but—"

"Wait," I interrupted. I was getting light-headed and it wasn't from the solvents. "What do you mean? Of course Cornell's still friends with you. I didn't say anything to him." Cold sweat started clamming my palms. "Oh, I did piss off Peter this morning. It wasn't on purpose. But I didn't do anything to Cornell. No Machiavelli, no Shan Yu—we agreed."

"I know you didn't." He rubbed a hand over the back of his neck. "It was my jackassery, not yours. There was a blowup at the student council table yesterday about Harper getting expelled and why the administration wasn't accepting character witnesses for her. Peter pointed out that Mendoza let me write an affidavit for Brandon and that we could do the same thing for Harper. You know how the student council gets. The lowerclassmen got involved and then everyone was telling Cornell that he let his girlfriend get expelled. It was a full clusterfrak." He tried to smile again, but this time it shriveled and faded. "I messaged Cornell after I got back from the library. That's when I got the full brunt of his secret swearing powers."

As much as it warmed the cockles of my heart to think about the student council table rallying together to fight for Harper's honor, I knew what this really meant. Ben had made himself clear to me in the park after the dance. *You can't ask me to give up my only fucking friends for you.*

And he'd lost Cornell anyway.

"Ben." My voice was hoarse. "I'm sorry."

"It's fine," he said, not quite looking at me. "And, hey, without the class credit we get for leadership, he'll take a dive in the ranking."

"That's not funny."

"I'm not joking." He did look up at me then and there was no hint of mockery in his eyes. "Once he resigns, one of us will be valedictorian."

The student council table was mostly empty. Jack appeared to be trying to make Peter read a catalog of some kind while Brad Hertz tried to chat up the junior officers. Cornell was sitting next to Mike Shepherd and the rest of the role-playing club. From our old table in the far corner of the room, I'd watched as Ben had come through the doors and spotted his two ex–best friends sitting together. He'd left without eating.

I'd wanted to go after him, but I had no idea what I could say to make him feel better. No combination of homework and comic books and making out in storage closets would fix his friendship with Cornell.

I sipped soup off the end of my spoon without truly tasting it. The revival of last week's watery minestrone seemed even worse today. Meg had stacks of her parents' psychology journals covering the place where Harper's tray wasn't. The inside of each magazine had been decorated in a Technicolor array of Post-its. Her fingernails kept riffling through the paper, never quite opening the pages.

"Have you developed the power of learning through osmosis?" I asked as she stroked another set of Post-it corners.

Her hand stilled and she hastily took a bite of the sandwich she'd been neglecting. "No. I can't focus. I have all of these journals and none of them has the answers I want."

"Then why did you bring them?"

"Because I still have hope."

A Tupperware container landed on the table next to my tray.

A cloud of expensive perfume filled my nose as Mary-Anne sat down beside me. Her hair bounced around her shoulders as she tucked her legs under the bench. Up close, I could see a shimmer of peach powder on her cheeks.

"So," she said, as though she often slummed it on our side of the cafeteria and started unprompted conversations with non-student-council members. "Do you guys not sit with us now? Or did you revise your seating schedule again? I cannot be alone with the boys and the babies for another day. It's total *Lord of the Flies* over there and the library isn't any better."

A tiny piece of onion slipped out of Meg's mouth. She stuffed it back in frantically.

"I think we probably sit here again," I said, trying not to look as shocked as Meg. "We only moved so that Harper could spend time with Cornell. Now that she's been expelled—"

"Ugh." Mary-Anne produced a pair of chopsticks from her jacket pocket. She snapped them apart and swirled the inside of the Tupperware. As my nostrils adjusted to the powdery sweet smell of her perfume, I caught a whiff of teriyaki sauce coming off her lunch. "That is such garbage. Harper would never do something that stupid."

I drowned a piece of celery with my spoon. "No arguments here."

"Cornell doesn't get it," Mary-Anne continued, nibbling a piece of rice from the end of her chopsticks. "If Harper really wanted to up him in the ranking, she would never have started dating him. Or anyone. It's too much of a distraction."

Meg groped her psychology journals again. "Maybe she didn't know how much work it was until she was in over her head." She flicked through the magazines, producing a worn copy that was laden with sticky notes and flags. She folded it open, displaying a page of tiny font under the headline THE WORTH OF TEEN LOVE. She tapped at a paragraph that had been meticulously highlighted and underlined. "It says here that high school relationships—romantic and platonic—are integral to adult identity development. The mistakes that we make now will inform the choices we make later in life. It's the basis of my entire thought experiment for this year."

Mary-Anne looked up from her teriyaki. "Your what?"

"Don't ask," I warned.

It was too late. Meg thwacked the journal down on the table. "I think the reason why Harper and Cornell didn't work was that they had no basis for their relationship outside of a chemical attraction to one another. It's an understandable mistake. On the surface, it looked like they shared the same ideals. They're both dedicated to their classes and their friends. But when Harper was removed from campus, she couldn't contribute to either of those things."

"She's still our friend, even if she doesn't go here," I said sharply.

"Yes," Meg said. "But it's not an active aspect of her relationship with Cornell. We were their buffer."

Mary-Anne narrowed her eyes at us. "You guys weren't going on dates with them, were you?"

"Of course not." I gagged, dropping my spoon. "They had a real relationship. They spent time together off campus. They loved each other."

"No," Meg stressed. She flapped a handful of journals at me. "They didn't. Every article I've read said that they didn't. It was just a hormonal reaction misconstrued due to an aggrandized notion of their basic compatibility. If they loved each other, they wouldn't have immediately broken up. Harper would agree that this is the only logical explanation for their failure as a couple."

I thought of Harper sitting in her flannel jammies, asking us whether either of us had heard from Cornell. She hadn't been wearing her indignant Spock face. She'd looked hopeful—like she was checking her work for a misstep in the equation.

"No," I said. "She wouldn't."

"She will," Meg stressed. "After she's had a chance to come to terms with her first failure. The shame of being expelled and being dumped—"

"And being framed," I said, raising my voice. "It's not her fault that she got expelled and it's not her fault that Cornell was too much of a coward to stand up for her."

"It's not our place to assign blame," Meg said, taking a generous bite of her sandwich. She covered her mouth as she chewed. "We'll love her no matter what. Because our friendship is based on trust and—"

"Wait," I said. All of my synapses fired at once, filling my head with a furious white-hot light. "You're talking like she actually broke into the homework portal."

Meg cut her eyes at Mary-Anne, who took another delicate nibble from her chopsticks.

"Meg." I must have yelled because the table of sophomores closest to us turned to look.

Meg rolled her eyes. "Well, she never said that she didn't do it."

"Yes, she did!"

Everything that had happened at Harper's house the day before played in front of my eyes at quadruple speed. Lunch, list making, going through pictures. Harper hiding her face behind a teacup. Harper hugging me before pushing us out the door.

The clatter of plastic forks and laughing conversations and the soft tide of textbooks being opened and closed started to press in on me. All our friends had been folded into pockets—across the room, across the campus, across town. All of it was wrong. Peter and Ben and Cornell shouldn't have separated. Mary-Anne shouldn't have been the third person at our table. Meg shouldn't have been staring at me with her blank therapist expression.

It wasn't supposed to be like this. There should have been more voices, more help.

"No," Meg said softly. "She didn't. I would prefer if it weren't true, but from the leads we came up with, the evidence points to—"

"Not her," I shouted. I brushed my hands over my hair. Thoughts were pinging around my head with so much force, I would have sworn I could feel them boomerang off my skull. "I don't believe you. Why would Harper risk everything to go up one place in the ranking?

She never cared about making valedictorian. You, on the other hand, went up six places when she got expelled. You care so much about your stupid thought experiment. Do you care about creating your adult identity more than you care about your friends? Because, in case you forgot, one of your best friends got expelled for something she didn't do and all you can do is sit there and dissect her relationship."

"I am trying to be prepared for whatever happens next," she shot back. "But we can't keep pretending that it's all going to be fine. There is a strong chance that it won't be."

I goggled at her. "Can you hear yourself? You sound like a robot."

"And you sound delusional." She stood, sweeping all of her magazines into her arms and throwing her bag over her shoulder with a sniff. "I can't deal with you when you're like this."

"I'm always like this!" I shouted as she started marching toward the student council table.

I put my head in my hands. A panic attack was creeping up my spine. My lungs went tight, working hard for the tiny molecules of oxygen polluted with perfume and soup steam.

Mary-Anne set her chopsticks down and gave a quiet *ahem* to remind me of her presence. As though I could forget.

"It seems fair that you should get to see my meltdown," I said without raising my head. "I was ringside for you throwing salad at the junior officers."

She made a tittering sound that I belatedly registered as a laugh. "Well, I was right. That dance was useless. The cricket team is stuck in their old uniforms and the band sucked. It was a total waste of a dress. I thought Jack getting cleared would save it, but then he ran off with you. . . ." She swept a fingernail under her lashes, erasing some invisible smudge. "I don't know why he keeps trying to make peace with Peter's friends. I've been telling him all year that it's a waste of time. He never listens."

My head popped up. "I didn't know you talked to Jack."

She leveled me with a droll stare. "I've been talking to Jack since sophomore year. Classic on again, off again. My literary agent said it's ruining my poetry. My last chapbook is apparently 'unpublishable.' No one wants to read about the prodigy having boy troubles. I'm supposed to be finding my adult voice, not pining." She wrinkled her nose. "Don't go blabbing about any of this. My shrink is on vacation and I have writer's block. That doesn't mean that I want everyone putting the pieces together. Some things are better when they're private, don't you think? Outside input gets so messy. Your friends judging you, making notes on you, comparing your rankings . . ."

She batted her eyelashes knowingly at me. The soup in my stomach boiled as I thought about Ben and I sitting on opposite sides of the student council table. *Oh, hell.*

"I don't have anyone to tell," I said. The truth of this was physically painful. "So, when Jack got suspended, did you think he'd actually cheated? From what people say about him, it sounds like something he's capable of."

"Most of what people say about him, he started himself. He did a paper on gossip last year for social psych that got really out of hand. I don't think he considered that the rumors would stick around. All that bullshit about making drugs and animal testing . . ." She rubbed her lips together in thought. Somehow, her lip gloss remained untouched by teriyaki sauce. "He could have hacked into the system, if he'd wanted to. He is a computer genius. But he's been working too much this year to have time for petty vengeance. He jumped up twenty places in the ranking in two months. Whoever messed with his grades cut him off right before he broke the top ten. He's trying to get a late acceptance to MIT to stay with Peter. It's so sweet that it makes me want to puke. I assume that's why he keeps trying to play nice with you all. Not that you've been very welcoming. He has this crazy idea that helping Peter's friends will prove that it would be okay for them to go to college together. He's been ignoring Brad and Nick all year. And me. Thus, our current off-again." She sighed and fluffed the back of her hair as though thinking too hard had deflated it. "He showed up at winter ball, kissed me hello, and then started asking if you and Meg had shown up yet. He was so freaked out about Harper getting expelled and Peter thinking it was his fault."

"Really?" I hadn't considered it at the time, but it had been strange that Jack had followed me out to the parking lot when I'd gone tearing out of the dance. Mendoza had pointed out that he had been risking a renewed suspension. Why would he have done that if he were guilty?

If the hacking had to be mathematically and emotionally reasonable, then it couldn't be Jack. Getting into the top ten wouldn't have done him any good if it hurt his relationship with his brother.

"Look, I know it's a long shot since you guys are, um, not together right now," I said. "But do you think that you could get a copy of the code Jack used to find the source of the probations?"

She flinched an unconcerned shrug. "Oh sure. At the very least, I could get a copy from Nick. He owes me a favor. I tutored him in French last year so that he could keep his scholarship. What do you think you're going to find in the code?"

"I don't know," I admitted. "But I have to look for something that proves that Harper didn't get herself expelled." I looked over at the student council table where Meg had planted herself next to Peter. "Since, apparently, I'm the only one of our friends who's worried about that."

Mary-Anne scoffed. "Meg's hypothesis is inherently flawed. If Cornell valued his grades over everything else, he wouldn't be trying to quit the student council." She paused, giving me a brief, bright smile. "Congrats on making valedictorian, by the way. Please don't let Ben get ahead of you. No one wants to hear *that* speech."

"Thanks," I muttered. I hadn't even begun to consider seeing my name at the top of the ranking list. It wouldn't get posted until we came back from winter vacation. It was a tenuous reality, a Bizarro world that had been created the second I'd left the winter ball.

Yikes. Even my inner monologue was making DC references. Everything was wrong.

I stared down at my lunch. "Do you mind if we sit here in total silence until the bell rings?"

"Sounds good to me." She picked up her chopsticks again. "Same time tomorrow?"

Why is Mary-Anne asking me to pass notes to you? Since
when do you write notes to Mary-Anne?

Buffy

Think of it as analog texting. It's old school. She's emailing me a copy of
Jack's code. Do you want a copy?
Also, if you're going to start passing me notes, you should work on
folding them. This looks like it got run over by a truck. Didn't you see
how tiny Mary-Anne folded hers?
Trixie (see how nice it is when you can read someone's handwriting?)

I'm crap at coding. Let me know the results?
I'll look into the art of origami after finals.
Can you get access to another storage closet?
Check yes or no.

Benedict Montgomery West

Your initials are BMW? Hahahaha!
You find a closet. That last one was gnarly.
Beatrice L. Watson

Your wish is my command. And my initials are classy as frak.

- B.M.W

✸ 26 ✸

I'd convinced my parents to give me access to the Mess website after dinner by telling them that my Econ teacher had sent out a study guide for our final exam. Since I didn't need the study guide—I had 104 percent in that class—the firewall would only show one download coming from my computer. If my parents were going to treat me like a common criminal, I had no choice but to act like one.

So far, I'd put up with being grounded with mute vexation. I'd always hated TV shows where surly teens went around slamming doors and screaming, *"I hate you!!!"* As much as the idea of slamming a door was becoming more seductive, I bit back the impulse. I stood patiently next to the front door while my dad gathered all his papers together in the morning. I waited alone at the edge of the parking lot after school until it was time for Mom to come fetch me. I didn't argue about what was on the radio or what they wanted to watch on TV after dinner.

I went to school. I ate lunch with Mary-Anne. I accepted the notes that Ben kicked under my desk in American Immigrant or slipped into my messenger bag as we passed in the halls. I came home and polished the final essays I'd started weeks ago and glanced at the review sheets that my teachers had passed out.

It'd only been two days, but I felt like my vocal cords were going to atrophy.

Not talking to Meg and Harper was hellish. I'd taken to sitting in the empty American Immigrant classroom before the bell rang rather than face the empty planter box at the front of the school. Meg had spent a day in the cafeteria with Peter, but then had disappeared into the library, probably to keep ignoring her homework in favor of her ongoing research into why Harper and Cornell had broken up.

It wasn't that Meg and I had never fought before. There'd been plenty of flare-ups in our group over the years. I'd spilled soda on her first copy of *The Fountainhead* and she'd given me the silent treatment until I'd ordered her an even fancier copy off the Internet. When we were freshmen, she'd told me I was too pudgy to wear Harper's bikini—which had been true, but we'd screamed at each other about it anyway.

This was new. This was a fight without Harper. Harper was always the deciding vote. Even if she hadn't been locked up in her fortress of solitude, she couldn't possibly have refereed an argument based on her.

All I could do was try to clear her name. My parents and Meg and Peter and Cornell and everything else could wait.

I turned up my TV. If my parents listened outside the door, they would hear the soundtrack to *Battlestar Galactica* and assume I'd fallen asleep while marathoning again.

There was nothing glamorous about searching through the thousands of IP addresses that had cleared Jack Donnelly's expulsion. From what I could tell, Dr. Mendoza had given Jack access to all the tracks of the senior homework portal. Every login, every piece of homework submitted, every email sent and where it went, all time stamped. There were no names attached, just line after line of student ID numbers and IP addresses.

Jack really did deserve all the extra credit for finding anything at all in the slurry. My eyes started to water almost instantly as I scrolled through page after page. I found my own student ID number and cross-referenced every email I'd sent since September. With only one class together, Harper and I hadn't used our school accounts for much this year.

I grabbed a notebook and started writing down student ID numbers. The Fake Harper had done a lot of damage. They would log in at one address and then submit an assignment in another immediately after. That would account for all of the plagiarism accusations. It wasn't clean work, but it was effective. The combination of school computers, home computers, and people checking their email from their phones meant that everyone's account was cluttered with different codes. The Fake Harper could have been using multiple IP addresses without anyone ever noticing.

I went back to my own account and checked the dates of each email I'd had with Cornell, Peter, and Meg. I fell into an easy patter, finding the student number of one of my friends, then tracing it in the list. Meg routinely submitted her homework from one address—the computer in her bedroom—and checked her email from another— her phone. Peter was the same. Cornell's account had the occasional blip address, but when I checked them, they appeared in multiple accounts. That had to be the school computers. And then there were the logins that the Fake Harper had left before the website crashed.

I sat back. Jack might have been able to delete any code that would have implicated himself or Peter, but he had no reason to cover for Meg and Cornell. Most of the Fake Harper's time stamps were in the middle of the night, so that ruled out anyone using Real Harper's computer to do the dirty work.

Except for Real Harper.

No. I couldn't go back down that road. I didn't care what Meg had said about Harper not denying Mendoza's accusations. I knew that she couldn't be responsible for this chaos.

My cursor hovered on the screen, waiting to be directed to

another student ID number. There was only one other person I emailed with regularly. Seeing the numbers, it was impossible to ignore. It was an almost daily barrage, one IP address on a loop.

I'd already accused everyone else that I cared about. If I didn't find anything, I'd never have to tell Ben that I'd searched his account.

Don't let me down now, hobo clown.

I typed in his ID number and picked up my pencil, tapping it against my notebook as I ticked through his logins. There was a home account and his cell phone, just like Meg and Peter. In September, he'd written emails to Peter and Cornell semiregularly. He got an email every Tuesday an hour after the student council meeting—Mary-Anne sending the secretary's notes. I quickly scanned her account. No sign of the Fake Harper. It was odd to be relieved by that. I'd never thought there'd be a day when I was comforted by Mary-Anne's innocence.

I scooted my chair closer to the screen. The last week of September, there was a random IP address logged in to Ben's account. That could have been anomaly. But then the Fake Harper started logging into his account. It never submitted homework. It never wrote an email. It just logged in and logged out. Over and over again. Sometimes it happened to overlap with Ben submitting something to the homework portal from his own IP address. Sometimes it showed up early in the morning or in the middle of the night. On weekends. On holidays.

I pulled up the calendar on my computer. The Fake Harper had accessed Ben's account on Wednesday afternoons when I knew he'd been at Busby and Tuesdays when he was at student council meetings. It'd logged in the night of the winter ball when we'd been at the park.

Fake Harper was spying on Ben West.

Dad turned on his blinker a split second before he swerved into the next lane. This was why I'd never learned to drive. I couldn't risk letting my father pass on his stunt-driving gene.

I closed my eyes and listened to the squeal of the windshield wipers. I wasn't positive that I'd managed to sleep at all. There hadn't seemed to be any reprieve from my own thoughts after I'd climbed into bed.

Whoever framed Harper was spying on Ben. They hadn't touched me and had only accessed Cornell's account twice.

This had to be what Harper meant when she'd said that even she'd believed she was guilty when Mendoza had shown her the code. The first, second, and fourth people in the ranking had been tampered with. Cornell's grades had been shifted. Harper's IP address was used. Ben was being watched. And my account was clean.

"I talked to Greg last night," Dad said, breaking into my thoughts.

I opened my eyes. Ahead of us, there were watery smears of red neon brake lights. I swallowed as we came to a short stop behind a station wagon.

"I know that you think that your mom and I have been too hard on you this week," Dad continued. He stretched in his seat as though he could spot the cause of the traffic. I kept my mouth shut rather than explain that the cause was the water pelting the ground. Sane people always drove slower in the rain. "And we appreciate you being a good sport about the whole thing. I think you took it better than either of us."

He chuckled and half-looked at me. I lifted an eyebrow at him and turned back to the road. It was a bad idea to let him make eye contact when he was behind the wheel. He got too intent on it and forgot that there was a world of metal on the other side of the window.

"We can't stop Greg from doing what he thinks is best for Harper," he said. His sigh fogged the windshield. He wiped it away idly as I reached down and turned on the defroster. "He says that she's been studying for her interview all week and that she's in a very good position to get placed at Marist."

I went rigid in my seat. Today was the day of Harper's interview. I wondered what else I'd missed since both of our groundings had gone into effect. Had she read anything other than the Bible this week? Had her dad realized that it was utterly impractical to live in a house without Internet access?

"It took some convincing," Dad said, unable to stop himself from smiling. "A lot of convincing. You know how hard it is to deal with Greg when he thinks he's right about something. I swear, he's got to be a Vulcan. You have always said that Harper reminds you of a blond Spock—"

"What's your point?"

"Greg said that Harper's interview is at two, so she should be out in time to come get you from school."

I forgot to watch the road. I twisted against my seat belt to face him. "I-I get to see her? For how long?"

"I couldn't get her out of her curfew. She turns into a pumpkin at eight o'clock on the dot. That should be enough time to make a trip to the comic book store and come back to our house for some quality time, right?" He flashed me a smile before sobering and remembering to drive. "You still can't gallivant, but I hate seeing you this sad, hon. Open the glove compartment."

The glove compartment door unlatched easily. It fell open, displaying a mass of old bills and insurance cards. My cell phone sat on top of the pile. I reached for it, not quite believing that it was there. I knew it was ten dollars' worth of plastic and computer chips put together by Chinese factory workers under terrible conditions and sold to my parents at a ridiculous markup. I knew that Meg's dad had published multiple articles about our generation being too dependent on technology and how it was rotting our developing brains.

But I'd never been happier to see its morally questionable, fingerprint-smeared screen.

"You need some time to decompress with your friends," Dad said, watching as I turned the phone on. It had a full charge. "We can even order you guys some Indian food. Tikka masala for Harper and extra samosas for Meg, right?"

The phone trilled and buzzed in my hand as a week's worth of texts came pouring in. Meg telling me about Cornell leaving the student council. Ben laughing about us getting kicked out of the study room at the public library. And one from ten minutes ago, from Harper.

I can't wait to see you guys this afternoon. Slurpees and Busby? We can bring a tarp to the park and make a waterproof fort?

I could feel the alternate universe I'd been living in wink out of existence. The traffic started moving again. Time started moving again. There was hope. There was a chance to make everything right.

And then I remembered that I hadn't spoken to any of our friends all week. Harper was expecting both me and Meg to celebrate the limited return of her freedom. Maybe she'd want to see Peter and Ben. Maybe she'd want to talk to Cornell.

How could I tell her that, in the span of a week, the group had torn itself apart?

How could I tell her that it was mostly my fault?

Me [7:22 AM]
It's Trixie. I need your help.

Unknown Number [7:24 AM]
How did you get my number?

Me [7:25 AM]
Mary-Anne.

Unknown Number [7:27 AM]
Ah. What do you need help with?

Me [7:29 AM]
Can you get everyone to the library at lunch?

Unknown Number [7:30 AM]
Everyone meaning your friends?

Me [7:32 AM]
They like you more than me right now. I have faith in your evil twin powers.

Unknown Number [7:34 AM]
You must be desperate.

✿ 27 ✿

Every table in the library was piled high with textbooks and laptops. The aisles were congested with people muttering reference numbers and trying to look things up on their phones without being caught by the roaming librarian.

I took the long way around the bookcases, silently cursing the Mess for not installing brighter lights. As I'd expected, the middle of the six hundred section was the aisle that finals forgot. I took a seat on the floor and wiped my hands against the carpet. I tipped my head back, reading the upside-down titles above me.

"Why animal husbandry?"

I jumped and grabbed onto the closest shelf to keep from face-planting into the carpet. Jack put his hands up in surrender as he walked toward me. He wore a plain black sweatshirt over his uniform. He considered me for a second before slipping the hood off his head.

"Good God, Donnelly," I breathed, clutching my chest as my heart slammed against my ribs. "This whole creeping-in-the-shadows thing has to stop." I peered around his legs, but there was nothing behind him except for more books and geometric-patterned carpet. "Where's everyone else?"

"I outsourced the job. It turns out that your friends don't actually like me more than you." He flopped down across from me. "So, why did you choose the animal husbandry section?"

"Because there aren't any classes on it. Urban school for geniuses; not a lot of interest in sheep." Not that you could tell from all the literature surrounding us. The Mess's generous benefactors must have been really dedicated to the idea of domesticated animals. "Aren't you curious about why I called a meeting?"

"Not particularly." He propped his elbow up on the nearest shelf, shoving a row of books back. "I figured you either wanted to talk about this Harper thing some more or gloat about being the new valedictorian. Either way, it doesn't really concern me."

"That's funny. From what Mary-Anne said, it seems both of those things concern you a lot. You worked really hard to make it to the top ten before the deadline for MIT applications. And Harper getting expelled didn't exactly ingratiate you to your brother—"

"Yeah, okay. Shut up a second," he said, too distracted to be truly insulting. "I think the others are here."

I clenched my teeth and folded my arms mutinously over my chest as the sound of thudding footsteps and spinning wheels got closer. B. Calistero came around the corner, his cheeks burning red as he skidded to a stop. I glanced at Jack, who scowled at me.

"What?" he asked. "You said your friends. I thought you liked the frosh. He follows you everywhere."

B's face went vermilion.

"Have a seat, B," I said. I was afraid he'd faint from all the blood in his body taking up residence in his skull. "Thanks for coming."

He tripped over one of the wheels on his rolling backpack. "No problem!"

He settled onto the floor, a few feet away from me. As he collapsed the handle of his backpack, Nick and Brad filed into the aisle—the former short and blond, the latter tall and curly-haired. Meg, Cornell, and Peter followed, wearing matching looks of confusion. Mary-Anne brought up the rear, her pink fingernails sunk into the sleeve of Ben's jacket. She caught my eye and immediately dropped Ben's arm. He took a large step away from her and looked from me to Jack and back again.

"Are you being held hostage?"

"No," I said.

"It looks like you guys are trying to bring back the feelings circle from Aragon." Brad snorted.

"Let's sit down," Peter said, sinking to the floor next to Jack.

Meg made a face. "Oh, I do not think so. Someone had better tell me what fresh hell this is."

"Keep your voice down," Jack said. "Haven't you ever been in a library before?"

"Don't you start with me, Jack Donnelly," she hissed, thrusting her hands onto her hips. "You sent your goons in before any of us had a chance to finish eating."

"We aren't goons," Nick grumbled.

"Henchmen?" Ben offered, ignoring the glare that Nick threw at him. "And why did they get goons and I got smacked upside the head by Poet Laureate Barbie?"

"Because you are more combative than the others," Mary-Anne said. She sat down on my side of the aisle, artfully tucking her legs to the side. She frowned at B and scooted closer to me.

I looked up at Meg, Cornell, and Ben. "It's not a trap. If you want, we can all go back to hating each other the second the bell rings. But I really need your help. Please."

Meg sank to the ground. "I don't hate you, Trixie. You're just the most bullheaded person on the face of the planet."

"There should be a book about that around here," I said, gesturing at the stacks. When her mouth twitched, I let myself smile at her. "You're not a robot. And I am a bullheaded demon monster."

"A minotaur?" offered B.

"The ancient Egyptians had a bull god, too," said Brad.

"Apis," Mary-Anne said.

"And this is what happens when you shove everyone from the top of the ranking list into one place," Ben grumbled.

I hadn't considered it until now, but it was true. The top nine people on the senior ranking list were here. I felt a twinge of guilt that I'd never talked to Ishaan Singh. He would have rounded us out to the full ten.

I sat up straight and clasped my hands together. I'd never started a meeting before. It seemed best to begin talking before anyone thought of another horned deity. "Okay. Last night I found out something really important—"

Cornell blew out a breath as he sat down next to Nick. "If this is about Harper coming to get you guys after school, it's fine. I already know about it."

I swiveled to look at him. "You do?"

Meg's leg shot out. She kicked Peter hard in the ankle.

"Ow," Peter whined. "That was my good leg!"

"I know it was," she snapped. "You weren't supposed to tell Cornell!"

"Why?" Peter sulked. He leaned forward to massage his ankle. "He deserved to know. I couldn't let him get blindsided. Just because he isn't my VP doesn't mean he's not my friend."

"He's your VP for another two weeks," Mary-Anne said idly. "Mendoza won't accept his resignation until after we get back from winter break."

"Uh, I can hear you," Cornell said, glowering. "So, if you want to cool it with the pronouns, that'd be great."

Ben sneered at him. "Hey, man, you peaced out. We've had a full week to adjust to your absence."

"This is not a student council meeting," I said. My temples were starting to throb. I reached up and adjusted my ponytail. "And this is not about Cornell and Harper's relationship."

Jack popped his knuckles. "Thank God."

"Because their relationship failed to crystallize," Meg said under her breath.

B's forehead creased into three margins. "But they were your control group, Meg."

"Ix-nay, Brandon," she whispered in a singsong.

Cornell turned on her. "Excuse me?"

"I'm really supposed to be in the office," Nick piped up, putting his index finger in the air. "I help Mrs. Landry with clerical stuff during lunch as part of my scholarship and—"

"I found more tracks in the homework portal code," I said loudly. "I can prove without a doubt that Harper isn't the hacker, but I need help figuring out who is."

That shut everyone up.

"It's too late," Cornell said faintly. He ran the flat of his hand against the grain of his scalp. "She's already at her interview at Marist."

"Jesus, Peter." Meg groaned. "Did you have to give him her entire itinerary?"

Peter folded his arms over his chest. "Yes."

"It doesn't matter," I said. "Jack was checking for IP addresses, not for time stamps. The person using Harper's IP address was logging in when Harper couldn't possibly have been near a computer."

Jack did a decent impression of his brother's confused face. "Most of the homework switching happened between midnight and three in the morning."

I shook my head. "But Harper's IP address was logging into Ben's account at all times of the day. Like when Harper was at the comic book store or on dates with Cornell or picking up her dad's dry cleaning. It didn't do anything in there, which"—I inclined my head to Jack—"is probably why you didn't notice it. It just logs in and logs out."

"Of Ben's account?" Peter echoed.

"Ben me?" Ben asked.

"Try to keep up, geniuses," Mary-Anne said.

"Why would someone change Cornell's grades, get Harper

expelled, and spy on Ben's account?" I asked, trying to hold on to the thread of the conversation with both hands. "Why go into first, second, and fourth place, but skip third?"

Ben turned to me, his lips pressed into a khaki line. "Are you sure they didn't do anything to my account?"

"Nothing that I could see," I said. "You haven't moved in the ranking at all."

He huffed a laugh. "Yeah, well, we can't all default into the valedictorian spot."

Cornell busied himself examining his fingernails.

Meg scrunched her nose. "They could have been trying to frame you and got Harper by mistake."

"One, two, four," B murmured. He combed the hair out of his face. "That's the beginning of a tetranacci sequence. Were there any attempts on number eight?"

"No," Jack said. "That's Brad. I checked his account when I was going through the code."

Brad punched him in the arm. "Thanks, man."

"If it were anyone but Ben," Mary-Anne said, "I'd think that someone was trying to look out for him. But since his only friends are here"—she quirked an eyebrow at Ben—"your parents wouldn't happen to be psychopaths who would destroy the futures of your classmates in the name of your ranking?"

"No," Ben said definitively. All the blood had drained out of his face, leaving him the same dingy off-white as his polo. "My dad's a technophobe."

"Your mom cares about your ranking," Cornell said. "She talked about it a lot when we were staying with her. All that stuff about how she and your stepdad were their class valedictorians . . ."

"She's on the other side of the country," Ben ground out. "She couldn't have taken over Harper's IP address even if she wanted to. Besides, if she rigged the ranking, she'd lose the ability to guilt trip me. And then what would we talk about?"

"Then I'm out of ideas," Mary-Anne said with a flick of her wrist.

"No offense, Benedict, but you definitely have more enemies than friends."

"That might have been true last year," Meg said, tapping a finger against her chin. "But not now. Ben has at least four friends."

"Do I count?" B asked.

"Oh," Meg said. "Of course. Five friends."

"Stop," Ben drawled. "You're making me blush."

"I told you this was going to turn into a feelings circle," Brad muttered to Nick and Jack.

"It's six," Cornell said stiffly. "It's been six all year. I don't register anymore?"

"Well . . ." Meg cringed. She wrapped a lock of her hair around her finger. "No. Obviously not."

"You did go sit with the role-playing club," Peter mumbled.

Cornell threw up his hands. "Where else was I supposed to go? Everyone else on campus thinks that I let my girlfriend get expelled so that I could stay at the top of the rank. The role-playing club are the only people who don't want to throw garbage at me when I walk through the halls. I didn't choose them because they hate Ben."

"It's just a sweet bonus?" Jack asked.

The bell rang, severing any additional remarks.

"Come on," Peter said, kneeling on his good leg to propel himself upward. "There's no point in being late to fifth."

Everyone gathered their backpacks. Jack helped Mary-Anne to her feet. He wrapped an arm around her waist and she swatted at him but didn't shy away. *On again.*

Cornell left without saying goodbye, his head down as he pushed his way out of the library. Meg watched him go, her mouth set into a tight pucker. She looked up at Peter.

"Why won't Mendoza take his resignation? He's not coming back."

"It's the bylaws," Ben said, scuffing his foot against the carpet. "You can't run a club without a vice president."

308 ★ LILY ANDERSON

"What?" I asked.

"It's a stupid rule," Peter said, leading the way out of the library. "The vice president is the deciding vote in a tiebreaker. Without him, we don't have a quorum. I tried to get it repealed. Mary-Anne's normally our tiebreaker anyway."

"Because you are all morons," Mary-Anne said, flinching as Brad stepped too close to her.

"But we can't have her as acting vice president without a vote and we can't run an election during finals," Peter finished.

"If any other club VP pulled this, the administration would let them fold," Ben said with a scoff. "But the bylaws were written by Marxist wannabes, so you also can't have any clubs without the student council, so—"

Something started slithering around in my brain. It was half a dozen thoughts, none of them quite able to link together. I stopped and squeezed my eyes shut until the sound of everyone walking away faded out.

There weren't enough people in the student council to run it. There had to be an emergency election. I pictured campaign posters. Peter would do his best to put his hand on the scale. He'd already chosen Mary-Anne. Mary-Anne had said that Ben had more enemies than friends, but that wasn't true. Meg had proven that.

No one's parents would break into the homework portal. No one's parents understood the pressure of the Mess. No one read the welcome packet. Ben's mom was on the other side of the country and couldn't have accessed Harper's IP address.

The hacking had to be emotionally and mathematically reasonable. Fake Harper needed motive and means. That was easy enough. School for geniuses, all crammed together. Hormones and broken relationships and everybody's limbic system growing too quickly to keep up with their prefrontal cortexes.

But the hacking had to be *spatially* reasonable. That's why Ben's mom couldn't have done it. She was too far away. Most people were too far away. Everyone commuted to the Mess.

A map of town unfolded inside of my eyelids. North, south, east, west. The park, the university, the Mess, the comic book store. It never could have been Meg. Meg was in my quadrant of town. So were the Donnellys. That's why Peter had to drive us to the winter ball. Cornell lived far enough away from Harper that he'd needed to drive to see her.

Fake Harper wasn't a mastermind. It had started methodically, but he or she had let emotions skew the data. There was too much evidence. There were too many footprints left in the code. Spying on Ben. Using Harper's IP address. Switching assignments. Between midnight and three in the morning—when parents wouldn't hear the hum of a computer or the click of keys.

I ran through the library. I could hear the librarian calling after me, but I didn't slow down, even as I burst through the doors and into the rain. Meg and Peter were halfway across the *M* mosaic with B scuttling behind them, his rolling backpack catching puddles. Ben was heading for the math and sciences building, his hands up to protect his hair from the elements.

I bolted, dodging through groups of people and slipping on the wet ground. I knew that I should go to Calculus and accept Dr. Kapoor's patent "Tardy Quiz." Now that I was holding down the valedictorian spot, I should have worked twice as hard to keep it. But I'd been number three for a long time. I was used to being third. I wanted to graduate with the rank that I'd earned, not at the cost of all my friends.

My messenger bag bounced painfully against my side as I caught up to Ben. I grabbed his elbow and spun him around.

"Who do you know who lives on the stone streets?" I panted. He looked confused and I shook his arm violently. "You know someone who lives across town. Harper's on Onyx. In order to use her IP address directly, someone would have to be on Onyx or Emerald or Agate. They have to be close to her and care about you."

His eyes were darting around, the same way they did in class when he was about to raise his hand. He scrubbed his hands over his face and cursed at the rain in English, French, and what might have been Orc.

I didn't have to wait for him to elaborate. I knew I was right. It was emotionally, mathematically, and spatially reasonable. "We have to get to the admin office."

He shivered and brushed some of the water off his face. His voice came out in a rasp. "He's not here. He was absent in American Immigrant, remember? And he wasn't in Gender Roles."

"How many classes do you guys have—" I cut myself off. It didn't matter yet, but it would. "We have to find a bus schedule."

Me   [12:32 PM]

I might be a little late to the parking lot. And I'm
definitely going to be grounded again. But I love
you both and I think I have a solution to everything.

✦ 28 ✦

I wished I'd thought to bring an umbrella. My clothes were soaked and Ben's hair had plastered itself to his forehead. Our uniforms drew the attention of the college students riding with us, but the driver took my money without question. I buttoned my jacket up to my neck as the bus puttered through the storm. Ben's leg wiggled next to mine as he stared out of the window at the buildings of the university.

Facts do not cease to exist because they are ignored. Aldous Huxley had said that in an essay once. He probably hadn't meant that being a genius sucks because you can't pretend that you never thought of the answers, but it worked for that, too.

I leaned over and pressed a kiss to Ben's cheek. A shadow of a smile crept over his lips. I took this as a solid sign that it was less likely that he was about to have a panic attack. He wove his fingers together with mine. He didn't let go, even as the bus dropped us at our stop.

"This way," he said with a slight tug on my hand for guidance. It was the first time either of us had spoken since we'd left campus.

I recognized the neighborhood from my ride with Meg on Monday.

The sidewalk was covered in a canopy of leafless trees. Most of the recessed driveways were missing cars.

We slowed to a stop in front of a large house with a sharply slanted roof. I craned to see the house behind it. I could barely make out a set of airy blue curtains in one of the windows. I wondered if Harper was behind them, practicing her apocrypha or if she'd already left for Marist.

Ben took a deep breath and wiped his face with the back of his sleeve before he rang the doorbell. He started to loosen his grip on my hand, but I held on fast. He glanced down at me in surprise and I rolled my eyes at him.

As I started to worry about whether or not anyone was home, the door creaked open, letting out a rush of blissfully warm air. Mike stood blinking at us in *Teenage Mutant Ninja Turtles* pajama pants.

"Greythorn? Trixie?"

"Hey, Shep." Ben squeezed my hand a little tighter. "We need to powwow."

Despite having known Mike for most of my life, I'd never given much thought to his house. I vaguely remembered his mother bringing cupcakes to school once, but he'd never had a big full-class birthday party.

I had not expected him to live in an issue of *Architectural Digest*. There were exposed wood beams and skylights and carefully chosen antiques. As the boys led the way past the living room and down a long hallway, I counted four Tiffany lamps and saw a painting that might have been an original Diebenkorn.

And then we turned a corner and stepped into a bedroom filled with NASA paraphernalia and a flat-screen TV displaying a paused video game. There was a half-eaten bowl of Top Ramen between two massive beanbags and a bookcase filled with *Star Wars* novels and D&D miniatures.

I felt myself relax. This was what I'd been expecting. This was common ground.

Mike leaned over and turned off the Xbox. The TV went to its blue AV screen, giving the room an eerie, cavernous glow.

"I hope my mom doesn't come home. I'm not allowed to have girls in my room." He went red under his acne as he shoved aside the bowl of ramen. "Go ahead and pull up a beanbag. Is there any chance you're here to give me Cline's notes from this morning?"

I sat on the nearest beanbag, which crunched and billowed underneath me awkwardly. I shoved an elbow into it to stay afloat. "He wants us to use MLA footnotes on the final instead of a bibliography."

"Oh. Cool," Mike said. He glanced over at Ben, who was settling into the beanbag beside me. "But that's not why you're here?"

"No," Ben said. "You know why we're here."

Even with the acne and the bed head and the cartoon jammies, Mike seemed much older as he sat down across from us. His face sagged as he stared at his hands, avoiding Ben's inscrutable gaze.

There was no point in tiptoeing. I was giving up the valedictorian slot. I was grounded again, probably for much longer than a week. I had to bet everything on being right.

"Hacking into Kenneth Pollack's account, I understand," I said to Mike's bowed head. "He's a douche and a bully. You knew that he stuck Ben's head in a toilet last year and didn't get suspended for it, so you decided to take it into your own hands."

Ben tossed me a look of confusion. I knew that he'd assumed that I would focus on Harper, but if he was going to leave this line of questioning in my hands, he was going to have to trust me.

"You found a way into B. Calistero's account to cover your tracks, used your own essay to frame him—because it's so obvious that no one would think of pinning it to you—and watched Ken get pulled off the basketball team." Mike twitched, but I kept going. I'd spent all week with the puzzle pieces scattered through my thoughts. It was easy to shuffle them into place now. "Cline's speech at the dance was wrong. Ishaan Singh did let his grades slip when he was suspended. He was fifth when you got into his account. Meg said so at the harvest festival. You needed his slot as wiggle room to start carving out the top four to your liking. You didn't want me, Harper, and Cornell to drop too far. You weren't waging war. You were playing chess. We were your major pieces. You wouldn't risk us getting knocked off the board. Our GPAs were protecting the top slot for Ben.

"But Jack would have ruined all that. He was supposed to be a pawn, but he started jumping ahead too quickly. It took him less than a semester to break into the top ten. It wouldn't be impossible for him to make it to valedictorian. So, you had to take him out, even though it would draw the attention of the administration."

"You forgot Alex," Ben interrupted icily. "He was so far down in the ranking, he didn't even factor. And Shep tried to get him expelled anyway."

Mike's hands had started shaking. I could see him clutching them into painful fists, his knuckles burning white. His teeth grit together, desperate to keep whatever was rising up in his throat from coming out. I'd never seen anyone look so petrified.

"Anyone could go into the ranking and shuffle people around," I said. I ducked my head, trying to catch Mike's eye. "Making Ben the valedictorian was only half of the goal. I bet you didn't even touch your own grades, did you?" He swung his head. "But if you succeeded in getting Alex expelled, the role-playing club wouldn't have a quorum. It'd either have to shut down or—"

"Or it'd need a new vice president," Ben said.

"The real vice president," Mike whispered as he forced himself to look at Ben.

"You kicked me out," Ben said, awestruck. "You had me voted off the board when I ran against you for treasurer. You hate to lose."

Mike wrung his hands. "We started this together. It's not right, running it without you. The game's not the same."

There wasn't a little fire in Ben's eyes. It was like Vesuvius detonating from inside Mount Doom on top of the volcano planet Mustafar. "You couldn't have shot me an email? 'Hey, come by on Friday to play a campaign.'"

"You didn't respond when I emailed you over the summer," Mike said so quietly that it was hard to make out the words.

"I was busy getting coffee for congressmen," Ben snarled. "And you apparently lost your shit, so I don't feel too bad about it."

"Enough," I said, keeping my voice level. "Ben, didn't you think it was odd that he volunteered to work the harvest festival?"

"Under the bylaws, all school clubs are required to work any event that could be classified as a carnival, bazaar, or moveable feast," Mike said. "The harvest festival is technically a carnival."

"The rest of the role-playing club didn't work the haunted house," I said, thinking of Mike standing at the entrance in his lab coat. "And you weren't required to go to the winter ball. But you knew from reading Ben's emails that he had to be there. It would have been in Mary-Anne's weekly reports from the student council meetings."

"You read my emails?" Ben roared.

Mike shriveled deeper into the carpet. "Not all of them."

"Just enough to know where you were going to be," I finished, looking at Ben. "That's why Mike came and sat with me at the dance. That's why he told you that I'd left with Jack. That's why he let Cornell sit with him at lunch. People who hate you don't go out of their way to see you. They don't make sure they pass you in the halls every day or take classes with you. They don't get close to your friends. They don't try to make you valedictorian. He's been trying so hard to make up with you—"

"He's been trying so hard that he hacked into the administration and got four people put on academic probation?" Ben shouted, leaping out of his chair and pacing the floor in front of Mike's bed. He looked deranged with his wet hair sticking up in odd cowlicks from where he'd tugged at it. "That makes no sense! That's the most asinine, roundabout, pathetic, completely fucking illogical thing that I've ever heard."

"No, it's not," Mike said. "You said that the only way your mom would fly all the way out for graduation was if you made valedictorian."

318 ★ LILY ANDERSON

Ben stopped pacing. His breathing was ragged. "You can't be the dungeon master of real life. My grades, my family are none of your damn business. I don't have to roll to your liking anymore."

"Don't you get it?" I asked. How was it possible for us to have the same IQ when he was so much slower on the uptake than I was? "Those are exactly the things that your friends care about. God, Ben, you know that I've been going crazy this week because of Harper's grades and Harper's family. That's what happens when you care about someone."

"Let's talk about Harper," he shouted. He pointed at Mike with a vibrating finger. "He got her expelled. He's the reason Cornell dumped her and you and Meg stopped talking and your parents grounded you. He did that, Trixie."

"I didn't . . ." Mike gulped and turned to me. "I didn't mean to involve Harper in this. I downloaded this software that would unlock the passwords to the nearest routers and their IP addresses. It wasn't like I went looking for Harper's house. The router had the name it came with from the manufacturer and the password was 'Sarah.' I thought it was the people next door. Their dog's name is Sarah."

My veins went cold. "Sarah was Harper's mom's name."

Mike put his face in his hands as Ben gave an unintelligible roar of rage and kicked the nearest bookcase. There was a tinkle of pewter statues falling over.

"West," I snapped without thinking about it. I'd almost forgotten the power of last-naming him. He immediately paused, glaring at me mutinously. "It's going to take too long for us to ride the bus back across town. Call everyone and tell them to get to Harper's."

"Everyone," he repeated flatly.

"I don't care what lie you have to tell Cornell to get him there. We can't fix this without the whole group."

He chewed on the inside of his cheek for a moment, undoubtedly trying to come up with a reason why this was not a rational request. Coming up short, he stormed out of the room, pulling his cell phone out of his backpack as he went.

"Please believe me," Mike whispered into his hands, which were still pressed against his nose. "I really was just trying to help Ben. I wanted my best friend back. It all went wrong and then it got worse and I—I never would have done anything to Harper."

"I know," I said. "I mean, you did get her expelled and didn't come forward when she was forcibly removed from campus, but we'll overlook that bit. Right now, I need you to promise me that you will help us put everything back the way it should be."

He lowered his hands, revealing his damp eyelashes. "I'm going to get expelled."

I wished I could tell him that there was another way for this to play out, but I knew there wasn't. The administration would be out for Mike's blood when they found out that they'd been duped into expelling their salutatorian for no reason. The Donnelly family would threaten to pull their funding if Mike wasn't punished for threatening their legacy. Not to mention the parents of all the other AP students, the basketball and cricket teams that had lost players, and all of our classmates who'd always thought that Mike was on the weird side.

It was a shame. Mike was on the weird side, but he was really just a nerd with too much time on his hands. He had thought that if he helped Ben, he'd get his best friend back. I understood that. I would have gone over to the dark side for Harper and Meg. I'd spent all week on the verge of it.

"Mike, what's your IQ?"

He took in a deep snuffle as fat tears started rolling through the nooks and crannies of his face. "One hundred and ninety-two."

The mad genius range. That stood to reason. "And where are you in the ranking?"

"Bouncing around the thirties," he said to the carpet. "I got bored in Gender Roles."

"Have you ever considered testing out of school? With your IQ and everything you learned at the Mess, you could walk into any high school on Monday and be done. They give credit for proficiency."

"Really?" He wiped his nose on the back of his arm in a long swipe. "Why haven't you done that?"

"Stockholm syndrome. But you should think about it." I leaned forward and patted him on the shoulder. With more than a little effort, I dislodged myself from the beanbag chair. "I'm gonna go make sure Ben isn't Hulk-smashing your living room."

Dad   [3:05 PM]

Got a call from your school again. This is a really
poor thank you, Beatrice.

Me   [3:07 PM]

I know. I'm sorry. I found out who framed Harper
and had to go get him to confess. He's being
expelled in the other room.

Dad   [3:08 PM]

WHAT?!

Me   [3:10 PM]

It's a crazy long story. I'm on my way to Harper's
now to tell her.

Dad   [3:12 PM]

How did you get across town without Harper
picking you up?

Me   [3:13 PM]

I gallivanted on the bus. Sorry sorry sorry. I'll have
her drive me home for dinner.

✦ 29 ✦

By the time Ben and I left, the rain had let up and Mike was on a conference call with his parents and Harper's dad. I couldn't endure listening to his sobbing confession again. While he had called Dr. Mendoza, I'd put in for another favor from Jack. First thing Monday morning, Nick would go into the administrative office and have Mike's transcripts sent over to Sheldon High. The Donnellys would get the pleasure of knowing that Mike was expelled and Mike would get to test out of school. He was eighteen. There wasn't any way for his parents to stop him.

I put my hands in the damp pockets of my jacket. My uniform had mostly dried while we'd been at Mike's, but my coat was a cold, clammy weight. Thankfully, it was a short walk around the corner. Harper's car gleamed in the driveway of the big white house. Peter's minivan was parked on the curb in front of Cornell's silver hybrid.

"God, I hope there are cookies," Ben said as we cut across the soggy lawn. "I would give my left hand for cookies."

I nudged him with my shoulder. "I'm the one who solved the case. If anyone gets cookies, it's me."

"Your case, my emotional trauma," he said, skipping the step up to the front door.

"Hey, your enemies list is down to just Jack and Ken Pollack. That's good news, right?"

I reached in front of him for the doorknob. The door swung inward, letting out the screams.

"How could you possibly think that I would be happy about that, you addlepated, impetuous jackass?"

I shoved past Ben and found Harper in the middle of the living room whacking Cornell with a wad of rolled-up paper. Cornell had thrown his arms up to shield his face.

"That's what we've been trying to tell him," Peter said from the couch in front of the window as Harper continued to abuse Cornell.

"He's been displaying symptoms of oppositional defiance this week," said Meg, standing safely back near the fireplace.

"You thought that I would break up with you over my grades," Cornell yelped, bobbing and weaving gracelessly as Harper's paper found purchase on the top of his head. "I had to prove to you that I loved you more than I cared about being valedictorian. You wouldn't take my calls."

"Because I was grounded, you feckless goon!"

"Oh good," Ben said, closing the door behind us. "More people pissed about the ranking. Can I go home now?"

"No," I said.

Harper spun around, her glasses crooked on the edge of her nose. She shoved them upward and pointed her swatting papers at me.

"And you," she growled. "I told you not to skip school again. I told you not to put yourself into any more trouble. This was supposed to be a nice day. We were going to get Slurpees—"

"And make a fort," Meg added.

"And make a fort," Harper wailed, waving her paper roll in a figure eight over her head like a lasso. "But, no. You two run off campus together for God knows what reason—"

"I don't think you're allowed to use the Lord's name in vain if you're going to go to Marist," Peter said.

"She's not going to Marist," I said, peeling off my jacket. "I just had Mike Shepherd expelled."

"I would have gone with baking Ben cookies before committing academic fraud," Harper said after I had finished explaining the events of the day. "But that's just me."

"God, I wish there were cookies," Ben grumbled.

"Personally, I think what Mike did was kind of sweet," Meg said.

"Trying to get five people expelled?" Peter frowned, stretching out his bad leg with a wince. "That's way more crazy than nice."

"Extreme, not crazy," Meg corrected. "He didn't even change his own ranking. It was totally selfless."

"Hallmark doesn't make a 'sorry I kicked you out of the role-playing club' card," Cornell said.

The Leonard household wasn't set up for company. Finding seating had taken almost as long as my explanation of what had happened once Ben and I had left campus. I was stuck between Meg and Peter on the couch. Harper and Cornell were a hand span apart on the brick ledge in front of the fireplace. Ben was on the floor with his back against the oak cabinet where the TV was hidden. It was a decent impression of himself—his knees akimbo, his head tilted to examine the room—but his expression stayed blank. I thought about pressing my nose into his cheek, kissing his jaw until his lips turned up in the corners.

But I stayed where I was.

"So, Mike framed everyone so that Ben's mom would come to graduation, Trixie's grounded again, and Cornell decided to destroy his academic future and possibly bankrupt the entire charter of the student government in the process," Harper said lightly. "You guys had a busy week."

"Leadership is a half-credit class," Cornell said. "It wouldn't ruin my entire future. It probably wouldn't even take me out of the top ten. I just wouldn't be valedictorian."

Harper turned to him with an impish smile. "I thought you were doing it to prove how much you loved me. Now it's only a half-credit class and a place in the top ten?"

"When we were in Mendoza's office, you said that I wanted to be valedictorian more than I wanted to be with you," he said, scooping up her hands and holding them between his. "I love you more than I love any place on the ranking. I tried to convince my parents to send me over to Marist, but they wouldn't let me. I could transfer myself after I turn eighteen and flunk out of there, too—"

"So much intellect, so little common sense." She rested her forehead against his. "I love you. Don't flunk anything that you don't want to."

"Okay." He nodded against her nose. "Does that mean you'll take me back?"

"I never let you go, you nitwit." She tipped her face to kiss him and Cornell's hand came up to shield them from view.

After the events of the winter ball, I had expected seeing the two of them together again to fill me with indignant rage. But there was no anger left in my body. They were so strangely comfortable together, even in knowing that everyone was watching them, expecting explanations. Beside me, Meg sniffled.

Ben didn't appear to be listening. He was looking up at the mantel, where a dozen pictures of Harper sat between various award statuettes. He seemed to shake himself out of his reverie, blinking rapidly as his eyes adjusted on Harper and Cornell.

"Harpo, are you going to come back on Monday?" he asked.

Harper extricated herself from Cornell and pushed her glasses up her nose. "The course load at Marist is much simpler than at the Mess. Really, I could do the same thing that Mike's doing and test out. It'd take a lot of work to make up for all the religion classes I missed."

After days of sleepless nights, frying my brain for answers, ditching school, and constantly fighting off the urge to cry, I had never stopped to consider that Harper could choose not to come back to the Mess. I'd been so desperate to make things right, to bring every-thing back to proper equilibrium. And what if it had all been a waste?

Harper flapped her hands. "And if I didn't come back then you guys could graduate with a higher ranking."

"Or we could never talk about the ranking ever again," Ben said. "That would work, too."

"I'm happy being number three," I said honestly. "Besides, Ben and I haven't tried to destroy each other in ages. Why bring that back?"

"Agreed." Ben yawned, closing his eyes. "The peace has been nice."

"Oh, please," Meg said. "You guys couldn't destroy each other if you tried. It's different now."

"Meg," Peter hissed, his eyes shining a warning at her from the other side of me.

She threw up her hands. "What? Are we really going to keep pretending that we don't know?"

"That was the plan," Cornell said, shooting Harper a nervous glance.

Ben opened one eye and stared around. "What plan?"

Harper gave a nervous cluck. I turned to Peter, who inspected the ceiling.

"Margaret?" Ben said. Meg blew a raspberry in return.

"You know," I said loudly, fisting my hands in my lap. "Consider-ing I found the way to revoke Harper's expulsion, I think I've earned the right to know what in the hell is going on here."

Peter, Meg, Harper, and Cornell exchanged another round of shifty glances. Cornell sat taller, his head tilted with a hint of haughty arrogance.

"It's just that you two couldn't be in the same place for five minutes without going nuclear," he said with all the diplomacy he usually reserved for ending student council fights. "And if we had to hear about the monkey bars one more time—"

"See, I needed a test group for my thought experiment," Meg

broke in. "I was planning on using myself and Ishaan, but the more I thought about him, the more I realized that it would be so inconvenient to date someone on the cricket team. Their games are always so far away. But then he got suspended and we were having so much trouble with you guys. There was the harvest festival debacle and the nerd duel and all of those miserable lunches." She rubbed her feet together as she wriggled into the arm of the couch. "And so we had a meeting."

"You had a meeting?" I repeated.

"A couple of meetings," Peter admitted.

"We thought that maybe you'd be nicer to each other if you thought the other person had a crush on you," Harper said.

"Enemies to lovers. It's a very common trope," Meg said in a rush. "It comes up a lot in regency and Victorian literature. Standoffish man, opinionated woman. I noticed it when I started doing my extra credit for Gender Roles. And I thought to myself, 'Well, there has to be a psychological basis for this plot.' And there is! Your putamen and insula light up when you're being faced with something you love or something you hate. Your brain literally can't tell the difference without context clues. By rewriting the negative preconceived notions of your prior relationship, you were free to see each other as positive stimuli!"

Silence.

"She sold it to us as sexual tension," Cornell said.

"Classic Elizabeth and Darcy," Meg said.

"I am not Mr. Darcy," Ben said.

"No . . ." Harper laughed. "You're the Elizabeth."

All of the air rushed out of my lungs. I felt like I'd been hit with a semitruck or a wrecking ball or Thor's hammer. I couldn't bring myself to look at Ben, who was motionless on the floor.

"The day in the park," I said. My face felt numb as I remembered being wedged under the tube slide, crying into a damaged comic. "When I heard you and Harper talking about how Ben was on the brink of suicide because he was in love with me—"

"Suicide?" Ben echoed.

"You did say you'd kill yourself if you had to spend more time with her," Peter said weakly.

"Hyperbole," Ben snapped. He reached for his backpack and dug around inside for a minute before pulling out a piece of notebook paper that was more tape than anything else. It looked like it'd survived a war. He thrashed it toward Cornell. "Then what in the hell is this?"

Peter made a choking sound. "You kept the poems? They were in the trash."

"What poems?" I asked.

Ben thrust the paper at Meg, who passed it to me gingerly. The page was covered in handwriting eerily similar to my own. Except I knew for a fact that I'd never written a sonnet, much less six of them. Whoever had written these had a patience for counting syllables that I lacked.

"What the hell is a *devinette*?" I asked.

"It's French for 'riddle,'" Ben said.

"I took three years of Italian," I said, shoving the paper back at Meg. I didn't want it near me ever again. "Those poems were obviously written by Mary-Anne. And I'm pretty sure they're about Jack."

"She did an excellent job matching your handwriting, though," Harper said. "Who knew she was an accomplished forger?"

"You know," Ben said stiffly, "I thought that Mike trying to get everyone expelled so that I could be valedictorian would be the worst thing that happened today. Congrats, guys. You really outdid yourselves."

"But it all worked out," Meg said frantically. "You two totally love each other. Under the stress of the last week, you crystallized into a perfect polymer. You surpassed the control group!"

"Hey," Cornell and Harper said.

"Love?" I spluttered, moving as far away from Meg as possible without actually ending up on Peter's knee.

"We don't hate each other, sure, but that's a little far," Ben added with a wince.

Meg muttered something that might have been the word *lying*. Distantly, I realized the downside of having a giant cat who operated as a polygraph. I never should have loaned her Ben's copies of *Saga*.

"Oh, please." Harper laughed. "You two are worse than me and Cornell."

"No one is worse than you and Cornell." Ben glowered at her.

"There's no point in denying it," Meg said. "Brandon has been keeping tabs on you. He agreed to help me with the statistics for the paper I was doing on my thought experiment. You really don't guard yourself with him the way you do with us. He brought back some really interesting data."

"She means that he called her screaming when he saw you making out in the library," Peter said.

"And in the storage closet in the main building," Meg said.

Peter snorted. "And in the girls' bathroom in the math and sciences building."

Ben caught my eye and I felt my cheeks burning. Damn B. Calistero and his superior spying skills. I should have known he would go rogue on me.

"There may have been some kissing," I said with as much tact as I could muster with my face on fire. "But that doesn't mean anything."

"Of course not," Ben agreed. "It's utterly meaningless."

Utterly meaningless? Way to go for the jugular, hobo clown.

"It was a hormonal impulse giving way to a physical manifestation," I said, trying to push down the jabs of annoyance cropping up in my brain. "Completely impersonal. It was a high-stress situation. It could have been anyone in that study room. Or storage closet." I coughed. "Or that bathroom."

"A fish," Ben offered. "Like a really big fish."

Cornell laughed. "Wow, you guys are bad at this."

"It's not like we haven't noticed the long lingering looks you've been giving each other," Meg said, a note of pity in her voice.

"And the constant texting," Harper said.

"Exchanging comic books and sodas when you think no one is paying attention," Peter added.

"It wouldn't be completely unfounded to say that we're friends now," I said. I glanced at Ben for confirmation and he gave a rigid nod. "Maybe even friends who have, in the past, kissed one another in regrettably public places. But that doesn't mean we're—"

"The lady doth protest too much, methinks," Cornell muttered.

"How about this?" Harper said, swishing her hair over her shoulder. "If Dr. Mendoza agrees to let me come back to the Mess—and I don't see why he wouldn't—I will agree only if you and Ben admit that you have been secretly dating for the last month." She cocked her head at Cornell for confirmation. "Fair?"

"Sounds good to me," he said.

"That's insane," I said.

"It's not, really. I would have a lot more free time at Marist. If I decided to go back to the Mess, it would be mostly for social reasons. I want to eat lunch and go to prom and take classes with my friends. But you and Ben continuing to pretend that you don't really like each other while you're also secretly dating sounds exhausting. Really, it's almost as bad as you guys actually hating each other. At least that was honest."

"You can't really be saying that you think we've been lying to you," Ben said. "You guys actually lied to us. You used us as guinea pigs for homework."

"Oh, it's much bigger than homework," Meg said. "I mean, it is the reason I jumped up in the ranking. Mr. Walsh was really impressed with my rough drafts. He counted it as four extra-credit assignments. But then my dad put me in touch with the editor of one of his journals. It's going to print in February. Brandon's name will be on it, too, of course—"

Harper cut across her. "We didn't lie to you. We lied within hearing of you. If either of you had actually asked any of us—or each other—about whether we were telling the truth, this never would have worked. You didn't ask because you wanted it to be true. You wanted Trixie to be in love with you and she wanted you to be in love with her. And now you are."

"So, you're welcome," Meg chirped.

"Also, sorry," Peter said.

"Mostly you're welcome." Cornell grinned.

The sound of a phone ringing gave all of us pause. Harper got to her feet and padded out of the room. Her voice floated in from the kitchen.

"Hi, Daddy! Yes, Trixie came to tell me. She was the one who figured it out. Do you think you could call her parents and let them know what happened? Fantastic, thank you . . . Now? Sure. No, I can take it. I know Marist would be a good fresh start, but I'd like to hear his offer. Okay. Love you." She poked her head back into the living room, her phone attached to her ear. "Yes, Mrs. Landry, you can patch me through."

She looked down at me imperiously and my organs all seemed to shift an inch to the left.

I was pinned to the spot. I considered how awful it would feel if Ben rejected me in front of everyone. Or at all. The way things were had worked out for us just fine. Why did we need to let other people in? Why invite an outside influence? What if letting other people see us ruined everything?

Outside input just gets so messy. Your friends judging you, making notes on you, comparing your rankings. . . .

I never should have let Mary-Anne into my brain as a phantom voice of reason. But she had made a valid point. If Ben and I were openly a couple, we'd be accepting the fact that everyone would immediately have an opinion about us.

Then again, Mary-Anne had been in on the thought experiment from the beginning. She'd known that nothing Ben and I did was actually going unseen. Our rankings, our lunchtime behaviors, our conversations had been under a microscope all year.

Everyone who mattered already knew. My best friends were all here, telling me that they'd known all along. They hadn't treated me or Ben any differently.

Which left Ben. Neither of us had ever said anything about what was going on because each of us assumed that the other was secretly harboring real feelings. But Ben had never been in love with me. And until that lie clicked into place, I hadn't noticed that my anterior insular cortex was on Ben West overload.

Now, I couldn't believe how obvious it had been. Staying up to pick fights or watch TV together, walking to class together, kissing and talking and being silent and wanting all of it all the time—that happy sickness had a name. I loved him.

Of course Meg's paper was going to print. The Great Thought Experiment worked.

She was never going to let me live this down.

I looked over at Ben, expecting the raw feeling in my throat to give way to real tears. His lips were pressed together so hard they'd disappeared, leaving a scarecrow frown between his nose and chin. He took a deep breath and reached into his backpack again. He swiped his thumb over the screen of his phone and plugged something into it.

My messenger bag buzzed. I took my phone out, aware that Meg and Peter were both reading over my shoulder.

Ben   [4:17 PM]
Hey. Do you want to come sit over here?

Me   [4:17 PM]
Should I go sit over there?

His lips reappeared in scoff.

Ben   [4:18 PM]
Why would I ask you if I didn't want you to?

I stood, moving across the living room slowly. Each footstep felt heavier than the one before. I sat down with my back against the TV cabinet. I looked at him sidelong, afraid that his face would show some sign of regret. He smiled at me and the freckle next to his left eye disappeared.

Harper gave an almost inaudible cluck as she made her way back into the kitchen. "Yes, Dr. Mendoza, I'm here. Yes, sir, it's very nice to hear from you. My father said you had news. . . ."

"A fish?" I whispered to Ben, trying not to draw attention to us. "You would have made out with a fish?"

"It would have been a hormonal impulse giving way to a physical manifestation," he quoted back sardonically.

"Right." I giggled. "We really are equally dumb, huh?"

He looped his arm around my shoulders and squeezed. "Yeah. But at least it's equal. I'd hate to be the smart one."

"Luckily, that will never be a problem for you."

epilogue

It was an uncomfortably warm Saturday morning. The combination of the TARDIS dress Meg had talked me into buying and the awful red polyester gown I was wearing over it didn't help. I was glad that I'd doubled up on deodorant. I could feel tendrils of sweat pooling under my sunglasses.

Ben had carefully arranged his hair under his mortarboard so that each little spike touched the brim. He had already unzipped his gown, revealing the Spider-Man T-shirt I'd given him for his birthday.

The ceremony had been long and mostly boring, although Cornell's speech had been oddly touching. He'd thanked the Mess for teaching him the value of hard work and making sure that law school would be a breeze by comparison. *"I have learned the true value of our motto*—fide et veritate. *Truth and loyalty. We surrender our pride for truth. It takes courage to be wrong. It takes courage to be right. I have been awed by the loyalty of those around me and I have worked every day to be better because of them."* He'd nodded to where Mike was sitting with the younger members of the role-playing club. He must have taken a day off from work to attend the ceremony. He'd spent the last couple of months as an intern at a video game company. He looked happy in the stands. *"I am a better person for having known my classmates. We are all better having been together."*

"I can't believe it's over," Ben said, examining the melee on the cricket pitch down below. There were hundreds of people on the field. They'd spilled out of the stands the second Dr. Mendoza had pronounced us Messina Academy graduates. There were people hugging and crying, pictures being taken, yearbooks being signed. Ben and I had retired to the top of the bleachers to avoid the fray after Mary-Anne had tearfully embraced me and made me promise I'd keep in touch.

Graduation, it seemed, made people crazy. I hoped B was taking notes on what he observed. He could write a killer Chemistry of Emotions paper on this next year.

"I'm going to have to find my parents soon," I said. "Eventually, my dad will realize that he's been taking pictures of scenery that I'm not a part of."

"Me too." Ben sighed, leaning back on his elbows. He kicked his white high-tops onto the bleacher below us. "I left my grandparents as a buffer, but I shouldn't let the parents stay alone too long. Mom's been extra weird this visit. She still thinks it's her fault that Mike broke into the homework portal. But at least you'll finally get to meet Olivia."

"I wonder if she'll like me," I said, thinking of the few pictures of Ben's sister I'd seen. She had Ben's large brown eyes and wild dark hair.

"She's four, Trix. Say something about unicorns and you're golden."

"Gender normative," I countered, poking him in the ribs with my elbow. "Haven't you given her comics yet?"

"I've tried. But she only likes Superman. I don't know what to do about being related to someone who doesn't like Marvel."

"Now you know how I feel talking to Harper." I laughed, looking out at the field again. The spire on the math and sciences building loomed tall over the gym, the sun beating down on the brick.

"It's weird that we're never coming back," I said. "I mean, I'm excited about college and everything but . . . it's weird, right?"

"Very." He nodded. "But we don't leave for school for another three months. We could always break into the cafeteria if we get nostalgic."

"We aren't breaking into the cafeteria," I said with a snort, scooting closer to him. He wrapped his arm around me and I rested my head against his shoulder, carefully avoiding hitting him in the eye with my cap. Both of us had become adept at ignoring the fact that it was too hot to sit this way. It was worth the extra warmth.

"I got you something," he said.

I snatched off my sunglasses and had to squint to see him as my eyes adjusted to the blinding light. "Is it the newest *Saga*?"

"You know they took a hiatus for the summer." He frowned, reaching into the pocket of his jeans.

"A girl can dream." I sighed. "Maybe you became really good friends with Brian K. Vaughan and convinced him to . . ." He held out his hand and I paused. "Oh. Wow."

Cupped in his palm was a Dalek statuette cast in pewter. I immediately recognized it as part of the set we'd been drooling over at Busby. I picked it up delicately, admiring its miniature plunger arm.

"I couldn't afford the whole set," he grumbled. "But you really wanted the Dalek, so I figured . . . Anyway, I hope you like it."

"Try 'love it,' you doof," I squealed, throwing my arms around his neck to kiss him. Our caps collided and we both laughed.

"Are we interrupting?"

I twisted around and saw Cornell grinning at us, his yellow valedictorian sash sliding down his shoulder. Harper, Peter, and Meg were following him up the stairs toward us.

"Aren't we always?" Meg asked. Even in dangerously high heels, her gown was at least three inches too long. She held it daintily over her ankles as she climbed.

Ben chuckled, reaching up and making sure that our hat incident hadn't ruined his hair. "Generally, yes."

"Look at my graduation gift," I said, holding the Dalek up for the group to admire. "Isn't it perfect?"

"Duh," Harper said, adjusting her glasses. "We were there when he bought it."

"We're very sneaky." Meg beamed.

I stuck my tongue out at them.

"Did you give Ben his gift yet?" Peter asked innocently.

"Gift?" Ben asked, turning to me with unmasked excitement. "I get a gift?"

"What kind of heartless demon doesn't get her boyfriend a graduation gift?" I asked, clutching a hand to my chest with false injury before scrambling to find my messenger bag. Meg had tried to talk me into using a purse, but none of them was big enough.

"I feel like I shouldn't answer that," Ben said. "But I'm not sure."

"Hush it, you," I said, pulling the small pink box out of my bag. I carefully undid the tape on the lid. It had taken a lot of planning—and bubble wrap—to make sure that the cupcake stayed intact. I held it aloft, pretending not to notice as everyone retrieved their cell phones. The frosting was perfect, a fluffy red buttercream, with a giant yellow number four emblazoned on the top.

Peter nabbed the first picture, perfectly capturing the moment just before Ben realized that there was a cupcake being launched into his face. Harper took the picture of the icing smearing across Ben's mouth and cheek. Cornell got me laughing and shouting as Ben wiped his chin on my hair, successfully getting a smear of frosting on one of my hair-sprayed curls. Meg was too busy falling over giggling to take any pictures at all.

Amid the chaos, Ben pried the smashed remains of the cupcake out of my hands and took a bite.

"How does fourth place taste, Benedict?" I asked.

"Like red velvet. My favorite." He grinned, his teeth perfectly white beneath the swirls of red and yellow frosting painted across the lower half of his face. "You know that this means that I'm going to grow the mustache back this summer?"

"You wouldn't dare," I breathed.

He leaned forward until we were nose to nose. Or as close to nose to nose as we could be given we were both wearing silly hats.

"It will be bigger and better than ever."

"You're gonna look gross." I reached up to scrape some of the frosting off his chin with my thumb. "Hey, West?"

"Yes, Beatrice?"

"I love you."

"I know."

"Hey," said Peter, shaking Meg's shoulder. "That's from *Empire Strikes Back*!"

"Oh, Cornell, our little athlete is growing up to be a real geek." Harper giggled.

Cornell braced his fist to his mouth, faking a sniffle of pride. "I promised myself I wouldn't cry."

Ben threw his head back with a laugh. I moved to shove him, but he caught my hand. "Love you, too, Trix."

He leaned forward, kissing me soundly. As I wrapped my arms around his neck, I could feel frosting creeping up my nose and my mortarboard smashing into his. I heard everyone complaining that we had pictures to take and people to say goodbye to and a pool party at Peter and Jack's house to get ready for.

But I was too frakking happy to care.